★

They were angry and brokenhearted and they wanted vengeance, and who could blame them? It took a lot longer than a day to get the story out of them in any sort of order, but their side of it was that little Jordan Ambrose was taken to St. Mary's Hospital here in town, where he got sicker and sicker for three days; then he was taken to the operating room, and in one hour and a half, he was dead. Even though I know little about medicine, it sounded fishy. But malpractice?

When I sent for the medical records of Jordan Ambrose from St. Mary's, they dropped on my desk like a load of dynamite.

———————————— ★ ————————————

"Most readers will want to hear more from the quietly charismatic hero of this poignant, penetrating, suspenseful debut, written in a style both easy and elegant."

—Kirkus Reviews

...was a spur that left them shaken, and they went
...vengeance; and who could blame them? It took a
...lot longer than a day to get the story out of them. It
...my sort of night—but then that is of it was that little
...orden Amhurst was... ...ed to ally. Mary's Hospital
...in terms... ...days later and when sometime
...the plant he was taken to the operating room, and
...is one...cated a half hour... ...ead, three hours [later]
...knew little about medicine, it made no difference, But
...difference!

When I read in the medical section, of, On the
...America Sept 30, last, will—through satthey-dash
...he a kind of by-path.

"Your need to will want to be a movie from the
...kindly diagnosis as cold as neon can yet
...penetration, suspense and story, written in a style
...between wry and magic."

—Kirkus Reviews

WILLFUL NEGLECT

MARY MORGAN

WORLDWIDE.

TORONTO • NEW YORK • LONDON
AMSTERDAM • PARIS • SYDNEY • HAMBURG
STOCKHOLM • ATHENS • TOKYO • MILAN
MADRID • WARSAW • BUDAPEST • AUCKLAND

For Alan, whose ethics have always
been impeccable.

WILLFUL NEGLECT

A Worldwide Mystery/January 1999

First published by St. Martin's Press, Incorporated.

ISBN 0-373-26297-3

Printed in U.S.A.

No writer ever really works alone, no matter how much he or she claims to. I would like to thank some of the kind people who helped me in the shaping of this novel.

My husband, for loyal support through many unpublished years, and for checking the medical facts; my fellow-writers of "Rejects," for listening so well; Phyllis Wood, for sharing her space and her estimable working habits; William Maltman and Beverley Johnson for providing legal background; Ruth Cavin and Carrie McGinnis at St. Martin's Press for guiding me gently through the publishing process; and especially my agents, Anna Cottle and Mary Alice Keir, of Cine-Lit Representation, for their enthusiasm, dedication, and tact.

I looked over Jordan
And what did I see?
A band of angels comin' after me.
—Old Negro spiritual

ONE

WHEN THE AMBROSES first appeared in my office that gloomy November morning, the clouds low and dark outside, nothing about them flashed any warning signals. They were ordinary-enough people. He was large and loose-limbed, with the look of an athlete gone to seed, his feet weighted to the ground, a slight potbelly, and an expression of great sorrow on his face. She was tall, slender, fine-boned, and angry. I recognized the anger in her eyes even before she spoke. That the Ambroses were black was the only unusual thing about them. Black people were not common in my office, in my town.

I leapt to my feet, anxious not to appear surprised, and stretched my hand across the desk. "Noah Richards. I'm pleased to meet you."

The words, hardly startling, seemed to make them uneasy. They glanced at each other with sideways cautionary flickerings; then Ambrose took my hand and smiled vaguely, a mere creasing that didn't relieve the grief in his heavy face. He was younger than I'd thought immediately. His large hand enveloped mine and it was warm and sweaty.

"Joseph Ambrose," he said, and dropped my hand quickly. "This is my wife, Angel."

Angel, I thought facetiously, what a heavenly name, but I didn't say it, of course. Angel Ambrose didn't seem to want to touch my hand; she stood glowering at me as though I was the enemy. Her head was small, poised precisely on a long, sinewy neck, with hair cut close to her head like a cap of velvet, her skin the warm golden brown of the autumnal maple tree outside my window. She gleamed in the dingy office, skin shining, eyes sparking that fierce anger. An avenging Angel, I thought, and didn't know how perceptive I was.

"Please sit," I said, waving to the functional chairs on their side of the desk, seating myself in the high-backed chair that had been my father's. Large and worn and comfortable, it enfolded me with some kind of security, retaining in its shape and scuffed leather the sense of a departed world.

The Ambroses stared suspiciously at the chairs and then both sat down suddenly, as if they didn't do so, they might change their minds and bolt from the room. Angel was graceful and swift in her movements and had narrow shapely knees that drew my eyes unwillingly. I concentrated on her husband.

I kept my voice gentle. "I understand you wanted to see me about your son?"

"Jordan." Ambrose's voice was unsteady, the graven expression of sorrow deepening on his dark face, blackening it. He folded his hands together, intertwining his thick fingers as though in prayer. He couldn't continue. He bent his head and stared at his hands.

"He's dead." Angel's voice was firm and loud. "He was five years old and he's dead, and we want to know why."

"Yes, Mr. Richards, that's about it," Ambrose mumbled, and he didn't look at me. "We want to know why."

It was always hard to get through the painful start of a discussion like this. I knew only what Bella, my secretary, had told me about their phone call. They'd come to talk about the death of their child in the hospital. Medical malpractice was what the Ambroses wanted to talk about. I had little taste for malpractice suits.

I cleared my throat. "Perhaps you'll tell me what happened. I know your son was a patient at St. Mary's. Can you tell me what was wrong with him?"

"He had a bellyache." Angel spoke rapidly, the words

falling over one another, a strong trace of the South in her voice. "Just a simple bellyache. I took him to the doctor and he wanted to put him in the hospital. For observation, he said. Said he had gastritis or something like that and it wasn't too serious. Our boy stayed there, in that hospital, for days and days, getting sicker and sicker, and then they took him to the operating room and then he died."

There was a dense silence in the room. The ticking of the brass clock on my desk grew loud and obtrusive. When I looked at Joseph Ambrose, he was an empty shell, all the light in him gone out.

"I'm so sorry," I said, and heard how inadequate it sounded. "So very sorry." Another leaden silence filled the space between us. "When exactly was this?"

"September fourth," Angel said. "Two-thirty in the afternoon of September fourth."

"This year? Just two months ago?"

"Two months ago," she echoed bleakly.

Slowly, Ambrose shook his big head from side to side. "And there ain't nothing we can do to bring him back, Mr. Richards."

I waited for them to tell me more, but they seemed struck dumb with remembering.

"I know how difficult it must be for you to talk about it, but you'll have to try to give me some details about his illness and his treatment. The point of this meeting is that you're not satisfied with the treatment he received, isn't that right?" Of course they weren't satisfied. Their child was dead.

Angel stared at me with contempt. "He's dead, isn't he?" I had the sudden uneasy feeling she could read my mind.

"Truly, you have all my sympathy." Truly, they did. The thought of anyone losing their child cramped my heart and I dared not even contemplate such an abyss. "But sometimes, you know, everything that's possible is done and still a life can't be saved. You do realize that, don't you?"

Sitting up straighter in the chair, Angel radiated an intimidating fierceness. "You don't understand. Them doctors did nothing. They just watched him die. I sat in that hospital room with him and watched them watch him die. They kept telling me he was okay, that he'd soon be better, but he kept on getting worse. The nurses were upset, too— it wasn't just me. One of the nurses got mad at the doctor, right in front of me. And then the surgeon rushed him off to the operating room and he died right there, on the table. Those doctors killed him. They didn't even let him die peacefully. They stuck knives in him and killed him."

Her words spun and echoed in the room. I sighed. "Do you have a death certificate?"

Ambrose reached into the inside pocket of his jacket and pulled out an envelope with a crumpled official form inside. I had to lay it on the desk and smooth it with two hands before I could read it. I could practically see the tearstains on it.

"This says bacteremic shock and cardiac arrest. It doesn't convey too much to me, I'm afraid. I think it means he had an infection and then his heart stopped. What did the doctors tell you?"

Angel's voice rose. "They told us lies, nothing but lies."

Ambrose sent her a warning look. "Hush your mouth," he said, surprising me. And she shot back at him, "I ain't here to hush my mouth, Joseph. I'm here to tell him the truth."

Struggling with the words, Joseph went on. "After he… Afterward, they told us his insides had got all twisted up because of the other operation and that gave him another infection, which was what made him sick."

"He'd had another operation?"

"Yes, sir, six months before—at the army hospital. They took out his appendix."

Clenching her hands into fists, Angel shook them at me. "And there wasn't nothing wrong with his appendix, either. The doctors at the army hospital told us that, after the operation. They said he'd had pneumonia, not appendicitis. So they were wrong, too. Everybody was wrong."

I was getting confused. I knew little about the intricacies of medicine. Sometimes it felt as though I knew little about anything anymore. "Now just a moment. Let's back up here. Your son was at the army hospital before? And then he was at St. Mary's? Why was that? Why did he go to two different hospitals?"

"I was in the army then, see," Joseph explained. "Now I'm out. Now I work at Bennetts Mill."

"Bennetts? What's your job, Mr. Ambrose?"

"He's supervisor of the supply shop," Angel said.

I was surprised again. Bennetts Mill, the biggest employer in our town, which wasn't saying much, is an out-of-date, anti-union plant, and I'd have thought the management far too entrenched in old-fashioned thinking to have a black man as a supervisor of anything.

"And you, Mrs. Ambrose? Do you have a job?"

I almost expected her to tell me she was a lawyer. Her combativeness reminded me of some of the women in my class at law school. It was important to know the Ambrose's status, what type of education they had, what expectations their child would have had, for when it came down to the dollars and cents of a child's life, God forbid, that's how a jury would calculate it.

"Oh, I work. Folks like us got to work. I'm at Sturtevants—in sales."

Which meant, I supposed, that she was a sales assistant. Sturtevants was one of the leading stores in the area, and that probably explained why her clothes looked so smart and expensive.

As they answered my questions, I jotted notes on a pad, aware that Angel Ambrose was watching what I wrote, screwing up her eyes to try to read my handwriting. It wouldn't be easy—I could hardly read it myself. "So, at the army hospital, they took out his appendix?"

"But there wasn't anything wrong with his appendix," she cried, as though I was slow in getting the point.

"Okay. All right. But after that, had he been well? Not chronically sick or anything?"

Joseph sighed, a slow, shuddering exhalation of breath that came from somewhere in the depths of his large body. He had sunk into the chair as though exhausted. It was only 10:30 in the morning. "He was well enough, until he got that bellyache. So Angel took him to see this new doctor...." His voice trailed away.

"A different doctor? Someone who hadn't seen him before?" They nodded at me. "And this doctor sent him to St. Mary's?" They nodded again. "And at the hospital, what did they think was wrong with him?"

Joseph Ambrose looked away from me, off into an unhappy distance somewhere, as though he wanted to drop this whole business right then. He seemed to have no stomach for the fight his wife was spoiling for.

"The doctors said they didn't know what was wrong. They wanted to observe him." Angel repeated the story patiently and clearly, as if she thought it would never get through to me. "They said they thought Jordan had gastritis or something. They said they wanted to watch him. They watched him until he died."

"Which doctor sent him to St. Mary's?"

"Clarke," she said, spitting out the name. "Tyler Clarke. He calls himself a pediatrician, and he sent my baby to the hospital to die. And then along comes the surgeon, a big fat guy name of Woods, who takes him to the operating room and finishes him off."

Quite suddenly, all the hard, brittle poise left her, and she started to cry. At first, she wept silently and facilely, the tears streaking down her golden cheeks and into her mouth; then she covered her face with her thin strong hands, the nails painted red like wounds, and began to wail loudly and noisily, gulping and choking. "Oh, my baby!" she screamed. "Jordy, my baby! My little boy! Jordy!" Her keening rose and shattered the quiet of the room, rattling the teeth in my head. Joseph went to her and cradled her head in his arms, and they rocked together, crying together, spilling their grief in my office.

THAT WAS IT; that's how it started. They were angry and brokenhearted and they wanted vengeance, and who could blame them? Their five-year-old son dead and they didn't know why. How would any of us feel if our child had died in a hospital with a horde of doctors and nurses looking on and seemingly doing nothing? Wrongful death was what they were talking about, and I had no idea if there was a case or not. It took a lot longer that day to get the story out of them in any sort of order, but their side of it was that little Jordan Ambrose was taken to St. Mary's Hospital here in town, where he got sicker and sicker for three days; then he was taken to the operating room, and in one hour and a half, he was dead. Even though I know little about medicine, it sounded fishy. But malpractice? Well, I didn't know. There are rules that govern whether something is medical malpractice. Though it wasn't my field, it wasn't anyone else's field, either, here in this town, so I felt obliged to do my best to fumble along and find out what had really happened to their little boy.

The Ambroses—at least Angel Ambrose—wanted to sue every doctor in sight. I didn't have much stomach for suing doctors. Doctors are human, like everyone else. One of my closest friends is a physician. He does his best. At least I've always assumed so. I have to believe doctors try their utmost. Two years ago, my own wife died in spite of the latest and greatest medicine had to offer, and I couldn't go on functioning if I didn't believe everything possible was done for her.

But when I sent for the medical records of Jordan Ambrose from St. Mary's, they dropped on my desk like a load of dynamite. I read them through once, then again and again. Despite my medical ignorance, those records read like a horror story from beginning to end, nurses charting a child getting sicker and sicker and physicians not answering the nurses' frequent calls for help. The records seemed to substantiate everything the Ambroses had claimed—that little Jordan Ambrose had died from malignant neglect.

It was then that the warning signs should have flashed. I don't get angry very often. I like to think of myself as a dispassionate kind of guy, always one step away from too much involvement, keeping emotions at arm's length because emotions cloud the issues. Anger and involvement don't help a clear mind, but those records made me hot under the collar. Damn angry. Mad as hell, in fact. It's easy enough not to get mad with the sort of legal garbage I'm called upon to perform 99.9 percent of the time. Dross, most of it. Boring, nit-picking, mundane, paper-pushing dross—divorce, wills, probate, taxes, real estate deals. After years of moving the property of affluent middle-class Americans around, I was beginning to get stale and dull, the blood definitely running cool. So I was almost glad to feel the anger grow in me, to recognize a real wrong that should be righted. I wasn't happy to read that tragic story just so I could feel a righteous anger returning, a flush of rediscovered youth, but I have to admit that it felt healthy to be really incensed about something once again.

But in spite of all that, I found it hard to believe that Jordan Ambrose's case could be so simple. A little boy can't just lie in a hospital and fade away with a treatable illness, not in this age of high-powered medicine and diagnostic aids. There had to be more to the story than I could read in the hospital records, some medical problem I wasn't capable of understanding, some reasonable rationale for the sad sequence of events.

I needed a trained eye the way a blind man needs a guide dog. I needed an expert witness, but expert witnesses are a very suspect bunch. There are those who make a living out of swearing whatever it is you want them to swear, like politicians. I wanted one who'd tell me the truth.

I took the records around to my friend Chauncey Carlsson, M.D.

TWO

CHAUNCEY'S OFFICE was on the other side of town, in a building a few other doctors built for themselves when they first started in practice, before Springwell went into its downward spiral. Chauncey was an old-fashioned general practitioner who had a special interest in allergies, which, God knows, everyone had in our neck of the woods. It was odd, in a way, that we'd both gravitated back to the town where we'd been kids together, because most people who left Springwell didn't return. I'd known him as long as I've known anybody, and though I'd been gone a lot longer than he had, he was one of the reasons it was all too easy to stay once I came back. I'm not sure I'd have survived Janet's illness without his support.

Walking in with no prior announcement, the day after poring over the mishmash of hospital notes, I hoped he wouldn't be up to his ears in patients. His office was warm and comforting—like his home—with a waiting room you don't mind hanging around in for the statutory half hour all doctors make you wait. There were fishing magazines scattered on small tables, a brightly lit aquarium with tiny psychedelic fish, the friendly glow of soft lamps. If I was ill, which I never am, I reckon I'd stop worrying once I got there.

I didn't have to wait half an hour. The girl at the desk buzzed him for me. He came rambling down the corridor, tall and thin in his white coat, fair hair crumpled and spiky, as though he'd been dozing, trademark stethoscope hanging out of his pocket. "Hey, Noah, what's up? This isn't official, I hope. Not sick, are you?"

"Not sick," I assured him. He threw an arm around my

shoulder, guiding me along the corridor to his office. Chauncey was only a couple of inches taller than I, but he was so thin and blond, his hair and skin so full of light in contrast to mine, that he made me feel short and dark and solid. Once we were as close as brothers, but there was never any mistaking that we sprang from different stock, Swedish on his side, Welsh and Irish on mine. As kids, we were in and out of each other's homes, went sailing and camping and hiking together, got into trouble together, and it wasn't until graduate school that we parted ways. It was hard to believe we'd reached the considerable age of thirty-six, hard to believe two such scruffy kids could ever mature into reasonably worthy members of society. The difference between us these days was that Chauncey was firmly anchored in life, settled, comfortable, while I was adrift on a sea of uncertainty, waiting for a fresh breeze to steer me in the right direction.

He led me into his consulting room, a small, cluttered space heaped with books and papers, the walls covered with medical school diplomas, residency program diplomas, medical society diplomas, photos of the family. One photo of Daphne, his wife, I particularly liked. Sunshine caught her soft hair in a halo; she was smiling into the camera with delighted candor. Whenever I went into Chauncey's office, that smile greeted me.

"You got me on a quiet afternoon, Noah. Just catching up on some journal reading."

Taking the thick folder of records out of my briefcase, I dropped it on his desk, making a dull thudding sound. "I'd like you to look at these, Chauncey. Help me to make head or tail out of them."

"What the hell is it?" He peered at the pile of paper, flipped a couple of pages. "St. Mary's?"

"A child died at St. Mary's a couple of months ago—in the operating room. You heard about it, of course?"

Pushing the stack of notes to one side with the flat of his

hand, he propped himself against the edge of the desk. "I did hear something about it," he said warily. "Not many patients die on the table these days."

"Know the details?"

He frowned, his eyes a startling blue, generations of Scandinavian genes in them. He should have been called Erik or Anders or Jan, like the rest of the males in his family. Chauncey was his mother's maiden name. "Don't tell me you're involved? Are you talking a suit?"

"Does that surprise you? Doesn't it sound like a suit?"

Coolly, he said, "Everything sounds like a suit these days, Noah."

"This was a child, Chauncey. A five-year-old kid. You can't be amazed that the parents would think of suing."

Getting off the desk, he moved behind it, sitting in his chair as if to put a distance between us. "You're asking me to look at these notes?"

"I've got to have someone look at them. I'm hardly a medical whiz myself."

He grimaced, as if a bad smell emanated from the records. He didn't touch them.

"You know which doctors were involved, don't you?"

"Who were they?"

"Come on, Chauncey! You must know. A town this size, you must know who was involved in this case. You said you'd heard about it."

"I didn't hear any details."

"Not even who the surgeon was?"

He was staring at me, eyes narrowed. At last, he said reluctantly, "Okay. So I heard it was Woods."

"That's right. Carl Woods. What sort of a surgeon is he?"

His pleasing face had turned quite unfriendly, thin and pinched around the lips, the blue eyes slate gray and cold. "Carl Woods is nearly retirement age. He's been a damn fine surgeon for many years. I hope no one's going to drag him into any courtroom now.''

The conversation was not going the way I had envisaged. ''Chauncey! A five-year-old kid is dead. What the hell are you talking about?''

''I'd never have thought it.'' The disgust was plain in his voice. ''You of all people, turning into a plaintiff's lawyer. Why in God's name couldn't you have stuck with tax law?''

I corrected him. ''Corporate law.'' He knew very well why I hadn't stuck with it. ''All I want you to do is to look at these notes and give me an opinion. Nobody's suing anyone yet. Nobody's suing you, for Christ's sake. You don't need to get so damned excited.''

Folding his arms tightly against his chest, he rocked back in his chair, squinted down his narrow, high-bridged nose. ''It's intolerable, Noah. These days, physicians are sued for anything that doesn't work out perfectly. People expect miracles. We're not miracle workers. We perform an inexact science. What works for one person doesn't always work for another.'' He thumped the chair to an upright position, unwound one arm, pointed a thin threatening finger at me. ''Wait until attorneys start getting sued. It's coming. Then you'll find out how it feels. There'll be some smart-assed lawyer on the stand, swearing a case was handled the wrong way, that you didn't live up to the standards and all that kind of bullshit. It's easy enough to say afterward what went wrong. Hindsight, Noah. It's a powerful argument in the hands of people who don't have to put their expertise on the line.''

''You haven't even read the records,'' I pointed out mildly.

''And I don't want to. These people are my colleagues, Noah. Go find someone else to do your dirty work.''

A chilly silence grew between us.

''Okay, all right. If that's how you feel. Maybe that's all

I wanted from you anyway—to tell me whom I should go talk to.''

Averting his eyes, he stared out the window, as if hoping I'd disappear if he didn't look at me.

"Look, Chauncey, there's this funny thing with the law. An attorney is constantly faced with things he knows nothing about. Those years of law school teach one something, I suppose, though I have trouble now remembering what it was, but out in the real world there are whole rafts of specialties with their own secrets. Ships sink, and we have to find out how ships should be built. Buildings collapse, and we have to find out about concrete and metal stresses. Doctors go to medical school and into specialties that take half a lifetime to learn, and then some jumped-up attorney like me who can't tell chicken pox from smallpox has to find out what they should have done and why. All I'm saying, Chauncey, is that here's a healthy five-year-old kid who's dead and a sheaf of notes from nurses who make a record of him getting sicker and sicker for three days, and no one is doing anything. Three days, Chauncey. Not half an hour, or even one day. Three days, for God's sake! In a hospital—*your* hospital. Your nurses. His blood pressure was dropping into his boots, he was complaining of pain, and they made numerous calls to doctors who didn't respond. Then he was rushed to the operating room, and in a little over an hour, he was dead. I just want to know what the hell happened, that's all.''

Chauncey pushed his chair farther away from me, refolded his arms, gazed at the diplomas on the walls as though he'd never seen them before, peered down his nose again, as if I were some kind of unpleasant growth that had sprung beneath his feet. The long strand of our friendship felt stretched, friable, about to break, and for a moment I was tempted to say, "Oh, forget it. Nothing is worth this.'' But I didn't. It seemed to me there was something more important than friendship at stake here, even if I couldn't believe we were testing the boundaries in this way. I waited.

At long last, he began to breathe more normally. His nostrils were still dilated, but his eyes became a more familiar color, and without more words, he leaned forward, pulled Jordan Ambrose's notes across the desk, and started to read.

He didn't offer any comment, just turned the pages one after the other, methodically. Eventually, he came to the operating room note, then made a small noise in his throat and shook his head, minimally, screwing his eyes up. Smoothing the folder with one hand, he turned back a few pages and read them over again. I could hear phones ringing down the corridor, the voices of the women at the front desk, the clatter of a typewriter, a soporific air of business as usual. I concentrated on keeping quiet, not daring to offer any comment, and studied Daphne's laughing face.

When I looked at Chauncey again, he was looking at me, his expression grim.

"What do you think?" I asked.

He closed the file, pushed it away. "I think it stinks."

"Stinks for or against a case?"

There was an unhappy, baffled look in his eyes. "I can't bear to think of you as a plaintiff's attorney, Noah. I see them as nothing but parasites on the body politic, nothing but ambulance chasers."

I was determined not to be riled. "Believe me, Chauncey, I haven't chased any ambulances. I'm not sure I even want the case, but I want your opinion of the nurses' notes."

He stared at the ceiling, closed his eyes, and said slowly, the words dragged out of him, "I don't understand why no one answered their calls."

"Tell me, Chauncey. Why aren't there any residents or interns at St. Mary's to answer calls?"

He regarded me with pity. "See how much you know?

St. Mary's is a community hospital, not a teaching hospital. There's not an intern between Seattle and Vancouver, or between Seattle and Portland, come to that. Most hospitals in this country have to manage without them. The docs at places like St. Mary's take all their own calls, the middle of the night, weekends, whenever. There are men around here who haven't had a night off for years.''

That's right, what did I know? My experience of hospitals was limited to the big city.

"It takes a toll," Chauncey said. "Suppose you had to drag yourself out of bed night after night? You can get so damn weary you don't know whether you're coming or going."

Could that be the reason, just sheer weariness? "I guess you should know what life's going to be like if you decide to be a surgeon," I said sanctimoniously.

"Easy for you to say, isn't it?"

Pulling the file back to my side of the desk, I opened the pages. "Will you help me with a few things?" I went quickly on before he had chance to refuse. "When the boy was first admitted, his temperature was a hundred and one and eight-tenths. Is that very high?"

His mouth twisted into the resemblance of a smile. I knew it was an absurdly basic question. "No, but it's abnormal, of course."

"When the doctor, Clarke, admitted him, he wrote, 'Abdomen rigid and tender.' What should that have meant to him?"

Reluctantly, Chauncey said, "That something was going wrong in the belly."

I turned more pages. "And here, this blood count. What does this mean?" I showed him the lab report.

"White cells twenty-one thousand," he said. "It's a high white count; means some inflammatory process was happening. Clarke calls for a surgeon then. That was the right thing to do."

"But the surgeon doesn't come until the next day. Not until ten the next morning. Why was that?"

Chauncey examined his fingers as though they could hold the answer to my question. "I presume Clarke didn't tell him there was any urgency to the case."

"And someone sends the kid for an X ray. That okay?"

"Sure. But no one seems to have read anything significant into the X ray. No one even seems to have read it." Sighing, he rubbed his hand across his face. "After that, Noah, things got serious. We're now into the second day of admission." Suddenly, he seemed to warm to the task of dissecting the notes, as though the problem was more compelling than blind defense. He stabbed a finger at the page. "The nurse on the evening shift reported the child complaining of pain and having a very rapid pulse, poor color, swollen abdomen. She palpated the abdomen and recorded how tense and tender it was, how lethargic the child was, how restless he was. How she couldn't get him even to suck on some ice chips. She called Clarke. That was at six in the evening. He didn't come. They called him at seven, again at eight, and he showed up around ten p.m. Apparently, he spoke to the surgeon again, but no one came. All night long, the nurses reported a child declining. Poor blood pressure, unresponsive, and so on. Now we're at the third day. The nurses made"—he ran his finger down the page—"five, six calls. Clarke saw him at six in the morning; Woods came in at noon and took him to the operating room. They got him there at about one o'clock. The surgery lasted one and a half hours. He died at two-thirty."

We sat silently for a while among the diplomas. "What about those nurses, Chauncey? You know them?"

"They're on the surgical ward. I rarely have patients there."

"You think they know what they're talking about?"

He shrugged, somewhat hopelessly. "I've no reason to doubt what they've written. They have no ax to grind."

Getting to his feet, he paced the small area behind his desk, two steps one way, two the other, looked out the window, his back to me. Eventually, he said, "Like a cup of coffee?"

"Just tell me, Chauncey. Don't drag it out. What happened? What went on in that hospital? Who was at fault? Not the nurses, it seems. Was it the surgeon? The pediatrician?"

As though he couldn't find a place to be comfortable, he returned to the chair, rocked, swiveled, fiddled with the journals on the desk. At last, through clenched teeth, he said, "Look, if I give you a name of someone to talk to, will you leave me out of it? I'm not happy with what I read here, Noah, but I've got to work with these men. I'm not qualified to criticize a pediatrician or a surgeon. Get someone from outside Springwell. Go to Seattle, where there are specialists falling over themselves." Searching around in the muddle of books and papers on the shelf beside his desk, he pulled out a thick roster and flipped through the pages. "There's a pediatric surgeon in Seattle named Randolph Sweigert. He's got a good name, attends at Childrens. He'll give you an unbiased opinion."

"Can I tell him you gave me his name?"

Chauncey was writing the number on a pink telephone slip, and for a moment he seemed to hesitate even about that. "Oh, sure, what the hell." He handed me the slip. "I hope you know what you're in for, Noah. You've got a hell of a lot to learn."

THREE

SPRINGWELL IS a little more than sixty miles from Seattle, in the foothills of the Cascades, a town straggling between the green-forested mountains that edge down almost to Main Street, a curving arm of Puget Sound a couple of miles to the west, a freshwater lake one mile to the east. When the weather is fine, approximately three months of the year, it's as good a place to live as anywhere, gently uncrowded, comfortably down-market. On lazy summer mornings, I sometimes slip away in my father's old dinghy, still moored at the dock, to fish the rich waters of the lake. On those early mornings, there will be bald eagles keeping watch from the high branches of the Douglas firs, herons stalking the shore, red-winged blackbirds nesting in the reeds; the only man-made sound disturbing the deep silence is the sputtering of the outboard. Fishing is one of the reasons I stay in Springwell.

But when it's wet and dark, as it was on the November day I drove down to Seattle, Springwell is the end of the universe, nowhere USA, a town dying with the lumber industry, decaying from lack of business and taxes to fix the streets. Only the fast-food joints and the gas stations flashing their hopeful signs around the freeway entrance offer any promise of life still left in the dim buildings scattered among the hills. That morning, the gray clouds hung low, wreathing in the dark trees, and I had a sinking feeling the sun might never return.

I was on my way to interview Dr. Randolph Sweigert, whose name Chauncey had given me so reluctantly. It was clear that Chauncey was unhappy with me, with the very idea of a malpractice case. I didn't need disapproval from

Chauncey, one of my few remaining friends. Even though
Springwell was a small town, I didn't know those doctors
who treated—or rather, didn't treat—Jordan Ambrose, but
Chauncey knew them, of course, and he didn't like it, not
one bit. Those are the difficulties for a small-town lawyer—
too limited a circle of acquaintances, too many people who
know you or one another, too many ways of making yourself unpopular with too few people. Maybe I should have
dispatched the Ambroses to Seattle to find a real malpractice lawyer, but I felt I couldn't let them go yet, not without
exploring some of the nagging questions. It was the first
time for a long time that I'd wanted answers to questions
about anything.

That morning, for my meeting with the surgeon, I wore
one of my L.A. lawyer suits. It didn't fit quite as well as
it used to, too loose now at the waist, drooping on the
shoulders, a sure sign that I wasn't eating enough or getting
enough exercise. But the sleek black turbo-charged Saab,
comfortable and fast, another relic of big-city life, still fitted
well, a possession that still gave pleasure. The only thing
in the car that didn't work was the phone, and I reminded
myself again to get it reactivated. Though why? How often
did I need it these days?

Whenever I drove the Saab any distance, I could feel
Janet in the passenger seat beside me, smell her perfume,
hear her laughter. We'd driven up from Los Angeles in this
car, too lengthy and tiring a journey for her, but one she
insisted on making. Perhaps she guessed it would be her
last chance to look at the mountains and valleys on the long
road from California. On that journey, she still had laughter
in her.

I hadn't been to Seattle for months. Seattle was where
everything was happening in the Northwest, the city growing and booming, new buildings thrusting from huge holes
in the ground, jackhammers at every intersection, the price
of houses skyrocketing. It wasn't at all the laid-back, rather

hick town I'd known as a student at the university. The noise, the dust, and the congestion on the downtown streets reminded me of L.A.—apart from the rain, of course. In November, the rain had turned the construction sites to ugly mud heaps, and I decided I didn't care much for cities anymore. Two years in Springwell had succeeded in turning me back into a small-town boy.

Dr. Randolph Sweigert's office was on the fourteenth floor of a medical tower with marble hallways and gleaming elevators that slid discreetly upward. The elevator disgorged me into a suite of sculptured carpets, upholstered chairs, and paintings that matched the furniture, and my first impression was that a lot of money had been spent there. I wondered if his patients got the same impression and argued about their bills. Some people must need to look as if they're doing well.

Randolph Sweigert seemed astoundingly young to be doing so well. He, too, was wearing a dark serious suit and a striped tie, as if trying to appear older and wiser, but he was pleasant enough, almost shy, with an eager-beaver expression, although puffy around the eyes, as if he hadn't had enough sleep. We'd already talked on the phone, and the records I'd sent sat in a neat heap on his desk, so there was no need to skirmish around too much.

Once I'd admired the view and made a quick study of the framed diplomas on the walls, I got out my notebook. "You understand, Dr. Sweigert, that we're talking off the record. What you tell me today is for my own information only." Most of what I wanted to know, I could probably have got from him on the phone, but I wanted to meet him and size him up—for future courtroom appearances, of course.

He swiveled uneasily in his plush upholstered chair. "As long as it's off the record. Frankly, I'm not too eager about malpractice cases. Is any physician?"

"Of course not, Doctor." I was soothing. "And don't

worry. If I need a deposition, it will be perfectly obvious. There'll be a stenographer present and the attorneys for the defendants. If it comes to that, of course.''

For a moment, he regarded me cautiously, sizing me up in turn; then he picked up the pile of notes, weighing them in his surgeon's hands, well-shaped, competent hands. "My first reaction is that I certainly hope it comes to that. Almost everyone concerned with the care of this poor child was grossly negligent. Except perhaps the nurses.''

"Really? It's as simple as that?" A surge of adrenaline tingled along my spine.

"As simple as that.'' He put the tips of his fingers together in the maddening way of people who are very sure of themselves.

"It never is, you know,'' I said. "Simple. Have you ever given testimony in a malpractice suit?''

He shook his head. He had soft close-cropped hair, like a young boy. "As a matter of fact, no.''

"Have you ever had a suit brought against you?''

He looked faintly outraged. "No.''

"That's good. So tell me why you think these doctors were negligent?''

Signs of distress flickered on his youthful face, a tightening of the lips, a twitch at the corner of his eyes. He riffled the pages of the records. "Where shall I start?''

"At the beginning.''

"The beginning? The beginning was at the army hospital where they took out his appendix. He didn't have appendicitis; he had pneumonia. If they hadn't operated then, when he didn't need it, he'd never have proceeded to the stage of an adhesion, from which he died.''

"An adhesion?" I asked. "What exactly is that?''

"A kind of scarring of the bowel. Sometimes the intestines form bands of tissue after surgery, which make it stick together, twist, and tighten on itself. Typically about six months later. So if he hadn't had that first operation... We don't have the records of that first mistake." He pointed a finger at me. "You should get them. And then, after that..." Gazing at the records, he shook his head again. "At St. Mary's, it's a tale of disaster. Frankly, I'm appalled at the lack of care and understanding."

He stopped suddenly and waited for me to say something.

"You're a qualified pediatric surgeon, aren't you, Dr. Sweigert?"

"Yes, sir, I am. I have my boards in pediatric surgery."

"So you'd be able to diagnose Jordan's condition better than someone who didn't specialize in children?"

I was uneasy that he was too adamant, too certain he was right. There's danger in being too sure you're right. You can't see the other side sneaking up on you.

"That child was deathly ill. Anyone should have recognized it. The nurses did."

"Why do you think no one took any notice of the nurses?" Those notes the nurses made, their calls for help, the increasing urgency of their summons loomed larger and larger in the issue.

Sweigert threw up his hands. "God only knows! But you'd be surprised how some doctors guard their territory, almost as though the very idea of a nurse suggesting a diagnosis is enough to make some physicians turn their faces the other way."

I could understand that. Like secretaries telling you how to run legal matters.

"What you should understand, Mr. Richards, is that rushing a patient to the OR isn't always the answer. Only in cases of severe hemorrhage can you afford not to wait. A patient has to be in reasonably good condition for surgery. By the time they got this kid to the operating room, his vital signs had deteriorated to such an extent that any operation was doomed to failure. Criminal, Mr. Richards. Absolutely criminal. They waited until he was in shock;

they didn't prepare him with enough IV fluids; they didn't even give antibiotics. God! They did nothing to preserve what life he still had left.''

I thought of Joseph and Angel Ambrose crying in my office. It seemed I'd found my expert witness, clearly committed to Jordan Ambrose's cause.

"So you'd be willing to swear a deposition to that effect?'' Of course he would. He was like Angel Ambrose—avenging.

Dr. Sweigert swung the chair violently, slowed it, glanced at his diplomas hanging on the walls. The pale young face crumpled; the clear eyes clouded.

"Well now, I don't know, Mr. Richards. Be a witness against fellow physicians? It's so easy when you're not there yourself. I wasn't there, I wasn't in on the case. There may be something I don't see recorded here.''

He came down off his high horse of certainty so quickly, I practically heard his heels screeching. Could he possibly be any use in the witness box?

"But you just said their conduct was criminal, Dr. Sweigert.''

He said quickly, "Off the record.''

I didn't try to hide my impatience. "Don't you have any sense of injustice, Doctor? No feeling those colleagues of yours didn't live up to the standards of your profession?''

Looking away from me, he locked his fine fingers together in some sort of agony. "These doctors practise in a small town.''

"There is one standard of care, Dr. Sweigert, whether you practise in Springwell or Seattle.''

"Yes, yes, I understand. But you must realize they don't have the access to the teaching, the sort of feedback we have here. They don't have residents and training programs.''

"So no one should have an operation outside of a large medical center? Is that what you're saying?''

"Of course not. That's not what I meant. Lawyers always twist words. Look, I'm not the defendant in this case."

"You wouldn't ever put yourself in such a position, would you, Doctor?" I laid my hand, palm downward, on Jordan Ambrose's hospital records. "Your standards are higher than these, aren't they, Dr. Sweigert?"

He seemed hypnotized by my hand. There was a long silence while he gazed at it; then he sighed, a sort of surrender. "My God, I would hope so. I hope I'd be able to diagnose and treat a case like this. Hell, I knew those classic symptoms when I was a second-year medical student."

"So you'll help me?"

I had many questions for Dr. Sweigert. I had to have some facts. I was fumbling around in the jungle of medicine, and so far I'd only received opinions.

He rearranged the papers on his already-immaculate desk, straightened the blotter, replaced the letter opener at an exact right angle to the blotter, then muttered, "Why did you come to me?"

"You're a well-respected pediatric surgeon—that's what I was told." I didn't mention Chauncey. "I fished around for a name and yours came up in my hand."

"There are plenty of others who'd make better witnesses than I would." I was prepared to believe that, but I'd liked his conviction when he thought he knew what was right and what was wrong. Feebly he said, "I wish you'd leave me out of it."

I smiled. Sympathetically, I hoped. "But that's life, Dr. Sweigert, isn't it? You can't be left out of it. That's what you deal with every day, isn't it—life and death? That's what we all have to deal with. Though I don't want to be philosophical, because it's not abstracts we're dealing with here. We're dealing with one specific death—Jordan Ambrose's. Five-year-old Jordan Ambrose. He didn't have time to get philosophical about life, did he?"

It was a while since I'd felt the cut and thrust of the courtroom under my belt, and I felt a dizzy rush of power as I attempted to inveigle young Sweigert with a Clarence Darrow act. "Look," I said, "I'm not accusing anyone—yet. I need some facts. I just want you to tell me, without condemnation, to the best of your medical knowledge, how it is that a healthy child can be admitted to a hospital and in that hospital get so sick that he dies of a straightforward, highly treatable illness. That's what you told me, isn't it? That the symptoms were straightforward? What is it that I'm asking that's so difficult?"

I didn't know how old he was. He had to be at least in his thirties, but he looked about twenty-four, insecure and unhappy and strangely unarrogant for a surgeon. "I just can't help putting myself in the place of those doctors," he said finally.

I nearly said, "Put yourself in the place of the parents," but I didn't. He wasn't a hostile witness and I needed his opinion as a surgeon, not as a parent. "Don't do that. Tell me how you would have gone about this case yourself. I'm not asking you to second-guess anyone. Tell me simply, so I can understand, what you'd have done that would have led you to a diagnosis. Because they never really made a diagnosis, did they?"

He fingered the case records with fastidious fingers, distressed. "To tell the truth, I could hardly bear to read these records. I pride myself on my profession, Mr. Richards. I studied hard to get into medical school. My wife worked to help me through my training. I earned a pittance as an intern. I was married and working ninety hours a week, busy saving someone else's life each time my wife gave birth to one of our children. My marriage fell apart because I was never at home with my wife and my children. All that, Mr. Richards, so I could acquire the expert knowledge to prevent a child like—what did you say his name was?"

"Jordan." I was half-afraid to interrupt and thereby let him talk himself out of it again. "Jordan Ambrose."

"So a child like Jordan Ambrose would get decent treatment, at least in my hands."

"Then you'll help me?" I persisted.

He sighed. "If you put it that way, I suppose I must."

It was rush hour when at last I drove out of Seattle. The freeway was clogged and very slow; rain dripped from clouds hanging about six inches above the thick stream of vehicles. Desperate for a drink, I considered waiting out the traffic in a bar, but the cheap joints near the freeway didn't appeal to me. Resigning myself to the car, I switched on the radio to get the road report, couldn't stand the commercials, turned the intrusive noise off, and thought about Sweigert. I'd won him over finally. No, the truth was, he'd won himself over. The struggle wasn't mine; it was his. Listening to his sob story, the story of his life interspersed with the facts of the case, I could hardly bear the thought of taking on another doctor. It had been a battle with Chauncey and a battle with Randolph Sweigert. Sweigert was on my side, but would I have the heart to make him testify? If I couldn't deal with him, outraged surgical knowledge and all, how was I going to manage the rest of them?

FOUR

WHEN I PULLED INTO the parking space beside my office, the lights were still streaming through the windows, which meant that Bella hadn't yet gone home. Sometimes it was hard to remember that just because Bella was there, it didn't mean my father was. Sometimes it was hard to remember Bella was *my* secretary now.

The rain fell in lashing gusts, soaking me in the few short yards to the door. On the door, the gold-leaf lettering still read RICHARDS AND RICHARDS, redone that way when my father talked me into joining him two years ago. Inside, Bella was tidying her already obsessively tidy desk, smoothing the cover on the computer, straightening the messages on the spike, making sure everything was neat and sterile, the way she liked it. She was dressed to go home, accusingly, raincoat buttoned all the way to the silk scarf at her throat, not a hair out of place in the same sleek hairstyle she'd worn ever since I first knew her. Bella herself hadn't changed in all those years: unmarried and childless, cool and efficient, somehow never young.

"Oh, Mr. Noah, you're back. Nothing important to report, just a few calls. They're here on the spike."

She removed my jacket from the back of a chair where I'd chucked it, shook the raindrops off, hung it on a hanger, and handed me the pink telephone slips as though I wouldn't find them myself. "Mrs. Carlsson called about an hour ago to invite you for dinner. Mrs. Ambrose wants to talk to you, and there's a call from Mr. Lance Todd, the attorney. Something to do with St. Mary's Hospital. Please return his call before you go home." She also seemed to believe I was incapable of reading the messages without her help. "Mr. Jack Probert wants to see you about updating his will, and Mr. Bigelow Harrison needs a real estate contract written up."

Bella had been father's secretary for the past fifteen years. She kept a proprietary hold on the practice, organizing me and the schedule and the books just as she had for him. I should have replaced her, politely, when he died, if only to make the practice seem like my own, but I didn't have the energy or the nerve or whatever it would have taken. Inertia had served as a motivation for a long time. The truth was that I couldn't manage without Bella, and the rest of the truth was that the practice would never seem like my own.

As I accepted the slips of paper from her, it occurred to me that the Ambrose case was one of the few not inherited from my father, and I was sure that fact had already occurred to Bella.

"Did Mrs. Carlsson say what they were having for dinner?"

Bella pursed her lips. "I wouldn't feel it my place to ask."

"As long as it isn't steak and kidney pie again. She seems to think it's my favorite thing. I haven't the heart to tell her I can't stand kidneys."

"It'd do you good, Mr. Noah. You look as though you need some decent food inside you, if you don't mind my saying so." I did, actually. Picking up the neat gray umbrella that matched her raincoat exactly, she announced, "Well, I'll be going now, Mr. Noah, if there's nothing else."

She always called me Mr. Noah, as if I wasn't quite worthy of the family name. I'd told her about it, but she hadn't taken any notice. Bella never took much notice of anything I said. She listened politely enough, but somehow she didn't hear me, as though she was expecting her true employer, my father, to come back from some mysterious

extended vacation. The only real innovation I'd effected in
the office in more than two years was to install a computer,
and even that met with serious resistance at first. After my
father died, I insisted Bella learn to use it, and now she
was a confirmed computer freak, excited about its capabil-
ities.

She put her hand on the door, her pale, earnest face glowing pink from the neon sign on the opposite side of the
street. "The answering machine is on, Mr. Noah. If you
can set the alarm before you leave?"

I held the door for her. As soon as it shut behind her, I
locked it and retreated to the inner office for a snort of the
scotch I kept in the lower drawer of my desk. The bottle
wasn't exactly hidden, just out of sight. Out of the clients'
sight but surely not out of Bella's.

I rang the Carlssons' house and Daphne answered.
Daphne was English, the reason she persisted in serving
steak and kidney pies. I put up with the pies because of
her radiant smile, kind heart, and nice English voice.

"Noah darling! Such a miserable day. Do come and eat
with us and cheer me up. Chauncey's seeing a patient at
the hospital and shouldn't be late, though he always says
that, of course. You might have to talk to me all evening."

I never minded talking to Daphne. It was other people I
wasn't too sure about. "Just the three of us?" I asked.

"Just us."

"It isn't that you don't have nice friends, Daphne. But
I'd prefer to do my own fixing up, you know."

"Well, I wish you'd get on with it."

She wasn't optimistic about my prospects for female
companionship, and she was right. I didn't have the heart.

"I've a few calls to make; then I'll be right over. And
thanks, Daffy."

"Don't call me that." She laughed, as usual, then hung
up.

I dialed the number for Todd and got a recording. Leaving my name, I poured another scotch, a smaller one. Reaction from the hospital had come quicker than expected. I wasn't ready to talk to them yet, but nothing is guaranteed to annoy more than unreturned phone calls. Jack Probert's will and Bigelow Harrison's real estate contract could wait until tomorrow. Sipping at the whisky, I called the Ambrose's number. The call was answered immediately by Angel, as though she'd been sitting and waiting for the phone to ring. She sounded brittle and cross, her way of speaking more foreign than Daphne's English accent.

"What's going on? I need some action, Mr. Richards."

"You'll have to be patient, Mrs. Ambrose. This will take time. Lots of time, I'm afraid. There's a great deal to learn before we can think of filing a suit. This could take months, you know." I should have said years. The wheels of the law grind very slowly, and expensively.

Once again, it was as though she could read my mind, even over the phone. "I don't care if it costs every penny we've got. I want those damn doctors to pay."

I'd explained it all before, the contingency basis, my fee coming out of any settlement. "You have to stop waiting, get on with your life, Mrs. Ambrose. Leave it to me now. I'll do my very best for you."

The righteous anger dissipated into pain, into plaintiveness. I thought perhaps anger was the easier emotion. "Joseph and me, we're really hurting, you know. I just want something to happen."

"I know," I said. "I understand." But I put down the phone knowing no one could begin to understand how they felt, the void that must be at the center of their lives. I had some inkling of the emptiness they had to live with every day, and I selfishly thanked heaven I'd never had a child to lose.

Entering the hours on the day sheet for Sweigert's interview, I wondered if I'd ever get compensated for my time. Contingency fees are all very well, but if a case never comes to fruition, it's time and effort down the drain. In the meantime, there would always be bills to pay.

At 6:30, a decent-enough hour to go to the Carlssons', I locked the office, remembered to set the alarm—though, God knows, there was nothing to steal—and crossed the street to the supermarket for a bottle of wine. Daphne and Chauncey lived farther along the same road that I lived on, in the same sort of comfortable old house. My house, like the practice, wasn't really mine, but my father's. The houses were built round the turn of the century—when Springwell was a flourishing lumber town—alongside the lake, where the lawyers and doctors and mill owners had always lived, north of the plants and the pervasive sulphuric odor of timber processing. The odor had gradually disappeared, together with the processors, and now only Bennetts remained to cut and shape raw logs into export lumber and occasionally stink us out when the wind changed direction.

As I came around the bend of the road, all the lights were on at the Carlssons' house. It glowed softly among the trees and the rain, an ideal welcome home at the end of the day. I envied Chauncey.

When I parked below the wide porch, the dogs raised their usual alarm. The front door opened, releasing a yellow stream of light to color the raindrops and glisten on the shiny planked surface of the steps. At the door, Daphne waited for me. She pulled the groveling animals away, put her face up for a kiss, and accepted the bottle of wine with feigned surprise. I always brought wine.

"Darling Noah, aren't you sweet? Chauncey isn't back yet. Don't you just hate November?"

Inside the house, alder logs crackled and flamed in the river-rock fireplace. The dogs collapsed, sighing, before the hearth, their brief sentinel duty done, and I stepped over them, spreading my hands to the flames. "November's fine in here," I said. "It's only outside that it's miserable."

Daphne was wearing a long flowery apron, and the flames and the lamps shone on her soft skin and hair. She looked good enough to eat. Chauncey, usually slow and deliberate in everything he did, had met her, a nurse in the hospital in England, when he was on a visiting fellowship, and he had snapped her up. It wasn't surprising he moved quickly for once.

"Help yourself to a drink, Noah. I'm drinking sherry, like a proper lady." She raised a small glass and the crystal winked in the firelight. "Here's to winter. May it go quickly."

I fixed myself another scotch at the cupboard in the corner that served as a bar, then filled the glass up with soda. I knew my way around their house as well as I did my own because I'd been coming here since I was a kid, when it belonged to Chauncey's parents. The old Victorian furniture had been replaced with English antiques and warm, soft colors, but the house felt as it always had, loving and nurturing. "Cheers!" Clinking my glass to Daphne's, I took a swallow of the whisky and suddenly didn't need any more of it.

I looked into my glass. "Sometimes I think I drink too much of this stuff."

Daphne sat on the sofa. The dogs reorganized themselves near her feet, and she absently caressed the nearest dog's ear. "I regard alcohol as a form of treatment in times of stress, don't you? Americans are so puritanical about it. I don't think you overdo it, Noah. You don't overdo many things."

Daphne was not judgmental, but she was watchful about my state of mind. "How've you been?" she asked. "Keeping busy?" It wasn't my professional activity that concerned her.

"Well, I'll tell you. Today, I went down to the big city. To interview a doctor in his big fancy office. Seattle's like a battlefield, mud everywhere, bulldozers thundering around like tanks. It used to be a nice, quiet, civilized town.''

She frowned at me. ''Not that malpractice case? You're not really going to take it on?''

So Chauncey had told her about it. ''First, I've got to explore the facts. Find out whether there is a case.''

''Malpractice is such a dirty business, Noah. Why do you have to soil your hands with it? Why don't you give it to one of the firms that specialize in that kind of thing?''

''Malpractice is no dirtier than any other side of the law, Daphne. Don't you believe people have a right to compensation when someone is negligent?''

She rubbed a foot against the furry side of one of the dogs, and it groaned in foolish gratitude. ''*Negligence* is a tough word, Noah. Medicine isn't an exact science. You should know that. Doctors are hardly ever sued in Britain. People have more respect for them there.''

''There aren't any contingency fees in Britain. Maybe that's why doctors don't get sued there.''

She made a face at me and, to her credit, laughed. ''Oh, that's a lawyer talking. You'd better have a jolly good case, Noah, or you won't win any points in this house, I can tell you.''

''I can hardly let that stand in the way, can I? It isn't as if Chauncey is involved.''

Horrified, she gasped. ''Noah! You wouldn't really take a case that involved Chauncey, would you?''

''I think I'd disqualify myself from that.''

''It'd break his heart if he got sued. And mine. He always does his best. I believe all doctors do the best they know how. It's just that things don't always work out perfectly. People aren't machines. You can't order new parts or oil something that's stuck.''

Standing with my back to the fireplace, the flames flickering on the comfortable room, the whole house seemed filled with a tangible sense of security. ''I wish I could talk this case over with you, Daffy. You were a nurse; you could tell me what you thought of the nurses' notes. They're the most striking thing on the record. But I shouldn't talk to you about it. Not unless I engage you as an expert witness.''

"Me, an expert about anything in this country? You've got to be kidding.'' When Daphne smiled, her whole face came alive, gray eyes alight, mouth widening and curving, tiny creases at the corners. "Well, if the nurses complained, then there might be something to it.'' She stood up and the apron fell around her ankles. Nice ankles, narrow, arching insteps. "I'd better see what's happening to the dinner.''

Casually, I asked, "What are we having?''

"Chicken.''

I breathed a small sigh of relief.

When she pulled the dish out of the oven, I declared it looked and smelled marvelous, which it did, and then poked my head through the door of the den. The boys were sprawled on the floor in pajamas, a noisy sitcom cacophony on television, and they were staring at it, mesmerized. Robbie was my godson, a small, skinny version of Chauncey, same floppy blond hair, same startling blue eyes and high Scandinavian cheekbones. His brother, Jeff, dark-eyed and dark-haired, was the inheritor of different genes. The boys reminded me of Chauncey and myself at their age, and as I stood in the doorway, admiring their graceful childhood awkwardnesses, the concentration in their clear eyes, I knew how I'd feel if something awful happened to either of them—something as awful as what happened to Jordan Ambrose. The thought jolted the breath out of my body and it was a moment before I could speak normally to them.

"Started skiing yet?''

"No snow,'' Robbie mumbled.

"Right. It's only November, isn't it? So what's up at school?''

His eyes glazed. "Not much.''

"Okay. I get it. You want me to leave?"

The matter of my staying or leaving obviously lacked interest for them. Their eyes turned back to the set, but I hovered over them a little longer, as though I might protect them from some unknown danger. Eventually, I closed the door and returned to the more stimulating company of their mother.

"Is it just me, or are they getting to be difficult conversationalists?"

Their mother laughed. "Be thankful for it. In the mornings, their mouths go nonstop."

"I guess if I had children of my own..." The words dropped heavily into the warm kitchen and I wished I hadn't spoken them.

Concentrating on something in a saucepan, Daphne didn't look at me. "You will someday, Noah."

"If you have your way, I will. And soon. At least you haven't invited anyone to dinner tonight with that in mind." She didn't take her eyes from the pan, and I was immediately suspicious. "Daphne! You didn't get me here under false pretenses again, did you?"

When she looked up, her face was flushed. "No, of course not. When did I ever lie to you, Noah?"

"Last week."

"I did not lie. I just didn't keep you fully informed, that's all."

"That's why people have to swear in court to tell the truth, the whole truth, and nothing but the truth."

"But then, we aren't in a courtroom, are we?"

"Did you or did you not ask anyone else to dinner tonight?"

A dimple appeared in the soft cheeks. "I did not."

"Why don't I trust you, Daphne?"

"Oh, Noah, I just want you to find someone nice. The world is full of wonderful women, just as alone as you. You're good-looking, you're kind and thoughtful, and you have a decent enough job, when you're not messing around with malpractice suits. It seems so silly to struggle on by yourself when you could make someone else happy.''

"So now I'm depriving some pathetic female of happiness by refusing to rush into another relationship?''

"*Relationship.* Such an overworked word. Anyway, who's talking about pathetic?''

"Daphne. Don't prevaricate. Don't plot; don't scheme. You want to know the truth?''

She lifted the wooden spoon to her lips, flicked at it with the tip of her tongue to taste the sauce, and rolled her eyes at me. "I don't know. When anyone says it like that, they usually have something unpleasant on their minds.''

"The truth is, I've already found the perfect girl for me.''

The pan went down with a clatter. "You have? Oh, Noah, that's wonderful! Someone I know?''

"There's just a slight snag. She's already married. Happily, I believe. To someone who also happens to be a friend of mine. Name of Chauncey Carlsson.'' It was said jokingly, of course, but in truth, I half-meant it. If Daphne were available, I wouldn't hesitate.

"Oh, Noah! Aren't you sweet?'' She chose not to make anything of it, but the tender flesh beneath her eyes went bright pink. She poured the sauce from the pan into a bowl. "Why can't you be serious?'' she said, and handed me the saucepan. Obediently, I took it to the sink and ran cold water into it.

"It's been two years. It's time, Noah.''

I swished at the copper pan with a brush until it was shining and clean and then washed the other things in the sink, a couple of white bowls with blue rims, a measuring cup, a carving knife. "If you'd let me live here with you and Chauncey and the kids, we could be a ménage à trois. Or would that be ménage à cinq? Not counting the dogs, of course. I'd promise to do all the washing up.''

She leaned against the kitchen sink and peered straight

into my eyes. I wished she wouldn't stand so close. Her flowery perfume made me feel a little dizzy.

"All right, so you don't want to talk about it. But wouldn't it be better if you did?"

I looked away. What was there to talk about? There was no mystery about Janet's death, a rapid and fatal leukemia that couldn't be stemmed even by taking her to Seattle to the Fred Hutchinson Cancer Center, world-renowned for treatment of the disease. A painful bone-marrow transplant hadn't worked. I'd quit the law firm in Los Angeles to stay with her, and it had been some sort of solace to move in with my father. But talking about it just left me exhausted. First Janet's death, then my father's. The two people I cared most about in the world.

I was rescued from Daphne's solicitations by the sound of Chauncey's car. The clatter of his feet on the wooden porch and his voice greeting the dogs fractured the cosy domesticity in the kitchen. For a while, it had seemed just like my own home.

FIVE

ST. MARY'S HOSPITAL, high on a hill above the edge of town, had a wonderful view over Puget Sound. But it was a square white nothing sort of place, a little run-down, like the rest of Springwell, a slapdash air about it, as though nothing of importance ever happened there. I couldn't imagine patients checking in with any kind of confidence.

I wanted to get the feel of it, walk the corridors, take a look at the place where Jordan Ambrose had been a patient. I hadn't been inside a hospital since Janet died, and as soon as I was through the doors, I wished I'd kept away. St. Mary's was as different from the Hutch as a minor-league ballpark from Fenway Park, but it was still pervaded by the same sickly hospital disinfectant, the same odor of forced conviviality and real desperation. I would never understand why anyone wanted to be a doctor or a nurse.

No one challenged me as I walked less than purposefully through the battered front entrance and along the hallway. No reason they should, of course. Dozens of people wander around hospitals all day. But I'd worn my country lawyer suit just in case, Brooks Brothers, tweedy and slightly shabby, unthreatening but authoritative. I waited at the elevator with a group of relatives and a nurse's aide in a white dress and white shoes who should have taken the stairs for the exercise. I knew she was a nurse's aide because the label on one huge breast said so. Patients' relatives are easily recognizable; they have the anxious, awed look that goes with the territory, a wariness, an expectation of bad news. Though perhaps that was just a projection of my own fears and expectations.

As the elevator doors creaked open, a spotty youth with

a baseball cap and a foolish dazed expression rushed in
with us and announced with astonishment, as though even
he couldn't believe what he was saying. "We just had a
baby. A boy. Eight pounds six ounces." He might have
been let out of junior high especially for the occasion.

The nurse's aide shrieked. "Oh, my, now isn't that wonderful?"

The little group of relatives muttered and clucked among
themselves. An elderly woman, carrying a stiff arrangement
of yellow flowers in a green glass vase, pronounced dole-
fully, "The Lord giveth even as He taketh away," and the
boy looked more confused. He said, "His name's Darrell,
same as mine."

"Darrell. That's a real nice name," the fat aide enthused,
and when the child father got off at the next floor, she
called after him, "You take care of that little son of yours
now, you hear?" She smiled happily and plumply, small
eyes disappearing in the flesh of her cheeks. "Isn't that
nice? It's always so nice to hear about babies."

I'd forgotten babies were born at St. Mary's, that it
wasn't just a place where children died. One of the relatives, a man in a blue-and-green Seahawks cap, cleared his
throat as if to spit. "He don't look old enough to be drinking beer, let alone fathering a kid," and the young woman
with him said scathingly, "I don't see what drinking beer
has got to do with it." He leered at her. "You wouldn't."
He took the older woman's arm and got off at the third
floor. We all got out together.

I knew it was on the third floor that Jordan Ambrose had
been a patient. I knew the name of the nurses who had
taken care of him, the ones on the day shift and the ones
on the night shift: L. E. Watson and J. D. Barnes and A.
Swetman. If I happened to run into any of them, I didn't
plan to talk to them—not yet. I merely wanted to see what
they looked like, what the place looked like. In a way, I
felt I already knew those nurses from the agonized notes

they'd written—particularly L. E. Watson. It was as if she'd written in red ink all over the pages, "Help! Help! Help!" Not that there was anything unprofessional about her notes, but I judged L. E. Watson and her colleagues to be allies in the case of *Ambrose v. St. Mary's Hospital, Dr. Carl Woods et al.*—when and if it came to that.

Directly opposite the elevator was the nurses' station, a three-sided arrangement of blue Formica counters, telephones, and chart racks, cupboards and chairs grouped behind. A fresh-faced girl with an ear clamped to a phone flicked incurious eyes at us as we emerged from the elevator in a group. Two nurses in white polyester pantsuits, stethoscopes hooked around their necks, pored over charts at the back of the station; an aide wheeled an IV stand into the glass cubicle behind them. Everything seemed calm, under control, normal hospital stuff. It made me shudder. I'd spent too many days and nights of despair in a place very much like this.

The relatives headed off down the corridor as though they knew where they were going. I followed more slowly, glancing in at the rooms as I passed. Most of the rooms had one or two names in the slot beside the door, and I caught glimpses of metal-framed beds, heaped coverlets, and television sets booming pap into the stuffy, soporific air. An old man in a terry-cloth robe shuffled by with a walker, carpet slippers scuffing, his face screwed into an expression that seemed to say the effort wasn't worth the trouble. My fellow travelers from the elevator were crowded into one room together, awkwardly, silently staring toward a bed whose occupant was out of my sight. After half a dozen more rooms, the corridor angled. I went around the corner, past a sluice room and a dressing station, and found the same arrangement of rooms stretching away to another nurses' station. On the left, a room seemed to be empty, no names in the slot, smooth, undisturbed white covers on the beds, so I stepped cautiously inside. It was a standard hospital room, two beds separated by a curtain on a runner, lockers by the beds, silent gaping television sets overhead, a sink in a corner, a toilet behind a door. The metal-framed windows had a long view down the hill, across dark treetops and over the town to the Sound. The water in the distance was pewter gray and white-capped, the shapes of the islands vague among sullen clouds. Standing at the window, gazing out, I remembered it was September when Jordan Ambrose was here, and I tried to think how different this view would have looked then. I wondered if he had ever looked out of this window as he lay dying. I wondered if Angel Ambrose leaned her head against this same cold glass and prayed for him.

I thought I didn't need this. I would find someone else to take the case.

From behind me, a crisp voice said, "Are you looking for something?"

I hadn't heard a footstep. I turned, almost guiltily. A young woman in a short white uniform and white stockings, straight fair hair knotted into a braid, was standing in the doorway, her hands on her hips. She was small and narrow-waisted and had smooth, shining skin, the very embodiment of health and professionalism. Immediately, I recognized she was my ally; her name tag read L. E. WATSON, R.N. She was so unexpectedly fresh, pretty, and young that she brought a surprised, involuntary smile to my face. In my mind's eye, L. E. Watson had been middle-aged, gray-haired, and motherly.

"Can I help you?" She frowned at me, apparently trying to decide whether it was sympathy or discipline I needed.

"As a matter of fact..." Hesitating, I threw aside my careful plan not to speak to anyone. "As a matter of fact, I was looking for you, Ms. Watson."

"For me?" Her eyes were hazel-colored and had dark flecks in them, beguiling eyes, their gaze direct and open even as they regarded me with caution and some suspicion.

"You weren't likely to find me in an empty room, were you? Why didn't you try the nurses' station?"

I attempted some rusty, unused charm. "Because I hadn't exactly planned on talking to you yet. But as you've appeared before me so miraculously, perhaps you could spare me a few minutes."

"Are you a drug rep? We don't deal with salesmen on the floors. You'll have to go to the nursing office, or the pharmacy."

Obviously, the charm wasn't working. Her manner was very brusque, and cool.

"I'm not a drug salesman." I offered my card, and she took it reluctantly. From the way she squinted at it, I judged she was slightly shortsighted, an appealing mix of capability and vulnerability.

She read the card and looked up with another frown. "An attorney? Why would an attorney be looking for me?"

"Because I'm the plaintiff's lawyer in the case of *Ambrose* versus *St. Mary's.*" I was, as of that moment.

"*Ambrose* versus…" The flecked eyes widened and she pressed her lips together. "You mean…Jordan Ambrose? The little black boy?"

"Yes, Ms. Watson. I mean that little boy."

Putting a hand over her mouth, she stared at me, shock and horror in the hazel eyes. For a moment, it seemed as though she was going to burst into tears, the eyes melting and swimming, a hectic pink flooding her cheeks; then she blinked quickly and made her hand into a fist, clutching it close to her lips. Her knuckles were white against her flushed face. She swallowed hard and at last she muttered, stammering a little, "There's going to be a case involving the hospital?"

"Very probably. The parents want to know what happened to their child, Ms. Watson. He died right here in this hospital and they don't understand why. What do you think happened to him?''

She fiddled nervously with the stethoscope at her neck, turned her face away so only the curve of her cheekbone and the nape of her neck, pale and vulnerable under the thick swatch of hair, were visible to me. ''I don't think I should talk to you about it.''

''Why not? You were there. You have nothing to hide, do you? Your notes are in his records. It can't be any surprise to you that the parents want to sue.''

As though she was thinking about it, she was silent for a moment. Then she said faintly, ''No. No, I'm not surprised. But I'm sure that I... You should get permission to speak to me about it. I'm just an R.N. I'm not the doctor in charge of his case. You're a lawyer, so you must know about that sort of thing.''

''I can talk to whom I wish when I'm preparing a suit.''

''Yes, but my...my position?''

She seemed absurdly threatened. Surely not by me? As if needing some kind of physical support, she sagged against the metal rail of the bed nearest the door, clenched and unclenched her hands, then wiped them down the front of the white uniform. ''I felt very bad about Jordan, Mr...um.'' She blinked at my card and brought it close to her eyes.

''Richards. Noah Richards.''

''Mr. Richards. But I don't want to talk about it. Not now, not here. I'm not sure I should talk to you about it at all, not...not before I've discussed it with...'' She gazed at me with despair. ''If you're going to sue the hospital, doesn't that mean I'd be involved, too?''

''You'll be asked to give evidence about those progress notes you wrote. You took care of him, after all. Your notes are very compelling, Ms. Watson. I'd like to ask you about all those calls you made to the doctors. Why no one came to see him.''

I waited for her to say something more, but she appeared stricken into silence.

I said, "Who do you think you have to talk to before you speak to me?"

She shook her head violently. Strands of fine blond hair floated out of the braid at the back of her neck. "I'm not sure. I'm not sure what happens under these circumstances. I've never been involved with anything like this."

My card fluttered out of her hand to the floor. She stared down at it and bent over the rail of the bed as though in pain, the color washed out of her face, her cheeks hollowed into such startling pallor, I thought she was going to faint.

Catching hold of her arm, I could feel the soft flesh above her elbow trembling under my hand. "I'm sorry," I said, and I was. "I didn't know it would upset you like this. We can talk anytime."

"Please, please don't ask me."

"There's nothing to be so alarmed about, Ms. Watson. Really. You have nothing to be afraid of."

But alarm and fear were what I smelled on her, and that confused me. Testifying in any form worried many people, but to this degree? I stooped to pick the card up off the floor and pressed it back into her hand, folding the unresisting fingers over it. "Why don't you call my office when you're ready to tell me your side of the story. You can call anytime. Will you do that?"

Taking a shuddering breath, she disengaged herself from me, her lips drawn into a thin line. Now she was so close, I could see she wasn't quite as young as I'd thought at first. The tiny lines around her eyes and mouth probably meant she was nearer thirty than twenty. But her skin was fine and clear like that of a girl in high school and her breath smelled sweet and fresh.

"Nobody's going to sue you," I reassured her. "Trust me."

I kept reassuring people, people like Chauncey and

Daphne and now this young woman, that I wasn't going to
sue them, when I was sure as hell planning to sue somebody. What point was there in being a lawyer if one didn't
have the stomach to take anyone to court?

She looked me full in the face. The fetching eyes had
thick fair lashes lightly brushed with mascara. If her face
hadn't been so tight with anxiety, it would have been soft,
and bright, and engaging. "Trust a lawyer? Is that wise?"
A small attempt at a smile didn't reach her eyes.

"You have to trust somebody, sometime."

As though she was chilled, she shivered and clutched her
arms together. "Trust is a funny thing, Mr. Richards. You
think you can trust someone and then you find yourself let
down. I need my job. I can't afford to upset the applecart.
None of us can." Backing away from me, she was poised
to run.

"You think you'd lose your job if you told me what
happened here with Jordan Ambrose? Why do you think
that?"

She was almost out the door.

"You're a material witness, Ms. Watson; no one can
prevent you from testifying. It's your duty to tell the truth,
the whole truth, and it's something you'll have to do if I
depose you." My words sounded pompous and belligerent,
not at all the way I wanted them to sound, not persuasive
and encouraging and reassuring. "Who did you mean by
'none of us'? The other nurses? Barnes and Swetman?"

A breath seemed to catch her throat. "Barnes and Swetman? Have you talked to them? Have you seen Nita
Barnes?"

"I haven't talked to anyone else. Not yet."

"Perhaps you should first *find* Nita."

"Find her? Why do you say it like that? Is she missing?"

Ms. Watson hesitated again, watching her words. Everything she said was being dragged out of her, reluctantly,
cautiously. "Nita hasn't been to work since that child died.

No one knows where she is. But I'm not suggesting anything, you know. She was very upset about it and she didn't ever come back, that's all.''

"She gave notice?"

"Not as far as I know. Why don't you talk to the nursing office?"

"I will. What about Swetman? Is she around?"

"Oh, yes, she's around. Why don't you talk to her?"

"I will. I'll talk to all of you."

She stared at me again, silently, then brushed the back of her hand against her forehead, her face pale and strained. "I must get back to work; they'll be wondering where I've gone."

"Ms. Watson, will you come and see me?"

"Perhaps. Perhaps not."

"I can always get a deposition, you know. You can always be called as a witness."

"Perhaps you'll have to do that."

"Don't make me do that." I wanted L. E. Watson on my side, not forced to testify as a reluctant witness. I certainly didn't want to have to bully and browbeat her. But she wasn't waiting to hear any more of my arguments. She fled the room—suddenly, whisking herself out of there like an apparition, a frightened apparition.

I hadn't even found out what the L.E. stood for.

SIX

ON THE WAY BACK from the hospital, I stopped in at Joe's Tavern for lunch. I'd been going to Joe's for lunch since I was old enough to drink legally, and even before. Joe's was an institution in Springwell, built around the turn of the century, when timber was a booming industry, and the scent of pine tar still lingered in the wide-planked floors, in the rough log walls. Huge handsaws hung on those walls from the days when logging was real men's work; they bore the brief history of the trade in razor-sharp teeth, in handles worn smooth by the sweat of men not so long dead. The saws were for decoration only now and were festooned with cobwebs, an indication of the state of the trade. Logging and fishing, the industries that built the Northwest, were disappearing fast, most of the old-growth forests gone and most of the salmon.

But it was quiet and warm in the large dim space at Joe's, with no jukeboxes or video machines to shatter the calm, and they knew what kind of beer I liked.

I sat on a cracked vinyl stool at the long bar and thought about L. E. Watson, about the fear in those beguiling flecked eyes, fear that was surely about something more than losing her job. Nurses could always get other jobs, even now, when nursing had also hit hard times. And what had she meant about the other nurse, Barnes? Find her, she'd said, as though it would be a challenge. It couldn't be that difficult. Springwell wasn't an easy place to hide in.

Without warning, a hand slapped me on the back. Startled, I spun on the stool and was more than a little surprised to find Lance Todd, attorney-at-law, standing behind me, grinning as though he'd run into a long-lost friend. Bon-homie oozed from him. Todd was as prominent an attorney as Springwell could boast of, and Joe's was much too downscale for him. And he was hardly my friend.

"Well, well, Noah Richards! Good to see you. Amazing we don't bump into each other more often, isn't it?" Clasping my hand firmly, he kneaded my shoulder with the other, pinning me to the stool. "Care to join me for a bite of lunch? Chew the fat."

I'd no particular desire to chew the fat with Todd. We hadn't met more than half a dozen times, and certainly not since he'd outwitted me in a real estate deal awhile back. Those negotiations still smarted. In my opinion, Todd's demands had smacked of greed and avarice and had killed my client's hopes of developing the property. He'd done neither my client nor his any favors by trying to get blood out of a stone. And then I remembered it was Todd who'd called about St. Mary's. I realized it was not mere happenstance that we'd bumped into each other so fortuitously.

I considered the offer of lunch for a moment. "Okay," I said. "Why not?"

He waved me over to one of the tables against the wall; I picked up my beer and followed obediently. Todd was the sort of man used to being obeyed. Fifty something, tall and lean and effortlessly patrician in his pale gray suit, buttoned-down shirt, and striped tie, he looked completely out of place in Joe's. In Joe's, he surely had to be at less of an advantage than in his own office.

Pulling out the heavy wooden chairs, we faced each other across the table. Todd smiled comfortably, leaned back in his chair, eased the knot of his correct tie, and gazed around with an air of interest. "Don't get in here too often. Not much of a tavern man myself. You know, Noah, I'd be more than happy to put you up for membership at the golf club."

"Thank you," I said politely. "But I'm not into golf."

His teeth were even and white and he had an expensive tan, a tan probably acquired on a course in Palm Springs or Hawaii. "You know very well that golf isn't the only purpose of a golf club, Noah. A golf club is somewhere for attorneys in small towns to find clients."

Suzie, the waitress, wearing a tiny tight skirt that would have been indecent on anyone a month or two older, bounced up to the table with a menu. Somehow Todd avoided looking at her legs.

"What'll you have, Noah? Lunch is on me."

"Thanks, but I'll buy my own. Always do. Try the chili; it's first-rate."

He sighed gently. "I don't have the digestion of a young man like you." He gazed briefly at the menu. "Make mine a roast beef sandwich, dear. On whole wheat. And a cup of coffee."

Suzie said, "The usual, Mr. Richards? Bowl of chili and a Heineken?"

"You've got it, Suzie."

Todd raised his eyebrows in amusement. "Apparently, they know you in here."

"It's very convenient to my office."

He placed neat gray elbows on the table and leaned close enough for me to smell aftershave lotion. Aftershave was unusual in Joe's. "Still in your father's old office, Noah? How's it going? Practice doing well?"

I shrugged. "It's a living."

Concerned sympathy creased the handsome face. "I was very sorry about your father, Noah. He should have had many more years in him. Such a loss to the community. And to you, of course. Still, it must have been a comfort to have had you in with him those last couple of years. He was a well-respected man around here. There's surely a lot of goodwill for you to capitalize on. Business could be a bit slow for a new man in town."

"You're forgetting I grew up in Springwell," I said.

"But you've been gone a long time. You were in L.A., weren't you?"

"L.A.," I agreed.

"You went to UCLA, didn't you?"

I couldn't imagine how he knew. "Yes, for law school."

"And then you were with Buckins and Brent, I understand. A fine firm. Your father used to speak of you proudly. Didn't you specialize in tax law?"

He knew a hell of a lot more about my career than was comfortable. I could hardly imagine my father exchanging little family confidences with Todd or anyone else. Obviously, he'd been checking up on me.

"Corporate tax," I said. "Very dull."

He sighed again. "I'd like a bit of dull corporate law myself, but Springwell's hardly the place to find that kind of practice anymore, is it? I'm surprised you haven't moved on by now, Noah. You could take your experience down to Seattle and they'd be falling over themselves to get someone like you. If ever you need any names, I'd be glad to help."

If ever I needed any names, I wouldn't be asking Lance Todd for them.

"You haven't moved on," I pointed out. "There must be enough business to keep you here."

"Ah, well. A few loyal clients, you know. Anyway, I'm much too old to leave now, whereas you've all your professional life in front of you. If I were a young man like you, I'd be thinking about somewhere else. Yes, it's very sad what's happening to our little town, Noah. Though if we pull together as a community, we may be able to attract new business to replace the old. I hear there's a chance one of the big names in computers might set up an offshoot within the city limits. Think of that, Noah. We could have a new Silicon Valley right here on our own doorstep."

For all his lawyer's suit and button-down collar, he seemed perfectly at ease on what I considered my turf. I made the effort to use his first name. He certainly used mine enough. "So, Lance, was there something particular you wanted to chew the fat about?"

Suzie flounced back to us in her tiny little skirt, plonked down a thick white mug, poured coffee for him in a dark frothing stream. He pried open the plastic container of cream with fastidious fingers and waited until she was out of earshot. "I'm sure you know what it's about, Noah."

He didn't hurry, stirring the coffee slowly, sipping at it. "It is, of course, about that unfortunate business of the child at St. Mary's. I hear you sent for the records."

At last we were getting down to it. "It was an unfortunate business, wasn't it? You're counsel for St. Mary's?"

"I'm privileged to serve in that capacity. Many local citizens are involved with the hospital in some way or another. Your mother, for example. How many years was she on the board of trustees?"

Surprised, I tried not to show it. "I've forgotten." I wasn't sure I'd ever known. My mother never made a big deal out of anything she did.

"Very civic-minded, your parents, Noah. Your father led that drive some years ago for the new operating suite at the hospital, you remember? Yes, of course you must. It took months of work on his part, a wonderful effort. That's the sort of leadership we lack nowadays. I'm sure we can look forward to equal involvement by you in the not-too-distant future." Pausing tactfully, he cleared his throat. "Of course, we're all aware of the recent tragedies in your life, and it takes a while to get over that kind of loss. But perhaps one day?"

"Perhaps one day."

"Good, good. Pulling together is essential in a small community like Springwell. And immensely rewarding."

Suzie arrived with the chili and beer and Todd's roast beef sandwich, and hovered for a hopeful moment. "Can I get you gentlemen anything more?"

He examined the sandwich, skewered with a toothpick and piled high with thin slices of beef, smiled at her dazzlingly. "This looks perfect, my dear." Unused to such polite charm, she retreated, giggling nervously.

"Of course," he continued smoothly—Todd was nothing if not smooth—"it's never been too difficult to raise money for the hospital. The town's always been very proud of it." He cut a delicate corner off the teetering mound. "And rightly so. Our hospital fulfills a vital need. It's been here forever. Most of the people in Springwell were born right there at St. Mary's. You were probably born there yourself, Noah."

The constant and somehow condescending use of my first name, as though he was my elder and better, was definitely beginning to grate on me.

"As a matter of fact, I was born in New York. My father met my mother at Columbia. They married as students and lived in romantic poverty."

He shook his head without disturbing a hair. "I'm disappointed. I thought you were a native northwesterner, born and bred. Like me."

I should have kept my mouth shut. "Now, Todd, as you were saying. About this case?"

He chewed thoughtfully. "It's not exactly a case yet, is it, Noah? Not until a suit is filed. I do hope you're not thinking of that. Communities like ours have a hard enough time keeping their hospitals these days. Life's tough for them, as it is for all of us. We're all in the same boat, aren't we? Struggling to make ends meet." Putting down his fork, he leaned close again, wrapping the two of us in a bond that must have appeared, to a casual observer, like professional camaraderie. "And you should think about the implications for yourself, Noah. Suing the local hospital is an uncomfortable situation for a local attorney. People are fond of their institutions. They can get upset when someone levels unwarranted criticism at them."

I gazed back steadily. "You surely can't think it unwarranted criticism to question the death of a five-year-old in the operating room?"

"A terribly sad incident. Believe me, I'm not disagreeing about that. But I think you'll find that nothing the hospital did contributed to that poor child's death."

"Have you read the records?"

"Of course. Naturally, there has to be an investigation of an incident like that. As counsel for the hospital, I've certainly read the record."

"Then I'm amazed you think you can defend St. Mary's. Everyone concerned botched everything from the beginning. Didn't make a diagnosis, waited until the child was so sick he couldn't tolerate an operation. The facts speak for themselves, Lance. Nothing about that child's treatment went right. What do you have to say about the surgery? About the surgeon?"

He frowned. "The surgeon?"

"Yes, the surgeon. Carl Woods."

"Oh, yes, Carl Woods." His eyes, briefly cautious, warmed to an open, frank gaze. "Carl Woods is a fine man, Noah, been in practice here for many years. He's due to retire next year. The board of trustees plan a big celebration for his retirement, they value him so highly. I'd like to think he'll be able to retire peacefully after so many years of service to the community."

"Peaceful retirement? You think that's what he deserves?"

He nodded emphatically. "I think that's what he deserves."

"He's a friend of yours, of course."

"He's my client, and also a friend. He's a friend of a lot of people around here, Noah." He paused. "Your father, for example."

I hope I kept the dismay out of my face. Suggestions of friendship with my father could only muddy the waters.

"It could be very tough bringing a suit against Dr. Woods in this town, Noah. There'd be a lot of sentiment for him and a great deal against the person suing him."

I washed the chili down with some beer. "Are you warning me off?"

Again he flashed the charmed smile. "Of course not. I wouldn't dream of such an idea. Just pointing out some of the difficulties you might face, that's all."

"Tell me," I asked, "what exactly have you said to the nurses?"

"The nurses? I haven't discussed anything with the nurses."

"You're telling me you haven't even asked them what happened? Haven't tried to find out what went on for three days with a child who died under their care?"

"It's not appropriate to talk to them, not unless a suit is filed. Which there won't be, will there?"

"You'd never want a case like this to come to trial, would you? Everyone would be anxious to settle out of court first. Without the unfavorable publicity."

He sighed forbearingly, as though he was dealing with a neophyte. Which he was, of course. "You know, Noah, hospitals and doctors are awfully tired of being threatened with nuisance lawsuits brought to frighten them into a big settlement. There's definite sentiment against settling these days. Plaintiffs' lawyers count on quick settlements, of course. It's expensive to bring a case, all those expert witnesses to pay, all those pretrial depositions, all that investigation. Consider the practicalities, Noah. Not just the upset and difficulties. How many cases are won in court? One out of ten, is it? Doctors and hospitals have their malpractice insurers looking out for them, paying their lawyers by the hour. Doesn't hurt them to drag it out, but it hurts the plaintiffs. And if a case does get to court and if by chance it's won, well, I'm sorry to say the death of a child doesn't warrant too much in the way of damages." He smiled again, sadly this time, and pushed aside the remains of his sandwich. "It hardly seems worth it, does it?"

I knew what he was saying was the truth, every word of it. The odds were always stacked against the plaintiff. And poor little Jordan Ambrose wouldn't warrant much in the way of punitive damages, especially now he was dead. If he'd survived, alive but damaged, it might have been a different matter.

I said thoughtfully, "The wrongful death of a child would probably fetch a million in this state."

He was shocked at my suggestion. "Noah, Noah! This isn't California. A hundred thousand is the most you could hope to get."

I was dutifully shocked in return. "A hundred thousand! For a wrongful death?"

"It's reality, Noah. Think who we're talking about here. A little black kid. What actuarial prospects does a black kid have? Rightly or wrongly, even in this state, a jury isn't going to award big damages to a black family. The young black male," he said, sighing once more, "is just not a good prospect. If I was thinking of bringing a case like this to trial, I'd be afraid a jury might decide this was just another kid who'd have grown up to sell guns and deal drugs."

We gazed politely at each other. I had to bite my tongue not to be rude to him. He was dealing, I knew that, and it was in my client's interests, as the books say, to listen to him, but I didn't want to listen to what he was saying. I understood the tactics but resented the implications. There was a right and there was a wrong. What happened to Jordan Ambrose was wrong and what Todd was offering now was insulting.

I wiped my mouth with the paper napkin. At the golf club, there'd have been cloth napkins. "If Jordan Ambrose had been allowed to grow up, he would have had many options. This isn't the Deep South of forty years ago and this wasn't a kid who'd have ended up on the streets. His father served in the military for twenty years, a Vietnam veteran. Now he's a supervisor at Bennetts. His mother is young and smart as a whip. This isn't a welfare family, Todd; it's your middle-class American family. They have perfectly good medical insurance, and if only because of that, their child was entitled to decent treatment. Who's going to get up in court and say these people aren't worthy citizens? I'll try the case in Seattle. They have a black mayor there. A lawyer, Todd, just like you and me.''

He shrugged, unimpressed. ''It wasn't very good insurance, you know.''

I stared at him. ''What?''

''Their medical coverage wasn't great. Some of those veterans' programs are distinctly lacking. It covered only thirty percent of the hospital bills. They should have gone to a veterans' hospital.''

''Oh, for God's sake!'' Getting to my feet, I pulled a wad of crumpled dollars out of my back pocket, threw a few on the table. ''Lunch is on me. I'll be able to afford it out of the damages we get.''

SEVEN

DOWNTOWN SPRINGWELL, all eight blocks of it, was washed in thin sunlight, the tree-lined streets too quiet for early afternoon—another ominous sign of economic malaise. Those streets were so familiar to me, I'd long ago stopped seeing them. It was an effort now to recall the Springwell of my childhood, the crowded stores, all those people on these same streets who knew me or my family. "Hi, Noah," passersby would call out. "How are you doing?" Or someone I didn't recognize would say, "You're Jonathan Richard's boy, aren't you? Sure look like him."

Nowadays, the sidewalks were empty and the cars going by were driven by strangers.

Occasionally, of course, I did run across somebody I recognized, or who recognized me. Older folk, mainly, parents of a distant, forgotten buddy. Now and then, someone my own age, dimly remembered from high school, greeted me with surprise in the grocery store or waved uncertainly across the street—a guy from the football team, a girl I may once have fancied, able to recall my face because they'd stayed home and not cluttered their memories with other places, other faces. But most of my contemporaries had left Springwell, gone to seek their fortune, or just a job, elsewhere. Those who'd stayed were the least memorable, the ones without ambition, their lives and mine having drifted so far apart, we could tell instantly we had nothing in common anymore. Of the real friends from back then, only Chauncey had deliberately returned. My own return was inadvertent.

The stores of my childhood memory had disappeared, too, like the friends from high school, like the salmon and the old-growth forests. A large Sears once stood at the corner of Main and Spruce, where everyone for miles around shopped for furniture, lawn mowers, and appliances. The building still existed, but it was chopped up now into cramped spaces full of tourist-type junk—T-shirts, carved seagulls on logs, plastic Indian totem poles. There were few tourists in August and none in November, and the bored purveyors of the junk stared through the smudged plate-glass windows, waiting for a decent hour to close up and go home. The sporting-goods store, an Aladdin's cave of rods and lures, spinners and reels, where we had renewed our fishing tackle and licenses every spring, had metamorphosed into a Dairy Queen; the bookstore on the other corner had faded into oblivion years ago, together with the teenage youths who'd lurked behind its stacks, hoping to pick up girls. Now such teenagers as there were in town looked for girls at the mall five miles away. The turn-of-the-century courthouse, a crumbling echo of the city Springwell had once hoped to become, was desperately in need of paint; the supermarket parking lot opposite my office was always half-empty.

Springwell was dying. In the last few years, a vital community had deteriorated into fast-food joints and second-rate retailers. It was no sort of place to have a law practice. Two years was enough. It was high time to pick up sticks, before casting myself into the financial pit of a lawsuit against the local docs. Money wasn't my problem. I'd made good money in L.A., and the ill winds that blew apart my family had left me financially secure. God knows, I hadn't wanted those inheritances, but it was resources such as those that would have to carry the long burden of a lawsuit like the Ambroses'. Someone and something had to pay for the months of work.

Up on the hill, the white bulk of St. Mary's loomed over the town. Todd was right again when he said the community needed it. I wondered about the state of its financial health.

It was time to talk to the Ambroses once more.

Back in the office, Bella was eating lunch at her desk, a small plastic container of salad, a carton of skim milk placed square in the middle of a paper napkin. Dutiful and alone, she was poised for action that might never come. The heavy responsibility for her weighed on me. Though why should I feel responsible? She didn't have to stay; she was quite as capable as I was of finding somewhere else to go. But the manner in which she chewed the Spartan food, the compulsive arrangement on her desk, and the barriers she'd drawn around herself made me aware, for the first time, that she might be equally as devastated by the upheavals in our little world as I was. I'd been too concerned about my own well-being to be concerned about hers. For fifteen years, Bella had been safe in this little cocoon. Maybe, after all, I *had* inherited a family retainer, someone for whom I'd be responsible for the rest of my life—or hers.

Rattling the door shut, guiltily, I told her, "You should take an hour off for lunch. Get out for some fresh air."

"In November? Where would I go? Anyway, someone should be here to answer the phone."

"Has anyone called?"

"No."

But there was a certain smug expression in her eyes. Carefully folding the paper napkin away with the container and the milk carton, she pulled a weighty bundle of files tied with red ribbon out of a drawer and pushed it across the desk toward me.

"You might be interested in this, Mr. Noah. It was among your father's papers."

I stared at it, and the typed title on the brown cover leapt out at me. Not the plaintiffs, whose names I didn't recognize, Arthur Westing, husband of Pamela Westing, deceased. No, it was the defendants' names that made my heart jump. Carl H. Woods and St. Mary's Hospital.

"What's this?"

"This is a malpractice case, Mr. Noah."

"One of my father's?"

"Yes. He brought that case against your same Dr. Woods."

"But I didn't think he ever dealt with malpractice."

She shrugged her narrow shoulders. "It was before my time, and we never had another. You're right—such cases weren't his preference. But I remembered seeing the papers, so I searched the storeroom for them."

Father's preferences were wills, probate, and real estate. "Gentlemen's stuff," he called it. The hurly-burly of the courtroom, the uncertainties, the pressures, and the deadlines were not for him. Nor did he care for the type of clients or the judges one had to deal with in a courtroom.

I flipped through the pages. "Did this go to trial?"

"The case was settled. Your father only spoke about it once, when we were reorganizing the files for storage. He told me the patient's husband was old and wouldn't have lived long enough to collect if they'd gone to trial. He didn't, either. He died just a few months later."

The pages and pages of records were too numerous and involved to grasp the essentials immediately. "What was the basis of the claim?"

"A gallbladder operation that went wrong. The surgeon cut something he shouldn't have and didn't find out until it was too late." The subject seemed distasteful to her, beyond the realm of polite conversation. "Not that I pretend to know anything about medicine. I was brought up a Christian Scientist."

Christian Scientist? Dear God!

Smoothing her immaculate hair with two hands, Bella leaned forward on the desk and looked up at me, the smugness gone from her cool eyes. "Mr. Noah, I've been reading the hospital record about that little boy. That poor little boy. It was terribly upsetting—didn't you think so? Why didn't anyone listen to the nurses? If they'd listened, they surely could have saved him, couldn't they?'' Quite suddenly, her eyes filled with tears, a startling sight. I'd never seen Bella anywhere close to crying, not even at my father's funeral. Her face that day had been tight and controlled, too proud for tears. Now, blinking and sniffing, she turned to hide such vulnerability from me. ''No one did anything until it was too late, did they? That's like Christian Scientists, sitting around and praying, expecting God to save someone. It doesn't work, Mr. Noah. Believe me, I know.''

I dared not ask what particular tragedy she was referring to.

''Are you going to take the case, Mr. Noah?''

''I don't know. I haven't decided.''

''I hope you do,'' she said vehemently. ''I hope you're going to get them all. They deserve it.''

That was an unusually strong opinion from the discreet, unemotional Bella. If only I could find a dozen like her for a jury.... Stretching across the desk, I grabbed her hand. ''Bella, you're a star! How could I manage without you?''

For a brief moment, she clung to me, a surprising, warm touch; then she drew her hands away quickly and folded them into her lap primly. Pulling a tissue from the box on the desk, she blew her nose.

She said, ''You know you can't use that in court, don't you?''

''But I can ask in deposition about other malpractice cases. It's all grist for the mill, Bella. Well done! You're a great right hand.''

She busied herself with the tissue. ''If you take the case, you'll need a couple of right hands. Your father found it too much for him, you know. He told me that. He said it was the worst task he'd ever had in his legal career.'' The color came and went in her pale face. "It won't be easy, Mr. Noah, especially with that type of client."

I was stung into disappointed anger. "What do you mean, 'that type of client'? I thought you were on their side."

"You have to face facts, Mr. Noah."

"Facts? What facts? The fact that a child died when he shouldn't have died? The fact that a whole slew of physicians didn't give him the sort of care we expect in this day and age? This isn't the nineteenth century, Bella; we aren't a backward nation. Those people had the right to expect their child to be treated properly in a hospital, and he wasn't. I hope you're not trying to tell me that because a child is black, no one's going to be sympathetic about his death."

Her back stiffened into rigidity, the color surging in her cheeks. The narrow line of her lips grew tight and defensive.

"I'm not trying to tell you anything, Mr. Noah. I'm sure you know what you're doing. It's just that it'll take a great deal of work, a case like that. And a lot of money. For instance, Mr. Richards had to pay for an opinion from a doctor in California. He didn't like it, he told me, not a bit, but he said it was the best five thousand dollars he ever spent."

That stopped me short. "Five thousand? My father spent that kind of money?"

"He said you had to be prepared to pay for good expert witnesses."

Staring at Bella, for once emotional and argumentative, her pallid skin flushed, her eyes bright and defiant, it occurred to me quite suddenly that my father told her many things he never told me. Sometimes it felt as though she'd known him a lot better than I had. In that instant, I found myself contrasting Bella's compulsive neatness and total loyalty with my mother's untidy distraction and decline.

Bella wasn't bad-looking, not really, not when one looked at her properly. She had nice skin and smooth dark hair. She might have been pretty when she was younger and less withdrawn. Into the corners of my mind crept a foolish, treacherous, unfilial thought. Was it possible—could it be possible—there'd been more than just a secretary-boss relationship between Bella and my father, alone together in this office for so many years while my mother was fading away in the house by the lake? Bella? My father? Twin souls of rectitude and rigidity? The idea was ludicrous, of course. Wasn't it?

Half-ashamed of myself and yet vastly diverted by the possibilities of unlikely sin and adultery, I retreated to my own part of the office and spent the rest of the afternoon poring over the old notes. My father's voice came clearly out of the ponderous, complicated, and unfailingly courteous questions, the repetitions, all the i's dotted and the t's crossed, the way he always worked. It was as though he were breathing over my shoulder. Once or twice, as the afternoon darkened into dusk and the light left the window, I almost expected to see him walk in through the door to turn me out of the chair that was rightfully his, to reclaim the secretary who was rightfully his.

Bella and my father? I tried to laugh at the idea, but instead, I found it touching and enviable. Everyone should have someone to love. My father, to tell the truth, had not been a very lovable man. Honorable, yes. Upright, yes. Careful, punctilious, and correct in his professional and paternal duties, but not a warm man. Someone to admire rather than to love.

Pushing the thoughts away, I tried to concentrate on the Westing case. It seemed straightforward enough. As Bella had said, something was cut that shouldn't have been cut. The cystic duct, apparently important. By the time the mistake was recognized, days after surgery, it was too late to save the patient. I read the expert opinion from the high-priced consultant in California. He sounded like Sweigert, confidently superior. Unfortunately, it was true I couldn't use the fact that Woods had been sued before if our case came to court. I wasn't sure, after all, how it was going to help. But it gave me the confidence to forge ahead. If my father had won against Carl Woods, I could, too—if only to prove it to Bella.

At the end of the day, I carried both lots of records home with me and sat up past midnight in the empty, echoing house with a bottle of scotch, reading the Ambrose case notes over and over. By 1:00 a.m., I could repeat the hour-to-hour progress of Jordan's hospitalization verbatim—who had been called when and how long it was before they came. I could follow the long absences and desultory appearances of the doctors, what they'd written on the chart and what treatment they'd ordered. It wasn't hard to remember the treatment, because there was practically none. I could say which nurse had recorded what sinking blood pressure and what rising pulse rate at what time, and I couldn't see why L. E. Watson was frightened. God knows, she and all the other nurses had sent enough alarm signals. And I was still no nearer understanding why the doctors hadn't listened.

The sad record of deteriorating vital signs was familiar enough to me—I, who had sat and watched a beloved wife slip away from this world with the same sort of signs. But at least I had the support of physicians and nurses who'd done everything that could be done. When the time came to let Janet go, even I knew that nothing else was possible. That was some sort of comfort.

At last, I went to bed in my lonely room, lay in the narrow bed, and stared at the ceiling, invisible in the dark. I tried not to dwell on Janet or my present celibate state, but my body suddenly ached for the feel of a woman. I supposed it was a good sign that I hadn't lost all sexual appetite, though what was the good of yearning for female flesh when I didn't have any interest in looking for another female? Daphne was right: It was time to get over Janet. Saying it was one thing. Doing it was another.

I turned on the light to chase the shadows away and told myself to think of the Ambrose case. I contemplated the lengthy work-up it would entail. If Father's suit against Woods was a yardstick, it would take expert opinions, reams of depositions, painstaking education in medical matters. Months of work stretching ahead of me, months condemned to stay in Springwell. And if I didn't take the case, where else would I go and what would I do?

Then something about the Westing case got me out of bed again. The file lay where I'd left it, on the dining room table, and when I turned to the back of the folder, I realized there was no conclusion, no mention of the settlement. Did Father really win? Why wasn't it recorded here? Tomorrow, I'd ask Bella to look for another file. It had to be somewhere.

I took some warm milk to soothe my troubled gut, aspirin for my aching head. The house creaked around me, full of ghosts. I tried to face the issues of the Ambrose case more clearly. To have a sense of outrage and a task to keep me from making a decision about my life was some help to me, I supposed. But was it the best thing for my clients?

EIGHT

A SLEEPLESS NIGHT and drinking scotch past midnight didn't make the next morning feel great. It was a relief to put aside the Ambrose case and attend to something else. Bigelow Harrison was coming in again to talk about his land deal, which should have been straightforward and wasn't, of course. Nothing is straightforward these days.

Bigs Harrison was an old client who'd inherited a parcel of land a few miles out of Springwell, toward the Sound. He wanted to develop the property, had fantasies of luxury homes around a golf course. "An upscale community," he called it. He reckoned it would lure well-heeled people from what Bigs considered the overcrowded and deteriorating cities to the south. "People want out of cities, you know, Noah. They're fed up with crime and high taxes. Here, they'd have clean air and water, no damned sirens going night and day. Peace and quiet and safety, that's what people want."

The plans were drawn up, the costs worked out, the profit he'd make. The problem was that he was fighting a losing battle with the state over three acres of wetlands slap in the middle of the property. *Wetlands,* the new environmental buzzword in the Northwest, replacing the spotted owl. Bigelow Harrison, whose family had been in the lumber trade, not the most conservation-minded business in the land, was in a constant and predictable rage over it.

A large man, thick-necked, red-faced, strong-willed, he came clumping into the office with more plans and more arguments. "Not one damn thing left a man can do without getting snarled in red tape. Soon they'll stop us taking a crap unless we get a say-so from some damn bureaucrat.

Where'd this country be today if people like me hadn't had the freedom to go ahead with plans like this? Would there be one single town, one single development? I'll be doing them a favor, giving work to all those damn builders and carpenters sitting around on their fannies collecting unemployment."

Bigs stayed with me because the family business had always been in my father's hands, but I wasn't totally sympathetic to his problems. The plans were attractive enough, if you liked golf courses and oversize houses, but we didn't need any more developments ruining pristine acreage and watersheds if they couldn't fulfill a few safeguards. I'd been urging him to go ahead with the environmental-impact statement the state was demanding. It was going to cost money, which he had, and without it, he wasn't going to get permission. He'd wriggled and protested and appealed for months and was getting nowhere.

"Do it, Bigs. That's my advice. Bite the bullet."

"Shit, Noah. It'll cost thousands. And at the end of it, the damn Corps of Engineers will probably say no."

"So, you want to drop the whole thing? Lose what you've already put into it?"

"Shit. Damn bureaucrats."

We'd been having roughly the same conversation for months.

He glowered at me. "Your father would've found some way around this."

"Believe me, Bigs, there's no way round it, not these days."

"When you think what it'd do for Springwell, it gets me spitting mad. Those people would go to the stores here, get their medical care here. Everything's here that people need, if only they'd let me get on with it before this poor dump of a town fades away under our noses."

Praising him for a civic-mindedness that wasn't completely convincing, I again urged him to make the appointment with the Corps.

He threw himself into the chair on the other side of the desk, scratched at his head with a calloused hand. "I'm going to have to find more investors. I can't handle this on my own anymore. There're a few people interested. You want to come in with me, Noah?"

I was taken aback. "That's decent of you, Bigs, but I don't have that kind of money."

"I'm not looking for huge amounts. Just want to spread the load a bit, get some moral support. I talked to a couple of the local docs about it. They're always looking for investments. I think doctors lend respectability to a business deal, don't you?"

"Doctors?" I said too sharply. "Who, for instance?"

He grinned. Bigs was like his nickname, big, and, when he wasn't on the subject of the government, pleasant-natured enough. He might have inherited a load of dough, but he was still a plain old northwesterner. "I'll tell you if you'll come in."

"Tell me who you're thinking of and I'll tell you if I want in."

He began mounding the papers together impatiently, then shrugged. "Well, I guess you'd have to know sooner or later. I talked to Carl Woods and his colleague Ginger Grogan. They're surgeons here in town, you know, and they're interested. It'd be good for their business, wouldn't it? All those home owners with good health insurance. We talked about setting up a development corporation. Of course, if you came in, you'd be our corporate lawyer, Noah. I'd make that clear."

Shit, I thought, shit and double shit.

"How come you chose those two in particular, Bigs? There are other doctors in town."

"Oh, I know them from the hospital board. Woods is a good guy. Grogan's a bit of an oddball, but he's got the right ideas about some things. Feels like I do. People aren't going to keep paying the kind of property tax to live with all that crime and violence down in Seattle. They're going to want to go somewhere. Why not here?''

''There's not so much crime and violence in Seattle.''

''You're damned wrong about that, Noah. Place is going to the dogs. Have you seen it lately? Full of blacks and Orientals and Hispanics. Crime's way up. That's what we've got to keep out of Springwell—deadbeats, drug dealers, school problems. No way we should let the same thing happen here as they've let happen down there.''

I didn't bother to argue with him. Bigs was fairly intransigent in his views.

''I didn't know you were on the hospital board,'' I said. It was beginning to feel as though every other person I spoke to had something to do with St. Mary's.

''Oh, well, got to do your bit in the town, haven't you? My mom was like yours. Thought the sun rose and set on the great god doctors. Maybe she was right, eh? So, are you going to join us?''

''I'll have to think about it,'' I said.

''Don't think too long, Noah. I'll give you a good deal. We'll make a fortune if we can just get the show on the road. But you know how it is. Got to get in at the right time. Strike while the iron's hot and all that.''

After he had gone, I thought about it a lot. If Bigs was involved with Carl Woods, I'd have to withdraw from one deal or the other. The choice was clear: the Ambroses or Bigelow Harrison. And Bigelow Harrison's business paid a number of the office bills.

It was certainly time to discuss matters with the Ambroses.

But instead of just picking up the phone to ask them to come to the office, I had a sudden urge to see where they lived, how they lived, which might make me understand who they were exactly—before casting them adrift. So at four o'clock, just as the light was beginning to fade from the afternoon sky, I drove south through the crumbling center of Springwell, past Bennetts Mill, belching sulfur into the gray air, out at the other end of town.

It was years since I'd been down that way. For years, I'd used the same route in and out of Springwell, off the freeway and along Spruce until the intersection, left and then right and then left again along the lake to the house. Even in a small town, it was possible to miss half of it. I was in more of a rut than I'd realized.

I don't know what I'd expected the Ambrose place to look like, but it was somewhat a surprise when I found it. The houses were small and undistinguished, 1950s spec-built, separated from one another by large yards, as though the spaces between houses were more important than the spaces inside. The Ambrose house was different from its neighbors only by virtue of the fact it was freshly painted, neater around the yard, the lawn smoother and greener, with sharply trimmed edges. Each shrub was carefully pruned, each flower bed weeded, as though the inhabitants in that particular house cared more for appearances than their neighbors did. That's what surprised me, I suppose. I'd have bet that Angel Ambrose wasn't a gardener and that Joseph was too downcast to be out tending his lawn. But someone was looking after it lovingly.

Driving past slowly, I did a U-turn at the intersection, then came back and parked. There were no lights or signs of life within the house. After awhile, I got out of the car and strolled beside the white painted fence, then turned and walked past again. Suddenly, the front door of the house flew open and Angel Ambrose came rushing down the path toward me, her heels clacking loudly on the bricks. When she got nearer, she stopped.

"Oh, it's you. I saw a stranger. I thought... What are you doing here?"

Her heels were very high, and she wore a bright red

jacket over a little short black skirt, stylish, out of place in this neck of the woods. She glowed and thrummed with that same barely suppressed rage I recognized from before.

Not altogether sure what I was doing there, I offered a feeble excuse. "I was passing and thought I'd call on you."

"Call on us?" Her lip curled. "Nobody calls on us. Nobody we want to call, anyways."

"I wanted to have a chat with you and your husband."

"I just came from work." She tapped one foot impatiently. "You going to come in, then?" Swiveling on the high heels, she headed back up the path without waiting for a reply, and I opened the little gate and followed. At the front door, she flipped on the lights, and I entered a large living room with pale chairs and carpet, elaborate drapes and dried flowers, as stylish and out of place in south Springwell as Angel's clothes. My old parka and unpolished shoes felt shabby and unworthy.

Shutting the door, she leaned against it and looked down her nose at me, as though I should know there were better things to do than roam around the countryside looking for someone to drop in on. "Joseph's still at work. Whatever it is you wanted to chat about, you can do it as well as if he was here."

"Do you mind if I sit down?"

I could tell she didn't want me to sit down, but she nodded curtly, and I chose the deeply cushioned sofa, trying to make myself feel welcome. On the table by my elbow was a large photograph in a silver frame, a studio portrait of a small solemn child with huge dark eyes. "Jordan?" I asked, although I knew it was, of course.

"Yes," she said.

The tiny shining face, the neat round head, the promise in the eyes all made me sad and immensely weary. I glanced up at Angel; she was hovering over me as though daring me to put my hands on the picture of her son. I said quietly, "He was a beautiful child."

"Yes," she said again.

She wasn't making it easy. I felt uncomfortable and intrusive, but even if it was perhaps unprofessional to come into their home like this, I was glad I had. This wasn't the home of people who had no other resources apart from me. They'd manage without me; I didn't have to save them. Then Angel, walking away from me to the other side of the room, took something from the pocket of her jacket and dropped it carelessly on a table near the window. With amazement and some shock, I saw that what she'd taken from her pocket was a small silvery revolver. It lay on the table, casually, like an ornament.

I shook my head in disbelief. "You carry a gun?"

She seemed surprised I should mention it. "Sure."

"Do you always carry it, or did you put it in your pocket just for me?"

"Someone stops, watches the house as if he was casing the joint. You never know who's out there."

"Around here?"

"Yeah, around here. Around everywhere. There's always someone out to make trouble. Can't be anywhere without trouble. Don't bother your head about it, Mr. Richards. Folks like us are used to it."

"You came out to...challenge me? If you thought I was up to no good, wasn't that a little unwise?"

She shrugged. "I ain't no coward. Gotta stand up to people, not let them get away with things."

No, she was no coward. "But you shouldn't go around with a gun. You might have shot me."

"Hell, everyone's got guns."

"Exactly. That's why people get shot all the time. But as a matter of fact, I don't carry a gun myself. Never have, never will."

Her lip curled again. "Then you're a fool."

"You got a license for it?"

"That what you wanted to chat about, Mr. Attorney?"

She made me want to laugh. She was spunky and feisty, and I couldn't help liking her. Angel was one of those people you either loved or hated, and she didn't seem to give a damn which it was. I hadn't come here to give a lecture on the right to carry weapons or the sense of it, but the very idea that she felt she had to keep guard with a weapon depressed and saddened me. Here? The Ambroses didn't feel safe out here? What the hell was the world coming to?

"There're a few things I needed to talk over with you, Mrs. Ambrose. About the case. You should know the hospital has made a tentative offer to settle. Not officially, you understand, but it's something you should think about."

"Settle? What do you mean, 'settle'?"

"They might be prepared to give you some money so the case doesn't go to court."

Glaring at me, she perched on the edge of a chair opposite, the short skirt riding high on her slender thighs, and pointed a long red fingernail at me. "I told you, it's not money we want."

"Money can make a deal of difference to life, Mrs. Ambrose. Buy another house, for instance, let you move somewhere you might feel safer. Start a new life."

"I don't want a new life. And it's not money I want."

Instinctively, my eyes went to the photograph. I sighed. "You want vengeance, don't you?"

"That's it, Mr. Richards. You got it."

Leaning forward out of the soft cushions, I gazed across the room at the golden skin, the high cheekbones like those of an Egyptian queen. The black eyes with their curly eyelashes glittered back at me, angry and unwavering. "Mrs. Ambrose, you need to understand that even if we go to court, you'll not get vengeance there. A court can't award revenge. It, too, can only give you money." I wasn't going to mention the sum of money that had been suggested. That could only add insult to injury, though, God knows, $100,000 might sound like a hell of a lot to the Ambroses.

"If there's a court case, it'll be in the papers, won't it? Spread all over the front page, here and in Seattle. I've seen some of those cases reported. Everyone would know what they did to our boy. Their names would be mud. That would be some revenge for me. Not enough, maybe, but some."

She wasn't a stupid woman. Or greedy, either, it seemed, because she didn't ask how much money I was talking about.

"What about your husband? What does he want?"

The red fingernail stabbed again. "Joseph will do what I want." I could believe that. "So we don't want any talk of settlement, understand? You're not even to talk to those motherfuckers about money."

I was startled into laughter. "I guess that's putting it pretty plain."

"As long as you get my meaning," she said sharply, and then she smiled at me, for the first time. The smile was briefly flirtatious and happy, with lots of even white teeth, transforming her face, the way she might have smiled at her child. "I like you, Mr. Richards."

My brain felt tired and old. "Well, don't like me too much. Because I also wanted to talk to you and your husband about taking this case down to Seattle. I can give you the name of good malpractice lawyers there who specialize in this kind of law."

She sat bolt upright on the edge of the chair, spine rigid, and fixed me with the sparking eyes. "Why?"

"Because you'll get better expertise. Lawyers who do this sort of work all the time have medical experts on their staff. They know exactly where to go to get good testimony; they have the resources to work up a case like this. Me, I'm only one man. There's a limit to what a one-man firm can accomplish."

It was only half the truth. The rest of the truth was that St. Mary's involved too many people I knew.

"You're saying you don't want to take our case? That's not what you said the other day." Her nostrils flared and there was no hint of the friendliness of a moment before. "I thought when we came to see you, Here's someone who doesn't care who we are, only about what's right. Now you're trying to wriggle out of it."

"No one's trying to wriggle out of anything," I protested. Wasn't I? "But I have to give you my best recommendation so you can pursue the process to the limit. My limit would come a lot sooner than a big malpractice firm's. I'd be remiss not to tell you that."

Folding her arms tightly against her breasts, she stared at me without speaking, waiting for me to continue. An implacable woman, an almost-frightening determination in her face, a strength and resolution I couldn't match.

"You want to think about it? Talk to your husband?"

"Joseph will do what I want," she repeated. "And I want you to be the one on the case."

I sighed again. "Why me?" I sounded like Sweigert in his plush office in Seattle. "What made you choose me?"

Gripping the arms of the chair, her fingers dug into the fabric. Suddenly, she seemed uncertain, averting her face so the glow of the lamp outlined the strong angles of her cheekbones, the velvet cap of hair. She glanced sideways at me, at the photograph beside me. "Can I tell you the truth?"

"The truth? Haven't you told me the truth so far?"

"About what happened to Jordy, yes." She hesitated. "But you're not the first lawyer we talked to. We already talked to some lawyers in Seattle. They listened okay, but after a couple of days they came back and said it wouldn't be worth it for them to do anything. Said it cost thousands of dollars just to work up this kind of case, and they said…" Her mouth twisted and she bit one side of her fleshy underlip with the strong white teeth. "They said we couldn't count on enough damages to make it worth their while. Said that when a child died..." She swallowed noisily. "Said if Jordy had had some terrible injury, then we might have gotten lots of money, but as he was dead..."

Bending her head, she spoke in a muffled yet furious voice. "It seems it won't cost those damn doctors near as much, because all they did was kill him." She put her hands over her face.

At least I didn't have to tell her that myself.

There was a long silence. She uncovered her face, raised her head. "Joseph, he said we should leave it be, that it'll bring nothing but more pain. He thinks we should have more kids—that's his idea of forgetting. That's not my idea. I'm going to make them pay for it, some way or other."

Then she said, "So I asked around, and I heard your wife had died in a hospital not all that long ago. She was young, they said. I thought to myself, There's someone who won't love doctors too much. So we came to you."

Her words sent shock waves through me. I shook my head to get rid of the sound of them. "You've got it wrong. My wife's doctors did the best they could...." I stopped. Whatever I said would only make her feel worse. Could only make me feel worse.

"Oh yeah," she said bitterly. "I bet they did. And I bet your wife was a nice white woman, wasn't she? Not a little black kid."

"Surely," I said sadly, "you don't think that, do you?"

Angel's glittering eyes held mine for another long minute. "Don't I? Then you tell me what I should think."

NINE

EVENTUALLY, I went home in the darkness of the November evening to the darkness of my own house. From the living room window, the lights of the Carlsson house gleamed like a beacon through the bare winter trees, and after a while I put on my jacket again and walked around the lake's edge toward it. A stray in search of a haven, of a sympathetic ear.

In single-handed practice, there is no sympathetic ear. I needed someone to listen, needed the day-to-day, face-to-face, jaw-to-jaw discussions, conversations, interactions, call them what you will, that come with other people. Lonelier, more desperate people than I hang out in bars, pouring words into strangers' ears, which are most likely deaf to any words except those inside their own heads. I hadn't quite reached that stage yet, but I understood their need. It's the permission to talk that is important, whether in bars or to colleagues or on a psychiatrist's couch.

If my late colleague, my father, were here, would he listen to me? Would he be sympathetic about the Ambrose case? Probably not. He'd probably tell me to leave it alone, not stray outside my province. He'd certainly say, "Don't get involved emotionally. Clients don't benefit when their attorney bleeds with them." Father wasn't a tilter at windmills or a champion of lost causes. He had enough sense to recognize the limits of his expertise.

I trudged along the empty road with automatic steps. The evening had grown raw and damp, a chill wind blowing straight down from Canada, numbing my fingers and face. All around, the trees were tall and threatening, the air laden with a primeval dankness of ferny undergrowth, the bulky unseen presence of the mountains looming beyond the lake. The weight of the wind heaved against me and thrashed at the branches of the firs and the hemlocks, whipping the surface of the water into small angry whitecaps. It was as though I was alone on the edge of the world.

I didn't have the self-sufficiency of my father. His independence was based on a deal of self-interest. He actually enjoyed wills and probate and real estate transactions, preferred solitary projects like fishing or gardening or poring over documents late at night, alone. He hadn't been a sharer. When I was a child, we'd go off fishing together, but even that seemed more out of some sense of paternal duty than out of any obvious pleasure in my company. He would sit silently for hours in the boat or stand thigh-deep in rushing water, absorbed in 'the gentle art,' as he liked to call it. He'd be astonished to find me still waiting when the time came to go home. The hindsight that comes with maturity told me my mother must have been lonely in her life with him. Not that she ever complained, at least not to me. Mother wasn't a complainer, not even when she was dying. Asked how she felt that day, she'd say, "Not so bad, considering." Considering what, Mother? That you were slipping away from a disappointing life? Did you have hopes the next one might be more entertaining, more companionable?

When Father and I practiced together—perhaps together wasn't the precise terminology; more separate and unequal, for I never felt quite equal to him—I'd almost begun to tolerate the paper pushing. A matter of survival as much as anything, getting up every day and going to the office just to have a reason to get out of bed. Father saved my thin skin by dragging me into the practice with him, and surely, if he'd lived, I'd have found the motivation to move on by now. If nothing else, he and I wouldn't have been able to put up with each other for too long. But that night, just over a year ago, when his sturdy heart failed at a Bar Association dinner, my fragile recovery from Janet's death shattered. Too many losses too soon. I kept on getting up and going to the office every day, just as before, because once more I'd lost the power to make a definitive move.

The road around the lake was so familiar to me that I didn't need to lift my head to watch the wet slick of pavement. There was no traffic to interrupt my thoughts and I didn't feel or hear anyone coming toward me until, all at once, without warning, a couple of huffing yellow dogs were greeting me, great slobbery grins on their foolish faces, tails beating enthusiastically, as though they'd been out searching for me. I looked up and saw Daphne in the middle of the road, laughing at me. Her smile was like sunlight come into the lonely night.

"You were so lost in thought, Noah, I expected you to walk right past me."

"What ever are you doing out on a night like this?"

"What does it look like? I'm taking the dogs for a walk. What are you doing?"

"Thinking. I was on my way to your house for some help with the thinking."

"Oh, good," she said. "I'll help. But let's keep going for a bit. The dogs haven't run enough yet."

So I turned around with her, back toward my own house, and we were blown along with the wind behind us. The dogs raced gleefully ahead, galloped back to us, and then took off into the night again. The moon came out from behind the black clouds and a fitful light glistened on the surface of the lake. I felt suddenly peaceful, and cheerful.

Daphne came nearer to me. "So, tell me, what were you so deep in thought about?"

She took my arm, her face turned up to mine so her words didn't get blown away in the wind, her eyes bright and interested, and soon I began to tell her the story of Jordan Ambrose. How angry and bitter his mother was, how sad his father was. How deeply it troubled me, because there had to be more to it than I could yet understand.

We walked far along the road, past my house among the trees, our heads close together. Daphne pushed back the hood of her jacket to hear me better, and the wind whipped her hair into feathers around her head. I couldn't help contrasting her milk white skin and wispy hair with Angel Ambrose's steely hair and dark gleaming face; Angel's eyes black and angry, Daphne's gray and gentle. Two young women, much the same age, living not very far apart, but from opposite ends of a spectrum, whose lives would only ever touch through the story of a dead child.

Daphne listened silently, sometimes standing still to hear better. At the end of it, after more silence, she asked point-blank, "Are you saying what I think you're saying? That because he was black, no one did anything?"

I hadn't dared put it into those words, not even in my own mind.

At the next bend of the road, the wind came blowing into our faces again and we turned to retrace our steps.

"Is it unthinkable?" I wanted to know.

"Unthinkable," she said.

"Maybe they just didn't know how to treat him. They aren't used to black patients up here in Springwell."

"Patients are patients, Noah. Inside their skins, they all look alike."

"But some people never get past the color of the skin, do they?"

"Doctors don't think that way. I can't believe that. I can't and I won't."

"What about those doctors, Daphne? You know them, don't you? Will you tell me about them? Chauncey won't. I need to know."

We were close to my house now. "Come in for a few minutes," I said. "Fill me in. You can have some of my scotch if you come in."

Her eyes shone in the moonlight. "Such an offer! All right. Just for a few minutes. I'll have to let Chauncey know where I am. He'll think I've been run over."

It was months since Daphne had been inside my house, and I guessed she wanted to see the condition of it as much as anything. She'd judge it, like a woman, as an indication of my state of mind.

We went in by the back door, which was never locked, into the kitchen with the vinyl floor tiles curling at the edges in too many places, past the dirty dishes in the sink, around the old pine table with newspapers spread all over, into the living room, where the furniture seemed shabbier than when I last looked at it. It was my parents' furniture, of course. Ours, Janet's and mine, was still in storage in California.

Daphne shed the shapeless parka and emerged in a T-shirt and jeans, her shape soft and round. She called Chauncey from the phone in the kitchen. "Just stopped by Noah's for a moment. Be home soon."

I wished she didn't have to be home soon. I wished she could stay here in the house with me forever. I poured the drinks, handed one to her. "Perhaps I should light the fire. It seems so cheerless in here."

She looked around the room. "A fire might cheer it up." It was said uncritically.

Fiddling with the kindling and the logs, which had sat unused by the fireplace for months, I crouched on my haunches by the hearth, watching the fire leap to life. Soon the flames began to lick the room into a semblance of comfort, and I fetched the copy of Jordan Ambrose's records and sat beside Daphne on the sofa. The dogs had been circling the room, sniffing and exploring, and now they crashed in heaps at our feet. The dogs, the fire, the drinks, Daphne, warming the cold place into a home again.

She said, "I thought you couldn't talk to me about this unless I was an expert witness or something."

I waved my hand. "Lawyer talk. You can be a character witness on behalf of these doctors. Explain them to me."

"I think I feel disloyal. Chauncey won't like it."

"But maybe you can shed some light on the mystery. Maybe make sense of it all. I certainly can't."

Opening the file to the notes I'd made about the sequence of events, I started to read out loud, but before I got to the second night, the nurses recording the falling blood pressure and rising pulse rate, the phone calls they'd made, Daphne took the pages out of my hand and read them silently to herself. I went to the sideboard and poured another scotch.

"Noah," she said at last, "this is shocking."

"Shocking," I agreed.

"I know most of those people. That makes it even worse, I suppose." She turned back the pages, frowned over them. "Tyler Clarke, the pediatrician. He's a little man, sort of ineffectual, not the most caring doctor in the world, I've heard. I don't take the boys to him. But Carl Woods, he's a nice guy and a pretty good surgeon, by all accounts. I can't believe he didn't do anything sooner. I mean, most surgeons leap to operate, don't they? That's one of the things wrong with the American system, in my opinion. Surgeons have to cut before they can make a living. I can't fathom why he waited so long, until the child was obviously too sick to survive an operation."

"What I didn't realize," I said, "is that surgery can kill you. I'm an ignorant layman. I thought surgery was the way to save lives."

"In my training in London, we were taught an old adage: Modern surgery makes the operation safe for the patient; it is now the aim of surgery to make the patient safe for the operation. This poor little sod was so ill by the time he went to surgery, he was destined to die."

"Just what Sweigert told me, except not as poetically." She browsed through the notes, her forehead creased.

"Oh God, it's so awful. Listen to what the nurses say. Here and here." I already knew by heart what the nurses had said. She stabbed her finger at the notes. "'Abdomen tense and tender, distended. Lethargic. Pallor around mouth. Rambling conversation. Skin clammy and pale. Unrecordable blood pressure. Pulse one eighty.' Those are signs of shock, Noah." Her eyes were appalled. "A lot of these notes are by the night nurse, Nita Barnes. I know her slightly. She's a good nurse, reliable."

"You know the nurses at St. Mary's?"

"I've volunteered there from time to time."

"Nita Barnes hasn't been back to work since. At least that's what one of the others told me—L. E. Watson. You know her?"

Daphne shook her head. "No. She called the doctors a lot, too, didn't she? She seems to have been on the phone constantly. I wonder why Grogan never went to see the boy? It says here he was sent for that first day, and they expected him to come, but he never showed up. He's the one who usually operates on the children, you know."

I'd almost forgotten about the no-show Grogan, but as he didn't even see Jordan Ambrose and didn't operate, the case wouldn't involve him.

"Carl Woods and Ginger Grogan are in the same office," Daphne explained. "If Grogan couldn't go for some reason, I suppose it's reasonable that Dr. Woods went instead."

She read and reread the notes, her glass of scotch untouched.

"Right at the beginning, the nurses make the diagnosis. You see, here. The admission note says, 'Abdominal pain, central Appendix out last February.' That's classic, Noah. He probably had adhesions from that previous operation."

I looked at her with respect. "You can tell that? And the doctors couldn't?"

"And I'm only a nurse, is that what you're thinking?

That's what these doctors must have thought, too, or why didn't they take any notice? Why don't you go and talk to the doctors yourself? Surely that's the best way to find out what they were thinking.''

''I can't talk to them. An attorney can't talk to anyone he's going to bring a suit against. Once I've made up my mind there is a case and I file a suit, I can get statements and depositions and maybe some answers.''

She looked exasperated. ''But that's daft! There could be a perfectly rational answer without getting as far as a lawsuit.''

''That's the law, Daphne. You've got to have some protection against self-incrimination. No, what I have to do is find other physicians of comparable skill and training and get their opinions about the treatment, if they think there was something wrong with it, and base my judgment on that. I got one opinion that day I went to Seattle, from a pediatric surgeon.''

''What did he say?''

''That the treatment was negligent. Actually, he used the word *criminal*.''

''There you are, then. Isn't that enough?''

''It's only one opinion. I need more than one. And before I get into depositions or anything like that, I'll have to educate myself about this particular medical problem. I have to know what questions to ask these doctors. And I have to prove malpractice, not merely incompetence.''

''Isn't it the same thing?''

''Not exactly. I have to prove they didn't live up to the standards of care. And the standards of care differ depending on the state. What applies in New York, for instance, may not apply in this state.''

She thumped the records on her knee, scowling. ''But they didn't do anything, so how can they have lived up to anything?'' Her eyes gleamed with outrage, spots of bright pink flaring on the skin beneath.

I smiled at her. It was wonderful having someone to talk to. "I don't have much trouble believing there's a malpractice suit here. Or rather, wrongful death—that's the correct designation. What I don't understand is the strange lack of response to the nurses. It's very odd, isn't it? If one of Chauncey's patients was in the hospital and the nurses kept calling him, wouldn't he at least answer in some way or other? Or send one of his partners? What the hell were they doing all that time?"

Daphne rested her head against the back of the sofa and shut her eyes as if to think better; papery eyelids closed, black lashes fluttering on the delicate skin beneath. I could lean on one elbow and gaze at her without betrayal. The firelight leapt in the room, touched red glints in her hair and flickered on her face, on the round shape of her breasts, the curve of her thighs in the blue jeans, and I had to look away because my heart, like the firelight, was leaping, too. I should never have asked her into my empty house, very foolish in my present vulnerable state.

"Chauncey doesn't like this one bit, you know," she said, and immediately I was alarmed and guilty. I snatched my arm away. Was it so obvious, this foolhardy hankering? She opened her eyes and looked at me sideways. "He can't bear the idea of anyone, let alone his friend, bringing a suit against St. Mary's. Or against any doctor, come to that."

"Oh, that," I said, stumbling. "No, of course not. Of course Chauncey doesn't like it." I shifted a safer few inches away. "I don't really blame him, but he understands I have to do what I think is right. I know this case is right, Daphne. The lack of care, the shrugging of shoulders, the whole wretched scenario makes me angry. Bewildered, too, but mad as hell."

She smiled, reaching nearer to pat my arm. "That's good, Noah. You need to get angry about something. You've been like an automaton, you know, ever since Janet, ever since your dad. Moving through life one inch at a time, not getting mad or upset or involved in anything. Just hanging on by your fingernails. I've been very worried about you.''

The warm, scented flesh was perilously close. If I moved my hand just a fraction, it would touch hers; if I leaned an inch to the left, my shoulder would be against hers; if she didn't stop smiling at me, her eyes tender and sympathetic, I might, at long last, kiss that curving mouth. Not just a platonic touch on the cheek between friends. But she did stop smiling, the smile fading slowly, a belated dawning in her eyes, as if she recognized for the first time the tightrope she walked with me. A tiny crackling silence filled the room, a pause that could have marked a sea change in our relationship. I knew that if I kissed her, it could be a beginning, but it could also be an end—an end to a friendship I cherished. To two friendships I cherished. I didn't think I had the nerve to risk that. But men are foolish, impulsive creatures and often take foolish, impulsive risks.

Daphne decided. She drew her hand away from my arm, stood up quickly and smoothly, and stirred the dogs with her foot. ''It's time we were going home. Chauncey will wonder what's become of us. Come on, dogs. Out into the cold night again.''

I got to my feet stiffly and awkwardly, wanting to apologize and not daring to say a word. Picking up her parka, Daphne thrust her arms into it, zipping up the jacket as though to hide herself inside it, and headed for the front door.

I couldn't let her go without putting things back together. I wanted to make everything ordinary again, the way it had been for so long; otherwise, something unspoken might always be between us. I chose very ordinary words.

''Thanks for listening, Daphne. I needed to talk to someone.''

She paused with her hand on the doorknob, her eyes forgiving. She, too, chose her words carefully. ''What are friends for? Maybe you can't talk to Chauncey about this case, but you can always discuss it with me. If it's of any help.''

I moved around her to open the door. The lock was rusty and unused, like me. The dogs went bounding eagerly out into the night, as though they had been shut up forever. The wind was dying down now and the moon was higher and brighter. Daphne pulled up her hood. ''You're doing the right thing, Noah. What's right is right; never forget that.'' She touched my arm quickly and then was gone across the porch and down the steps. I watched her fade away into the darkness.

I should have walked her home. Nobody was safe in the dark anymore, not even in Springwell. But the dogs would watch out for her, and I was the one who wasn't safe.

''What's right is right,'' she'd said. I knew she meant more than just the Ambrose case.

mn it, I *was* angry! Angry and bitter and frustrated
rightened about my future.

ad to sit down then, had to rest my forehead on the
en table. My eyes focused on the whorls and curliques
e once well-scrubbed pine, my mother's table in my
r's house, and I wanted to bang my head against its
wooden surface until something other than my heart
. I tried taking deep sucking breaths, tried to slow the
ng of my pulse, the pounding in my chest, tried to think
something, anything, of solace. Into the raging of my
rt floated only one small bubble, which wasn't much
nfort. That it was L. E. Watson's face, which I'd trans-
sed on my beloved wife's. Not Daphne's. God forgive
e, with all my other problems, my senses were stirring at
st and I found myself coveting my friend and neighbor's
ife.

Closing my eyes, I knew this was some sort of nadir.
here had to be a reason for going on, but I couldn't think
what it was.

At that moment, the telephone rang in the kitchen. It rang
so infrequently in the house nowadays that the sound sent
shock waves through me, disturbing me in my pit of despair. I lifted my head and stared at it balefully, with no
intention of answering. A moment ago, I'd wanted to hear
another human voice; now I didn't want to speak to anyone.
I wanted to drink beer and scotch until I slept without
dreams. But the phone continued to ring, jangling around
the room, shredding my already-ragged nerves, and at last,
reluctantly, I reached for it. It could, after all, be Daphne.

"Yes?"

An intrusive silence stretched at the other end of the line
until I almost dropped the receiver back on its hook. Then
a female voice, not Daphne's, said hesitatingly, "Mr. Richards?"

"This is Noah Richards," I replied curtly. Was Noah
Richards, I thought. Only God knew who I was anymore.

TEN

ONCE SHE HAD GONE, the creaking house was very empty.
The remains of the wind sighed and moaned through the
window sashes, an echo of loneliness.

I even missed the sounds of the dogs; a dog would be
company, silly, adoring dogs like Daphne's, but not even
the most adoring dogs are any good at conversation. Talking to a dog isn't much better than talking to oneself. Another human voice was what I needed. Turning on the television, I flicked through the channels, but, as usual, there
was nothing that appealed to me, so I turned it off again,
then searched through the rack of CDs and found a favorite
recording of *Rosenkavalier*. I raised the volume on the
stereo so the pure, lilting voices would fill the empty rooms.

Janet liked opera. Loved it. She'd dragged me, protesting, to the opera in Los Angeles and then in Seattle whenever she could leave the hospital. Said it made her forget,
for a while, the sentence hanging over her. I'd been making
grateful contributions to the Seattle Opera ever since, but I
didn't have the heart to go afterward. Now I missed it because I'd learned to love it, too. The spectacle and the music were yet another part of my life that had disappeared
with Janet.

It was late and I hadn't eaten; I knew sleep wouldn't
come if I didn't eat something. Opening the refrigerator, I
peered into its cold white interior. The shelves held nothing
of any surprise or interest. In the days when Father and I
were together, I often fixed dinner for the two of us. Father
had never learned to cook a thing for himself, but he'd
putter about the kitchen with me, set the table, share a beer,
and chat about inconsequential daily events. It was com-

panionable and comforting, two solitary men together, even if we did avoid talking about those matters closest to our hearts, how adrift we were, how to get our lives back on a steady course again. Though now I wondered whether it was a mistaken assumption that he missed his wife as much as I missed mine. Father believed time healed all wounds, and time had indeed taken care of his, felling him after two martinis and a dinner of prime rib.

I had to find some way of taking care of my wounds. Drinking scotch and allowing time to pass didn't seem to be working too well.

Taking a beer from the refrigerator, I popped the top and watched the chill liquid frost the sides of the bottle. The beer was cool and bitter down my throat and didn't taste particularly good.

The first act of *Rosenkavalier* partially drowned out the emptiness. I grabbed a couple of eggs to beat into an omelette and resolved not to think about Janet or Daphne or Jordan Ambrose or my father; as I held the smooth white eggs in the palm of my hand, I suddenly found myself wondering if L. E. Watson liked opera. Ms. Watson? The voice of conscience in the hospital records? Where had she sprung from? Maybe it was the sound of Sophie singing in the other room. Ms. Watson reminded me of Sophie, delicate and light, innocent when everyone around her was scheming and devious. Was Ms. Watson innocent? Or was it merely the shining hair and clear fair skin, the transparent hazel eyes with the dark flecks in them? But I was grateful it was she who'd come to mind, because she was a far less tormenting thought than the others that insisted on crowding in on me. What might L. E. stand for? Laura? Lydia? Lily? I'd once known a girl called Lily, a fat and rather stupid girl. The beguiling L. E. Watson couldn't possibly be the owner of a name like Lily.

Names always belong with the people we've known. It hurt to hear the name Janet. For two years, I'd forced my-

self not to dwell on her name or her face. N[...] in the kitchen, "Janet, Janet, Janet," as if I [...] myself against the sound of it. I tried to [...] face, and it became oddly mixed up with the [...] Watson's. The same fragile blonde look, [...] around the eyes. Janet's eyes were brown and [...] her blond hair not entirely natural. She used a [...] it, streaking ashy lines around her temples, th[...] filled with the tang of peroxide. The bathroom [...] smell of nail polish and talcum powder and t[...] beguiling female scents I hadn't smelled for two [...] My dulled senses missed not only my wife b[...] femininity she brought into a male existence; p[...] drying on the towels, perfumed soap, earrings sca[...] the dresser, silky nightgowns, scraps of paper by [...] phone with numbers no one recognized, dresses c[...] the closet, bra straps tangling the underwear in the [...]

Standing in the middle of the cold kitchen with [...] of curdling eggs in my hand, I mourned those trivi[...] almost as much as the person they came with. Jane[...] brought frivolity into my life, a frothiness. She was [...] hearted and airy, a counterbalance for my innate seri[...] ness, for all those inherited depressive Welsh genes. [...] laughed at me and with me and lifted my spirits. I had [...] known how much joy was lacking in my world until s[...] took me in tow, pulling me along with her sunny Californ[...] temperament—a temperament that came from being bor[...] into sunshine, from waking every day to blue skies and [...] warm weather. Without Janet, I was in danger of becoming like my father, humorless and gray like the skies of the Northwest.

Suddenly, I felt dizzy with rage and pain. Rage? I was angry with Janet? For dying? For leaving me high and dry like this, under gray skies, making omelettes alone in an empty house that didn't belong to me? For forsaking me? Abandoning me? For leaving me joyless and unhappy?

There was another silence, as though the caller was as reluctant to speak as I was. It struck me as idiotic that someone who didn't want to say anything was calling someone who didn't want to answer.

"Who is this?" I demanded.

A feathery sigh. "Mr. Richards, this is Lauren Watson. We met yesterday at the hospital."

"Lauren…" Startled out of self-pity and irritation, I almost laughed. "You mean L. E. Watson?"

"Yes. That's right."

Lauren. An unusual name, a name I hadn't thought of. "How strange you should call, Ms. Watson. I was thinking about you a few moments ago."

"You were?" There was more silence, and I was afraid she'd been scared off by that careless remark.

Hastily, I said, "Is there something I can help you with?"

A breath drew inward very close to the mouthpiece. I could practically feel it in my ear. "I'm sorry it's late, not your office hours, but I had to call before I changed my mind. I've been looking at the phone all evening, trying to pluck up courage. I don't think I can sleep unless I talk to someone about…about what you wanted to know."

I heaved a sigh of…relief, was it? Or was it a sigh of resignation? By talking to me, she was keeping me on the reluctant path of the Ambrose case. "I'm glad," I said. I suppose I was. "But you didn't have to pluck up courage to speak to me. I won't bite, you know."

As though she had to get it out before she did change her mind, the words began to tumble over one another. "That child should never have died, Mr. Richards. We knew it was all wrong at the time. We knew it should never have happened. All of us, on different shifts, we kept asking for someone to come and look at him. If you're a nurse and see something wrong, there's so little you can do about it, you know, only ask for a doctor to take care of it. And if no one comes... He was so terribly ill, anyone could tell that. It was quite the most awful thing that ever happened to me in my nursing career.'' She was speaking so quickly, her breath catching, that I had to concentrate, pressing my ear hard against the receiver. ''I feel so guilty. We...I should have insisted someone did something.''

Recognizing the despair and misery in her voice, I thought it was a mercy she'd called and dragged both of us from black holes. Trying to reassure her, I said, ''No one is going to blame you, Ms. Watson. It seems to me, reading those notes, you did everything you could to get help.''

''I certainly blame myself.'' She stuttered and stumbled over the words.

''Don't,'' I insisted. ''Don't blame yourself.''

''But I can't help it. How would you feel? And Nita...she was dreadfully upset. She took care of him, you know, both those nights when he was so ill. I told you she hasn't been back to work since, didn't I? She was so angry at Dr. Clarke, they had a terrible row the morning the child went to surgery. When I called her to tell her about the operation, she could hardly speak. And no one's seen her since. I'm worried about her.''

''You've tried calling her?''

''Yes, yes, several times, but there's never been an answer. I've left messages on her machine and she hasn't returned my calls.''

There was a frantic quality to her voice now.

''What makes you so worried? Maybe she just decided not to work at the hospital anymore.''

There was a long pause. ''I don't know. I just think...'' The voice trailed away.

''What do you think, Ms. Watson?''

''You said you'd try to find her. Will you, Mr. Richards?''

"Of course I'll try. It can't be that difficult, can it? You're not imagining she's…harmed herself?"

"Oh, no, I didn't mean that. Not at all. Nita's the last person who'd do that sort of thing. It's just that she's gone. Disappeared."

"What about the other nurse? Swetman."

"Annie Swetman? Oh, Annie's fine. She was more dumbfounded than angry, you know. She thinks doctors can do no wrong. She's not the confrontational type. She works all kind of extra shifts; she really needs the money. She'd be afraid of losing her job. I don't think she'd talk to you."

"But you'll talk to me?"

A slight pause. "I'm talking to you now, aren't I?"

"I mean officially—at my office. We could go over the records and you could explain those notes you made and what was going on at what time, that sort of thing."

"Can't we just talk on the phone?"

"No. I have to talk to you in person."

The light whispery breathing was so near the receiver, it was as though she were in the room with me. At last she said, "I'd like to get it over and done with while I'm in the mood."

"What, tonight?" I looked at my watch. It was past ten o'clock.

"It *is* a bit late, isn't it?"

It would help shake off the dust of despair to meet with the delightful Ms. Watson. But where, at this time of night? My office? A bar? Her home? Tempting, but unprofessional and unwise. I wanted a coherent account, not one dragged out of her in an inappropriate setting. Hoping I wouldn't lose her again, I said firmly, "Come to my office tomorrow." I didn't need to look at my appointment book; I'd make time for her anytime. "When do you get off work?"

Another long pause, as if she was still debating it. "I could come straight from the hospital, I suppose." She sounded reluctant. "Four o'clock. Is that all right?"

"Four o'clock would be just fine, Ms. Watson. You know where my office is?"

"You gave me your card," she reminded me.

"If I can get hold of Nita Barnes, you could both talk to me together. That would be very helpful. Why don't you give me her number? Address, too."

"Wait," she said. "I have to look for it."

The receiver went down with a clatter. I strained to hear the sounds of her place, whether anyone else was there or whether she, too, was alone, but all I could hear was Sophie singing in my own living room. It was difficult to believe L. E. Watson would be alone.

"She lives out in Fairview. One two two five four Grant Drive. Her telephone number is five-five-five-nine-four-eight-seven." I repeated the numbers, writing them down carefully. "Listen, Mr. Richards, I hope you find her. I can't stop worrying." Then she laughed slightly, a small strained sound. "Perhaps it's nothing. Perhaps she's gone on a trip to Mexico or somewhere. She's always taking trips she can't afford." But she didn't sound as if she believed it.

"There you are, then. That's probably the answer. Nothing to worry about. See you at four tomorrow, Ms. Watson. Lauren. And thank you for calling. You did the right thing."

"Mr. Richards?"

"Yes?"

"You won't tell anyone I called, will you? It's important. I don't want anyone to know. Please."

It was back, that edge of fear in the thin voice. I said soothingly, "No one will know. Everything you say to me is confidential. Lawyer-client privilege."

"Thank you. And Mr. Richards?"

"Yes?"

"I hope you get him. He deserves it."

She hung up before I could ask exactly whom I was to get.

The third act of *Der Rosenkavalier* filled the house with joyous melody. I picked up the half-beaten eggs and whipped them into life again, no longer at a nadir. I had rediscoverd an appetite. For life, I hoped.

ELEVEN

LAST NIGHT'S STORM had washed the sky pale and clear and left a dusting of snow on the torn volcanic peaks of the Cascades; across the Sound to the west, the Olympic Mountains reared out of the water, near enough to reach out a hand and touch. After the lows of last night, this was a day to lift the heart, a day to get out of town.

"I'm off to Seattle," I announced to Bella. "To the university library."

Getting out of town might put a few things into focus. In the night, I had dreamed, not of Janet or Daphne or Lauren Watson, but of Jordan Ambrose and his photograph. And yet, when I woke, I was still ambivalent, resolved one moment to pursue his case to the utmost and damn the consequences, convinced the next that the Ambroses would be better off with another attorney, an attorney out of Springwell, away from pervasive local influences.

Bella pointed to the entry in my daybook. "You're supposed to be seeing Mr. Probert at twelve-thirty about rewriting his will."

Damn Mr. Probert. Crossing off his name, I wrote in Lauren Watson's. "This young woman is coming to see me at four o'clock. It's to do with the Ambrose case. I'll need at least an hour with her. Tell Jack Probert it'll have to be another day. Say I'm sorry but that I had to go to Seattle on a case. Maybe that'll impress him."

Bella was not amused. "Keeping appointments is important, Mr. Noah."

Did she have to set herself up as my keeper? As long her salary was paid, what was she complaining about? So, maybe I was becoming a little obsessed with the Ambrose case. A little obsessiveness is good in an attorney.

Before leaving, I tried Nita Barnes's number. I hung on the line, listening to the distant ringing tone, and knew no one would pick up the receiver; an empty house somehow lends the tone an echoing, lonely quality. A mechanical click interrupted and a voice said, "No one is here right now. Please leave your message after the beep." I understood then why Nita Barnes might have gone to Mexico. She had the distinct sibilant English of a native Spanish speaker and I was surprised that neither Daphne nor Lauren Watson had thought to mention it. In the lily white community of Springwell, Hispanics were as rare as blacks.

I didn't leave a message on the machine. Before I could speak, a lot of clicking and buzzing intruded and the line went dead. The tape was full, which meant that Nita Barnes hadn't picked up her messages for a long while.

Leaving the office and Bella's disapproval behind, I drove the Saab fast down I-5, past the black-and-white mountains and the blue glittering Sound, the radio station playing golden oldies. Oldies at that radio station meant the Beatles, Jimi Hendrix, Peter, Paul and Mary, and I hummed along with the tunes, my cares released for a few hours. At four o'clock, the delightful Ms. Watson would arrive in the office, and for the time being I didn't have to listen to Jack Probert change his mind yet again. Jack Probert had already rewritten his will three times in the past two years, a symptom of eroding faith in his wife's fidelity.

The new glass skyscrapers of Seattle came into view, shimmering in the near distance. Swinging off the freeway to the UW campus, I parked in the underground lot, climbed the echoing concrete stairs, and emerged on the barren brick square at the heart of campus. I'd hardly been back here since my undergraduate days; the sight of the square and the muddled Gothic architecture made the intervening years fall away into an eternity, as if someone unconnected to me had once studied here, had once been fired with all kinds of unlikely ambitions, somewhere in an unimaginably distant past. The setting was the same, Mount Rainier still snowy and majestic at the end of the vista of fountains and lake, George Washington's statue still pigeon-spattered. It was I who had changed, of course. It was virtually impossible to reconstruct myself as that bearded radical youth full of passion and involvement, impossible to understand how he'd gone from that optimistic point in time to a one-man law office in a dying logging town. The journey seemed immense and puzzling.

The passing students appeared to be a different breed from my day, no longer in scruffy jeans and hiking boots, but prepped for the corporate world in chinos and loafers. I thought students should look more radical, but I knew that was an old idea. Nowadays, one had to be ready to conform. I thought I preferred the free-form youth of my day. But in the library, the musty aroma of books and damp parkas and disinfectant was quite unchanged, the small coughs and rustles and suppressed giggles exactly as always. It was, however, the wrong place. Medical texts, I was informed, were kept at Health Sciences.

Health Sciences was on the far edge of campus. Walking over to it on leafy paths, the sunshine and blue skies nearly made me change my mind; it was much too nice a day to spend indoors, especially in Health Sciences.

I'd never been inside the huge Health Sciences building before, had never asked what mysterious experiments went on in the warren of laboratories, didn't want to know now. Even the library reeked of formaldehyde and disease. The librarian weighed me down with a pile of thick textbooks, at once simple and yet incredibly complicated, containing descriptions of bowel obstruction, as if the authors had first read the notes from St. Mary's. Soon I was deep, too deep, into terms that demanded a medical education: *differential diagnoses, loss of extracellular fluid, air in the small bowel, fluid levels in the abdomen.* I gazed with scant understanding at murky reproductions of X rays, impossible for a layman to decipher. But after three hours, though I certainly wouldn't have pretended to be able to diagnose the condition, I had some inkling of what it was all about.

There were drawings and descriptions of the surgery, which made me queasy. The black-and-white illustrations of operations, devoid of blood and flesh, seemed deceptively simple, small mechanical feats of engineering, yet it was difficult not to picture real people under those scalpels, difficult not to wonder how anyone had enough courage to wield the knife in the first place, to slice through living flesh and stem the spurting blood. The text warned of dire consequences and danger, and I decided surgeons must need to be convinced of their own omnipotence and infallibility, or else how could they do such things to people? Did they never lose their nerve? Was that what went wrong with Carl Woods? Had he lost his sense of omnipotence?

God knows, I sympathized with that.

Having absorbed as much as was reasonable for someone with no stomach for that type of knowledge, I emerged from Health Sciences with relief and wandered up University Way, known for some reason as the Ave, in search of coffee. A hangout for students, the Ave was a little tidier and cleaner than in my day and the once-pervasive aroma of pot no longer lingered in the doorways. But it remained a general muddle of T-shirt shops, hamburger joints, popcorn stands, record stores, and junk dealers, all the down-at-heel pandering to student tastes and finances. Along the sidewalks, as in the old days, scruffy characters left over from the sixties still meandered in odd flowing garments, with nowhere to go, nothing to occupy their time, the same empty look around the eyes.

I felt eons older, an interloper, an outsider, fixed in orbit. Along the Ave, in the half-world between campus and real life, I contemplated those long-ago choices that changed real life for me. If I hadn't chosen UCLA for law school, I wouldn't have interned with a California firm. If I hadn't interned there, I wouldn't have met Janet, the graphic artist commissioned to make renderings of a disputed property, her watercolor drawings far more beautiful than the case ever was. I fell in love with the drawings first, then with the artist, who looked like a cheerleader, bouncy and blond and full of energy. If I hadn't married Janet, her particular tragedy wouldn't have become mine. If her particular tragedy hadn't been leukemia and the Fred Hutchinson Cancer Center hadn't been the place to treat it, I wouldn't be wandering the Ave today like a lost sheep. I wouldn't have the Ambrose case. It would be in the hands of someone who'd deal with it in a competent manner.

A twisted path had led me to the middle of the Ave. In the middle of the Ave, it came to me that I'd chosen California in the first place to avoid ever having to work with my father.

So how the hell had I ended up there after all? With Bella around my neck like an albatross? Easy to make the excuse of Janet's illness, easy to say my father's office had been a refuge in time of stress.

I had a sandwich and a cup of coffee among today's less-than-radical student body and knew I'd only given lip service to being radical. It was difficult being the only child of a strong-willed parent, but I couldn't make the excuse that I'd gone to law school just to please my father. The knowledge of law had fascinated me; the power of a law degree had attracted me—the power to right things I thought were wrong. The trouble was, I could hardly remember what it was I once thought so wrong. Until today, back in the seedy surroundings of my youth, that long-ago ambition to become a public defender had been quite forgotten. The salary that Buckins and Brent offered had flattered me; it was seductive to be wooed by one of the best law firms in Los Angeles. I didn't think I regretted it. Each

TEN

ONCE SHE HAD GONE, the creaking house was very empty. The remains of the wind sighed and moaned through the window sashes, an echo of loneliness.

I even missed the sounds of the dogs; a dog would be company, silly, adoring dogs like Daphne's, but not even the most adoring dogs are any good at conversation. Talking to a dog isn't much better than talking to oneself. Another human voice was what I needed. Turning on the television, I flicked through the channels, but, as usual, there was nothing that appealed to me, so I turned it off again, then searched through the rack of CDs and found a favorite recording of *Rosenkavalier*. I raised the volume on the stereo so the pure, lilting voices would fill the empty rooms.

Janet liked opera. Loved it. She'd dragged me, protesting, to the opera in Los Angeles and then in Seattle whenever she could leave the hospital. Said it made her forget, for a while, the sentence hanging over her. I'd been making grateful contributions to the Seattle Opera ever since, but I didn't have the heart to go afterward. Now I missed it because I'd learned to love it, too. The spectacle and the music were yet another part of my life that had disappeared with Janet.

It was late and I hadn't eaten; I knew sleep wouldn't come if I didn't eat something. Opening the refrigerator, I peered into its cold white interior. The shelves held nothing of any surprise or interest. In the days when Father and I were together, I often fixed dinner for the two of us. Father had never learned to cook a thing for himself, but he'd putter about the kitchen with me, set the table, share a beer, and chat about inconsequential daily events. It was com-

panionable and comforting, two solitary men together, even
if we did avoid talking about those matters closest to our
hearts, how adrift we were, how to get our lives back on a
steady course again. Though now I wondered whether it
was a mistaken assumption that he missed his wife as much
as I missed mine. Father believed time healed all wounds,
and time had indeed taken care of his, felling him after two
martinis and a dinner of prime rib.

I had to find some way of taking care of my wounds.
Drinking scotch and allowing time to pass didn't seem to
be working too well.

Taking a beer from the refrigerator, I popped the top and
watched the chill liquid frost the sides of the bottle. The
beer was cool and bitter down my throat and didn't taste
particularly good.

The first act of *Rosenkavalier* partially drowned out the
emptiness. I grabbed a couple of eggs to beat into an omelette and resolved not to think about Janet or Daphne or
Jordan Ambrose or my father; as I held the smooth white
eggs in the palm of my hand, I suddenly found myself
wondering if L. E. Watson liked opera. Ms. Watson? The
voice of conscience in the hospital records? Where had she
sprung from? Maybe it was the sound of Sophie singing in
the other room. Ms. Watson reminded me of Sophie, delicate and light, innocent when everyone around her was
scheming and devious. Was Ms. Watson innocent? Or was
it merely the shining hair and clear fair skin, the transparent
hazel eyes with the dark flecks in them? But I was grateful
it was she who'd come to mind, because she was a far less
tormenting thought than the others that insisted on crowding in on me. What might L. E. stand for? Laura? Lydia?
Lily? I'd once known a girl called Lily, a fat and rather
stupid girl. The beguiling L. E. Watson couldn't possibly
be the owner of a name like Lily.

Names always belong with the people we've known. It
hurt to hear the name Janet. For two years, I'd forced my-

self not to dwell on her name or her face. Now I said, aloud in the kitchen, "Janet, Janet, Janet," as if I could inoculate myself against the sound of it. I tried to conjure up her face, and it became oddly mixed up with the unbidden Ms. Watson's. The same fragile blonde look, but different around the eyes. Janet's eyes were brown and dark-lashed, her blond hair not entirely natural. She used a lightener on it, streaking ashy lines around her temples, the bathroom filled with the tang of peroxide. The bathroom also used to smell of nail polish and talcum powder and toilet water, beguiling female scents I hadn't smelled for two long years. My dulled senses missed not only my wife but all that femininity she brought into a male existence; panty hose drying on the towels, perfumed soap, earrings scattered on the dresser, silky nightgowns, scraps of paper by the telephone with numbers no one recognized, dresses cluttering the closet, bra straps tangling the underwear in the wash.

Standing in the middle of the cold kitchen with a bowl of curdling eggs in my hand, I mourned those trivialities almost as much as the person they came with. Janet had brought frivolity into my life, a frothiness. She was light-hearted and airy, a counterbalance for my innate serious-ness, for all those inherited depressive Welsh genes. She laughed at me and with me and lifted my spirits. I hadn't known how much joy was lacking in my world until she took me in tow, pulling me along with her sunny California temperament—a temperament that came from being born into sunshine, from waking every day to blue skies and warm weather. Without Janet, I was in danger of becoming like my father, humorless and gray like the skies of the Northwest.

Suddenly, I felt dizzy with rage and pain. Rage? I was angry with Janet? For dying? For leaving me high and dry like this, under gray skies, making omelettes alone in an empty house that didn't belong to me? For forsaking me? Abandoning me? For leaving me joyless and unhappy?

Damn it, I *was* angry! Angry and bitter and frustrated and frightened about my future.

I had to sit down then, had to rest my forehead on the kitchen table. My eyes focused on the whorls and curliques in the once well-scrubbed pine, my mother's table in my father's house, and I wanted to bang my head against its hard wooden surface until something other than my heart hurt. I tried taking deep sucking breaths, tried to slow the racing of my pulse, the pounding in my chest, tried to think of something, anything, of solace. Into the raging of my heart floated only one small bubble, which wasn't much comfort. That it was L. E. Watson's face, which I'd transposed on my beloved wife's. Not Daphne's. God forgive me, with all my other problems, my senses were stirring at last and I found myself coveting my friend and neighbor's wife.

Closing my eyes, I knew this was some sort of nadir. There had to be a reason for going on, but I couldn't think what it was.

At that moment, the telephone rang in the kitchen. It rang so infrequently in the house nowadays that the sound sent shock waves through me, disturbing me in my pit of despair. I lifted my head and stared at it balefully, with no intention of answering. A moment ago, I'd wanted to hear another human voice; now I didn't want to speak to anyone. I wanted to drink beer and scotch until I slept without dreams. But the phone continued to ring, jangling around the room, shredding my already-ragged nerves, and at last, reluctantly, I reached for it. It could, after all, be Daphne.

"Yes?"

An intrusive silence stretched at the other end of the line until I almost dropped the receiver back on its hook. Then a female voice, not Daphne's, said hesitatingly, "Mr. Richards?"

"This is Noah Richards," I replied curtly. Was Noah Richards, I thought. Only God knew who I was anymore.

branch of law has its own mysteries that require experience and skill to crack, and I used to relish challenges. Perhaps I also relished proving to my father how much someone was willing to pay me. Though now, somehow, it felt as if he'd won a battle I wasn't quite aware we'd been fighting.

But my father wouldn't approve of the Ambrose case. The Ambrose case was about a wrong. Cheered, I went back to my car on campus and drove north.

Five miles south of Springwell, the exit marked Fairview reminded me of Nita Barnes, and I swung off the freeway. At the first gas station, a laconic youth in greasy overalls directed me. "Left at the light in the middle of town; go till you see the school; turn right. That's Grant Drive."

This was meadow country, open fields and small hedge-rows, sunny and pastoral, the Cascade foothills with their oppressive dark evergreens away on the other side of the freeway. Fairview was on old 99, the highway to Canada before I-5 was built, and its reason for existing evidently ceased at that time. Along the road into town, abandoned gas stations rotted in various stages of disrepair; a single light marked the center of town. But on each side of the road, the homes were neat and trim, the paint recent, as though the owners cared, and at the right-hand turn by the school, the reason for caring became obvious. All of Puget Sound lay before me, the towering background of the Olympics, sharp-toothed and freshly dusted with a new covering of snow, the islands clear in the near distance. Far below, marine traffic braided the shining water, a huge container ship, a Washington State ferry, a green-and-black tug towing a couple of barges. I could see all the way up the Sound, almost to the Strait of Juan de Fuca, to Vancouver Island and Canada. I nearly ran the car off the road looking at the view.

I drove too far along Grant Drive, had to reverse and backtrack. The hand-painted numbers on the mailboxes eventually identified 12254 as a small blue house set back from the road by a long driveway. What I hoped to find there, I wasn't sure. Satisfy my curiosity, perhaps, get some sort of answer for Ms. Watson. I parked on the road and walked up the driveway.

It was a cheap little house, poorly constructed, the blue paint thin and peeling on the siding, no sign of life and no number on the cracked wooden front door. I banged on the door, felt the hollow core of it under my fist, didn't expect an answer and didn't get one. Turning to admire the extraordinary view again, I pictured a sturdy house here with wide decks and long windows to face the Sound and Olympics and catch the western sun. That sun, already sinking fast, streamed almost horizontally into my eyes and onto the small dusty windows, and I put my hand against the glass to peer inside. I saw a couple of couches with flowered throws, a television set, a pile of magazines on the floor. Then I went round to the back of the house, away from the view and the sunshine, into the shadows, passing a sagging wooden garage that a good wind like last night's should have brought down. At the back was a sloping, scraggly yard, wooden steps up to the back door. The steps were rickety and creaky. I rattled the handle of the door, stared into the small kitchen, which was clean and tidy, nothing of note. Nita Barnes was definitely not at home.

I turned to leave.

At the foot of the steps, a man stood, watching me.

He was tall, thin, and immobile and he wore an army fatigue cap pulled down over his eyes. One hand held a steel chain attached to a thick-necked dog and the other hand was deep inside a loose green parka. His sudden and silent appearance so startled me, I let out a sort of yelp, like a dog myself, and flattened my back against the door.

"Christ!" I said. "Where did you come from?"

The dog bared its teeth, its strong curving legs straining against the chain. The owner didn't answer. Below the cap, his bony jaw moved rhythmically, as though he was chewing tobacco, and there was a distinct smell of menace to him. When at last he did speak, his voice was aggressive and threatening. "What the hell do you think you're doing there?"

I pushed away from the supporting door. "This isn't your house, is it?"

"Never mind whose house it is. It sure as hell ain't yours. What do you want?"

"I'm looking for Nita Barnes. She lives here, doesn't she?"

The jaws worked compulsively, and I fully expected a stream of tobacco juice to come shooting out at me. He said, "So what do you want with her?"

"Not that it's any of your business, but I'm an attorney. My name is Noah Richards. What's yours?"

"Never mind what my name is. I'm not the one who's trespassing, am I?"

"Aren't you? How do I know that?"

"How do I know you're an attorney?"

I reached into my inside pocket to get one of my cards, and he immediately snarled, "Get your hand out of your pocket."

"Listen, don't speak to me like that. You want to see my card or not?"

Jerking at the dog, he backed away a couple of feet. "Okay, if it's really a card. But don't try anything funny, mister. I got a gun pointing right at your gut." He made a threatening motion with the hand inside the parka.

I gaped at him in spite of myself. "A gun?" Did everyone but me carry a gun in this part of the world? I thought of asking him if he had a license for it, as I'd asked Angel, then thought better of it.

"The card, mister."

The situation felt like something out of a second-rate movie. But he was real enough, and there was something dangerous and feral about him, as if he occupied a different world from mine. The set of his shoulders, the angle of his head, the regular unceasing movements of the lower jaw all made me think of one of those automatons, programmed for destruction, in those same second-rate movies. I itched to leap off the steps, smash my fist into his face to stop that compulsive chewing movement, even if the thought of touching him made my flesh crawl. But a gun changed the complexion of things. Another reason why I hated guns—they made a fight unfair. I was about to tell him to go to hell when he shifted the hand in the pocket and I decided it might be wiser not to bait him. God knows what his reaction might be. He wasn't like a normal human being. Putting my left hand high in the air, I dug around with the right in my inside pocket, pulled a card out, held it up between thumb and finger. "See. Just a common business card."

Lunging forward, he grabbed it from my outstretched hand. He reeked of paranoia. I got a better look at his face under the shadowing cap: long, heavy jaw, thin lips, high cheekbones. My hand, I was surprised to see, was quite steady.

The steel-trap jaw chewed faster. "Okay, so what does it say?"

"Can't you read?"

"Don't be funny, mister. Just tell me."

I shrugged. "Noah Richards, Attorney-at-Law, five five six oh Elmer, Springwell, Washington nine eight seven seven three. Telephone number: five-five-five-five-seven-two-three. Home number: five-five-five-seven-eight-nine-one."

I still couldn't see his eyes, but the tight shoulders relaxed slightly, his spine slackening as if a steel rod had been removed. He did spit then, a stream of black tobacco juice in a sideways shot, not at me, but at the ground near his feet, feet encased in heavy working boots, like a logger, laced high around the ankles. I couldn't imagine how he'd crept up so silently in them.

"An attorney, eh? So what do you want with the girl?"

"None of your damned business, whoever you are. Who are you?"

There was a brief gleam of teeth under the shadow of the cap. "Just a friendly neighbor, keeping an eye on the property around here. You never know who's wandering about. Looked to me like you was breaking in."

At least he'd begun to address me like a human being now. I eased back against the door, put my hands in my pockets. "In the middle of the afternoon? In broad daylight?"

"That's when break-ins happen, ain't it? When everyone's at work. If you're really a lawyer, you'd know that."

He kept his eyes fixed on me, the lower half of his face still engaged in that incessant chewing. I'd no intention of leaving the porch until he moved away, and he didn't appear to have any intention of moving. The dog sat alertly at his feet, ears pricked, teeth eager, a pit bull cross of some kind, the stereotypical dog for a gun-toting nutcase. The light was fading fast from the sky and a small chill wind sprang up, whispering among the trees. I felt a long way from home.

"When did you last see Miss Barnes?" I asked.

He shrugged as though it was of no interest. "Ain't seen her for weeks. Don't have nothing to do with her anyways. You know her?"

"No. But I want to talk with her."

"What she been doing? She in trouble with the law?"

"What makes you say that?"

Rolling the juice in his mouth, he spat again, sideways. "Cheap Mexican trash. They're all alike. Nothing but trouble."

"She's a nurse. At St. Mary's."

"Bet she's no real nurse." There was contempt in the

uneducated voice. "You know what they're like, those wetbacks. No schooling. No nothing."

If I were Nita Barnes, I certainly wouldn't want this guy as my neighbor. No one would want him as a neighbor. "She's an R.N.," I stated categorically. I knew that was true. I remembered how she'd signed her notes.

"Coming here, taking jobs away from citizens of the United States, going on welfare. They ought to be put on a truck and sent back where they came from."

"Well," I commented, "I'm sure she's happy you're keeping such a good eye on her house for her."

Another brief flash of teeth glinted in the shadowy face. "It's not her house. Anyways, it's her I keep an eye, not just the house."

If he gave me the creeps, God knows what he did to her. "So whose house is it?" I asked.

"Someone who should know better than to rent it to Latino trash."

Another silence ensued. There was the incongruous sound of birds singing in the shrubbery at the end of the sloping yard. The dog rattled its chain, showed the whites of its eyes. "Keep my card," I said, for want of something else to say. "If you see her, ask her to give me a call."

He shook his head. "I don't talk to her."

"Then give me a call yourself if you see her. What's your name? So I know who's calling."

"I ain't going to call no one. When are you going to leave?"

I was only too anxious to leave. I pushed myself away from the support of the door, eyed the dog. "Back off with the dog. He looks jumpy to me."

"Don't worry about the dog. I got him well under control."

He had the dog as much under control as he had himself—on a tight leash. I didn't trust either of them. When

I put a cautious foot forward, the dog immediately stood on all fours, hair rising stiffly at the nape of its thick neck.

"Back him off," I ordered. "Otherwise, we'll be here all night."

He jerked at the chain and the dog sat again. "See, he knows who's boss." He took a couple of steps backward, but the dog didn't take its eyes off me.

I was so angry, I felt nauseated. I didn't even want to keep my temper, could feel the heat in my face and at the back of my neck, the blood tingling in my fingers. I had to dig my hands deep in my pockets not to lash out at him. Coming down the steps slowly and deliberately, at last I could see his face clearly, and I took a careful look at it. It was thin and bony and curiously expressionless, protruding cheekbones and pale-washed eyes with barely visible eyelashes and eyebrows. Under the cap, his hair was surely very light. He was taller than I was by several inches, and though I wasn't totally convinced about the gun under his jacket, I wouldn't have bet on it. I would remember the face.

Hating to turn away from him, or from the dog, I could hardly walk backward all the way down to the road. The hair at the nape of my neck prickled at the thought of the two of them behind me. When I did look up the driveway in the last remnants of the setting sun, he was still watching, the chain in his left hand, the right hand in his pocket, and as I climbed into the security of the Saab and slammed the door, the ominous shape remained motionless, rigid as a statue, at the top of the slope.

So much for the fair citizens of Fairview. I accelerated away fast and wondered how many more there were like him, ruining the beautiful scenery. I hoped Nita Barnes had returned to Mexico, for her own sake.

TWELVE

DUSK HAD FALLEN by the time I swung into the parking lot by the office; the lights streamed out in welcome. I was immeasurably relieved to be back there. At precisely the same moment, a small red Datsun drew up alongside and Ms. Watson got out, caught in the friendly light. Smaller than I remembered, she wore a big dark coat that swamped her, and with the fair hair pulled away from her forehead and tied in a ponytail at the back of her neck, she looked no more than a high school kid.

When I spoke her name, she shot a startled glance over her shoulder, that same apprehensive look I'd seen at the hospital. As I held the office door open for her, she hesitated, as if she might yet change her mind; then she pulled the folds of the coat around herself protectively and ducked past my arm.

Bella sat neat and tidy at her desk, providing the office a reassuring legitimacy. "Anything urgent?" I asked.

Predictably, she shook her head. "Hold the calls," I commanded, as though dozens of clients were beating at my door, and I ushered Ms. Watson into the inner sanctum. The tired old room appeared almost warm and comfortable at this time of day, the glow from the lamp on the desk spreading a patina on the ancient furniture, hiding the wear in the shabby rug. Ms. Watson let me take her coat. Under it, she wore not the white uniform, but a long skirt almost to her ankles and a bulky sweater that hung loosely on her shoulders, as if she'd recently lost weight. She perched cautiously on the edge of her chair, eyes flicking around the room, on guard among the layers of sweater and skirt. The lamplight shone on her blonde head and smooth white forehead.

I wanted to put her at her ease, wanted to ask her if she liked opera. I also badly needed a drink. Opening the bottom drawer, I brought out the bottle of scotch and set it in front of me. "Before we start, I'm going to have a drink. Would you like one? Scotch?"

She was taken aback and pulled her mouth down in distaste. "Thanks, but I never touch hard liquor. I can't bear the taste of it."

"Mind if I do?"

She shrugged slightly. "Feel free."

Pouring a healthy slug into the glass, I tried not to knock it back too quickly. I wanted to get rid of the taste of the guy in the cap.

"How long have you worked at St. Mary's, Lauren? You mind if I call you Lauren?"

She smiled briefly. The smile took away the wariness, made her face gentle and pretty in the soft light. "Lauren's fine." She shifted in the chair. "I've been at St. Mary's eighteen months."

"And before that?"

"You want a resumé?"

"Sure."

"Well, I got my nursing degree at the University of Washington six years ago. I was at Childrens Hospital for a couple of years; then I went to Harborview and worked in the ICU there."

I made a quick calculation. If she graduated six years ago, she would be about twenty-eight or twenty-nine now.

"Childrens?" I asked. "Do you know Dr. Randolph Sweigert?"

Her face brightened. "Oh, yes. He's one of the attendings there."

"If you worked at Children's, you must be familiar with the treatment of children?"

The brightness faded from her face. "I guess so."

"And the ICU at Harborview? That must have been hard. Rewarding but hard. May I ask why you left?"

There was a subtle change in her expression, a closing up, a return of the insecurity. She lowered her eyes. "I moved up here to be near my sister. She lives in Springwell."

"Harborview's a busy hospital. You'd have seen a lot there." Harborview was the trauma center for the Northwest, a branch of the university. It took the burns, the road accidents and gunshot wounds, the overdoses, all the detritus of twentieth-century living.

She sighed, a fluttering sound. "Yes. I saw a lot. And I needed a change. You can get burned-out in high-powered places like that, you know. All the waste of life. All those machines. Half the time, it felt we were just keeping people alive so their organs could be donated. I got to feel like a piece of machinery myself."

She seemed too small and fragile to have labored in the trenches of such a battlefield.

"So you came to St. Mary's?"

Her eyes wandered away from me, back again, her mouth curving downward. "I thought I'd like to work somewhere where death was ordinary, you know. Death is part of a nurse's life, isn't it? I didn't expect anything like…" Her voice trailed away.

I poured another slug of scotch. I couldn't get rid of the encounter at Nita Barnes's place. "Tell me about Nita Barnes," I said.

"Nita? What do you want to know?"

"She's Hispanic, isn't she?"

Ms. Watson seemed surprised I'd ask. "Yes, I suppose. Her name's really Juanita. But she's been in the States for years. She used to be married to an American."

"And isn't anymore?"

"Divorced or separated. She never speaks of it."

"Did she ever say anything about unpleasant neighbors? People making threats?"

She stared at me. "Threats? What sort of threats?"

"I don't know. I was hoping maybe you could tell me. She never said anything to you?"

Lowering her eyes again, she huddled into the layers of clothes. "Nita and I aren't exactly friends, you know. Just coworkers. We don't see each other outside of the hospital." Her voice dropped. "Has someone threatened her? You think that's why she ran away?"

"You believe she's run away?"

"I don't know."

"Well, she certainly wasn't at home when I went there today. There was no sign of her, but I found this guy checking out the visitors. He wasn't exactly friendly and he wasn't kindly disposed toward Hispanics. He said something about the person she rented the house from. You don't know who that is?"

She clasped her hands together, knuckles tightly laced. "From one of the doctors at the hospital. Dr. Grogan, I think it is."

"Grogan? You mean the surgeon? Dr. Woods's colleague?"

"Yes. That Dr. Grogan."

"How did she come to rent it from him?"

"There was a notice on the board in the hospital cafeteria."

I don't trust coincidences. Most events have cause and effect. It seemed too much of a coincidence that a witness had gone missing from a house owned by one of the doctors at St. Mary's. On the yellow pad, I circled and bracketed the names of Barnes, Grogan, and Woods.

I said, "He might know where she's gone. I could ask him."

Her fingers clutched and unclutched. "What sort of man are you talking about? This neighbor?"

"Oh, the backwoods type, fatigues, pit bull. Just some bullying punk." But that wasn't how I thought of him. He'd been threatening and dangerous, and the encounter had unsettled and rattled me, left a nasty flavor. I finished off the scotch, fingered the records on the desk, then opened them at random.

"What I really want to talk to you about, of course, Lauren, is Jordan Ambrose."

I looked up at her and she was completely motionless in the chair, as though frozen. She made a small sound in her throat; all the color had vanished from her cheeks, the pupils of her eyes were black and huge, blotting out the flecked irises. She stared blindly around the room.

"I shouldn't have come. It was stupid of me to come." She shrank inside the huge sweater. "There's too much at stake for any of this."

I hadn't asked one thing to do with Jordan Ambrose.

"Miss Watson. Lauren. If someone's told you not to speak about Jordan Ambrose, you must tell me. No one can prevent you talking to a lawyer, you know. That's obstruction of justice."

She wouldn't look at me. "I can't afford to lose my job."

"You can always get another. Nurses as well trained as you don't have trouble getting jobs."

"You don't understand."

"No, I don't. And can't, not unless you tell me."

Gripping the arms of the chair, she slid out of it, backed toward the door. Always trying to escape me.

"Has someone spoken to you about this case, Lauren? Just tell me and we can sort out the problem together. Someone at the hospital? Another lawyer? One of the doctors?"

She paused, the flecked eyes widening, and reached for her coat.

"Dr. Woods?"

I thought she was going to leave without saying anymore, but then she said, "No, of course not. Not Dr. Woods."

"Then who?"

She was struggling with the coat, and I went to help, putting my hands on her shoulders as I did so. Turning her head away from me, avoiding my eyes, she pulled the collar around her face, took a deep, shaky breath, and then suddenly the words came rushing out of her as though a dam had broken. "You can't know what it was like in the operating room with that baby. I was there. I saw it. How he dwindled away during the operation, how they opened his chest and massaged his heart, then unhooked the machines and went away, and he was left there, his little body gray and limp and torn." Tears brimmed and spilled down the stricken face. "You could say we murdered that little boy. All of us. We're all guilty."

"Not murder," I protested. "That's too strong a word."

"Is it? I wish to God it was. I wish I could help. But please don't make me."

Holding her by the shoulders, I turned her to face me, and her body was stiff and resistant. "As soon as I described that man at Nita Barnes's house, you panicked. Who is he? What does he have to do with you, Lauren?"

She put her hands over her face.

"Has he threatened you, too? Is that it?"

But she kept her hands clamped over her face. I couldn't force her to speak. I couldn't even force her to stay. When I dropped my hands, she darted into the outer office, and by the time I got to the front door, she was already in her car, slamming through the gears, not even turning on the headlights until the intersection. I had to stand and watch her go. I'd wanted to stop her leaving and hadn't been able to. I wanted to find out what was troubling her and hadn't known the right words.

I WAS A LAWYER, not a policeman. It wasn't my job to delve into the secret lives and consciences of the employees of St. Mary's. Was it?

I stood for a long time mulling over the day.

Bella was gone, her desk tidy, cover on the computer, pencils and pens put away in their plastic holder. A pile of papers sat beside the computer with a note in thick felt pen. "10:00 a.m. appt with Jack Probert to set up a living trust." Bella was doing her best to keep my practice going.

I groaned at the thought of Jack Probert and his often-changed will, but it was, after all, my bread and butter. Reluctantly, I shuffled through the papers, the complications of Jack Probert's family life, the names penciled in. Tomorrow I'd have to see him, couldn't put it off again.

Taking the papers into my room, I poured another drink, thought about Lauren Watson, gazed into the whisky glass.

I wasn't usually in the office this late, not these days. In L.A., we frequently worked late, the norm for ambitious young associates, and when we worked late, we'd sometimes help ourselves from the fancy bar in the conference room, then top the bottles up with water. Every week at the Friday general meeting, someone would grumble about the deteriorating quality of the scotch. We'd smirk behind our hands, a smart-assed bunch of young attorneys, believing we were conning our elders and betters, but now, alone in my own office, sipping my own undiluted scotch, I knew they must have been wise to us all along. I felt a sudden jolting pang for the companionship of those days, the people along the hall to laugh with, the paralegals and secretaries and associates my own age. In those days, I didn't mind working late. Now, when there was no one at home waiting for me, I was out of the office by six o'clock most evenings. One of the smaller ironies of life.

Bella's draft of the Probert trust was word-perfect, of course. It should take less than an hour the next day. Also in the pile was Bigelow Harrison's real estate deal. For another hour, I tried to concentrate on the problems, making a note to call Bigs the next day. If for no other reason, I had to talk to him about this partnership with the surgeons.

I turned to the Ambrose file.

Law firms grow because one person can't keep all those balls in the air—real estate deals, living trusts, cases like the Ambrose case. Ahead of me stretched weeks and months of depositions and opinions and investigations. A suit has to be fully prepared beforehand. Dangerous to file without being fully prepared, without being ready for any question that may come up or any answer that might be given. I'd need another surgical opinion, preferably from out of state; depositions from Woods, the surgeon; from Clarke, the pediatrician; from the nurses. I'd depose Lauren Watson; then she'd have to talk to me.

It wasn't just a drawn-out, daunting task. It meant there wouldn't be time for anything else, nothing to earn Bella's salary, let alone my own, nothing to pay the rent on the office or the telephone bill.

And right now, suddenly, I was ravenous, as though the gastric juices had decided to flow after months of quiescence. On the desk, the brass clock showed nearly nine o'clock. Shoving the bottle back in the drawer, I closed the Ambrose file, turned off the lights, and went in search of food.

The easiest and closest place was Joe's. I didn't need the car, but I took it anyway, trying to tell myself I would return to the office afterward. In truth, there was nothing to go back for. If I was going to find answers to Jordan Ambrose, I needed to get out of the office.

In Joe's, the large dim space was almost empty. I never went there at night, disciplining myself to go home instead of hanging out in bars. Home was dull but safe. I imagined Joe's would be full of life in the evenings; it was always crammed in the old days, awash with beer and laughter and argument. So I was surprised to find only two couples at the tables and just four men squatting in a massive row on the bar stools, drinking silently, eyes riveted on the TV above their heads. It was a relief, in a way, not to be on the outside of a horde of others having a good time, but a half-empty tavern has a dispiriting feel. I slid behind a table, my back against the rough log wall, ordered a New York steak, medium rare, and a Heineken, and idly watched the soporific blur of the game on the box, the sound too low to hear the commentary.

It was a few minutes before I realized that one of the men at the bar was Joseph Ambrose.

The recognition came as a shock, as if someone from my past had reappeared inconveniently. Joseph Ambrose, with his aching face and defeated shoulders, was an insubstantial figure in my mind, a mere appendage to the avenging Angel. He was someone I didn't want to think about. I certainly hadn't expected to find him here and didn't need him to see me, not now, just as I was getting the taste of the day out of my system. I considered slipping away, but my steak was already ordered. I leaned into the shadows against the wall and hoped he wouldn't turn his head and spot me.

His black face was difficult to see clearly in the dim tavern light. I wouldn't have thought I'd have recognized him, but there was something unmistakable in the set of his head, even under the cap, something in the shape of his shoulders and the long graceful arc of his spine. He sat at the end of the row of men, oversized like himself, and now I saw they all wore similar jackets with BENNETTS MILL stenciled on the back in faded yellow. They sat together and yet apart, exchanging the odd comment about the game but otherwise seemingly alone with their thoughts. Superficial buddies from work, I guessed, without much in common. I admitted to myself that it was a small surprise to see Springwell mill workers drinking in the company of a black man.

The steak arrived at the same moment the game ended on the box. The men at the bar shifted and turned and, inevitably, as I had known he must, Joseph Ambrose swung on the bar stool, followed the waitress with his eyes, and saw me. I knew he'd seen me, even though I avoided looking at him. I could feel his eyes on my face. The men were talking and laughing together, as if it was safe to be easy and friendly now it was time to leave. "Load of garbage," one of them said—about the game, I supposed. "Well, back to the doghouse." Slapping hands, they moved to the door. Joseph said, "There's someone I wants a word with. See you guys later, okay?" I looked up then. The men were watching him watching me and they stared curiously. The doors swung and crashed behind them and I was left alone with him.

I swallowed a chunk of bread.

He came lumbering over to my table. "Mind if I sit here a minute?"

I waved to the seat beside me.

"Join me in a beer?"

He took off his cap, laying it carefully on the chair next to him. The cap left a deep crease across his forehead, as though he wore it most of the time. "Had enough," he said simply. "I'm not much of a one for drinking. But the guys asked me to have a beer with them and watch the game." He gazed at the door as if he wished, after all, he'd gone with them.

"Guys from the mill?"

"Yeah. Not bad dudes. Once you get to know them." He shifted his gaze back to me. "Took awhile."

I lifted my glass. "How've you been, Mr. Ambrose?"

He massaged the crease in his brow. With his buddies, he'd been smiling, but now the melancholy was back, flattening the light out of his eyes. He looked older, graven lines in the thick black flesh, touches of gray in his hair, a slump of age in the heavy body.

"To tell the truth, Mr. Richards, not so good. I came with the guys because it's better than going home, and that's a fact. Angel, you know, she's hell-bent on this suing business and she won't let it alone, not for one damn minute. You gets tired of hearing the same old tune. And the thing is, Mr. Richards, begging your pardon and all that, but I ain't so keen on getting mixed up with lawyers."

I dug a fork into the mess of potato and sour cream. "Very wise of you, Mr. Ambrose."

"Yeah, maybe." He sighed into his belly. "But it ain't just that, you know. I got me a decent job here and I don't want to screw it up. Ain't so easy to find work these days. I was lucky. A buddy in the army, white guy, he's a pal of the foreman at Bennetts and he put a word in for me. I was sort of surprised, to tell the truth, that they gave a job to a dude like me. But the foreman, he was in Nam and he likes vets."

He wanted to talk and I resigned myself. "How long were you in Vietnam?"

"Two-year tour. Got to be sergeant." He slapped his arm where the stripes would have been. "Ended up running the supply depot down at Fort Lewis. That's how I could handle this job I got now, same sort of deal, organizing inventory, keeping stock. The army was good to me, but, well, I'd been in twenty years. Long enough, I reckon. Got me a pension and all. Angel wanted me to get out while I could still get a job on the outside." He sighed again. "But to tell the truth, I miss the life. Had a lot of good buddies in the army. Now it's just me and Angel. A wife ain't the same as a buddy, you know."

I concentrated on my steak.

"The thing is," he said, "if it gets out we're suing the hospital and those doctors, life won't be worth living at Bennetts. I won't have no job no more. Easy to get rid of folks, you know. Guys get laid off every day."

Putting down my knife, I leaned closer to him, trying to read his eyes. "Has someone been telling you that?"

"No. But it don't take a genius to work that out."

"Listen, Joseph. I think you've got a case. But don't let me talk you into it. It's up to you and Angel. If you don't want to go on with it, then don't. It's your decision. But you should discuss it with her, not with me. Because it's the two of you who have to decide."

He rested his thick forearms on the table and gazed past my left ear. "But what do you think about it?"

I thought about it for a long moment, looked squarely into his sad face. "It's easy for me to tell you to stand up for your rights and not let anyone intimidate you. But I hear what you're saying. This is a small town; they stick up for one another here. Maybe you should think about getting another job somewhere, out of Springwell."

Bending his head over his arms, he stared at the table. "I got another family, you know. Grown kids. I was married real young, first time. I got a boy at Texas A&M. Doing very fine. First one in the family to go to college. Plays defense on the football team. He's good enough, they say, to make the pros, but if he don't, he's getting hisself a college education. And then I got two girls getting an education, too. Yessir, not so bad, considering. Their mama ran off when they was little, took the kids with her. She didn't like the service, always on the move, never knowing where next, so one day she ups and leaves, just like that. Walks out while I'm gone and never comes back. Women sure can be a pain, Mr. Richards. Think you're doing right by them and then all of a sudden they're off, no explanations, no nothing. You married, Mr. Richards?"

I shook my head. It didn't need two of us telling stories of the women who'd abandoned them.

"Well, maybe you're smart. Angel and me met when I was stationed down in Georgia. Real sweet baby, she was. Thought I was real lucky, and I was, you know, finding me

a fine young lady like that.'' His face brightened for a moment. ''But sometimes I wonder if Angel ain't too young
for me. Or I'm too old for her. She's got all this energy,
fizzes along like some sort of motor, always full of gas.
'Drive and ambition,' she calls it. And the truth is, Mr.
Richards, these days I sorta feel like putting my feet up
and just hanging out. I'd go back south, live off my pension. We could live good there, living's cheap down south.
But Angel, she won't hear of it. She likes it up here, likes
her job. Thinks we can make something of ourselves, but
I say to her, 'What is there to make? We got more than
enough to live on if you don't want to live too fancy.' She
was sure she would make something of Jordan, poor little
bugger. She reckoned he'd have a better chance up here
than down south, and maybe she was right. But now? Now
I say, what the hell's the point?''

I wanted to help, wanted to ease his burdens, yet I wasn't
at all sure the road we were embarking on was the best
way to accomplish that. But I knew it was the road Angel
was determined to take. Joseph Ambrose, it seemed to me,
was between a rock and a hard place, damned if he went
ahead with the case, damned if he didn't. If he went ahead,
he'd need stomach for the fight, and it didn't look to me
as though he had much stomach for anything. If he tried to
drop the case, I guessed it would cost him his marriage. It
might also cost Angel her revenge, because, right or wrong,
a jury calculates a child's worth on the worth of his parents'
lives. It's unpleasant to face some of the truths of our society. I knew the child of a black couple would fetch less
in the courts than the child of a white couple, even less if
there wasn't a deprived father as well as a deprived mother.
I could hear myself making the argument. ''Ladies and gentlemen of the jury. The death of her child cost this young
woman not only her son but her marriage, as well. The
damage to her life is incalculable.'' I could see the smart,
vibrant Angel in the witness chair and knew she would

never touch the hearts of a jury as Joseph would. She didn't touch my heart as he did.

"Angel needs you," I said. "She needs to pursue this case. It's important for her. Do you think you could really walk away from it? Forget about what happened?"

The black eyes glistened for a second, quickly went flat and expressionless. "I won't never forget, Mr. Richards." He shook his head. "No, sir, I won't never forget. But she's talking vengeance, Mr. Richards, and I'm not into that. Vengeance ain't what I'm looking for."

"What are you looking for, Joseph?"

He turned his face away from me for a moment, as though he was thinking, and sighed again, deep into his soul. "Peace and quiet, I guess. Just a bit of peace and quiet."

I pushed my plate aside. Somehow I'd eaten everything. "'The peace that passeth all understanding,'" I said.

"That's from the Bible, ain't it?"

"Death. That's the only real peace we get in this world, Joseph. Until then, we've got to fight the good fight."

I was telling him what I needed to tell myself.

THIRTEEN

THE NEXT MORNING, I woke too early, much too early. Weekends were already long enough. Watery sunshine was seeping between the drapes at the bedroom window and I lay in bed, trying to decide what to do with the day. The pale bright light decided me. I would go fishing.

In November, the weather in the Northwest is hopeless for everything except steelhead fishing. It's too late to sail and too early to ski, but it's just right for steelhead, because November is when they run. The wettest, dreariest days are the best for catching the elusive sweet-fleshed fish, and if a sunny morning like this didn't offer great hope of success, anything was better than idling around the house. I would take the dinghy up to the river at the north end of the lake.

It was almost nine o'clock before all the small puttering tasks that are half the fun of fishing were finally completed: spark plugs cleaned, rods checked, the dinghy's tank topped up with oil and gas, a thermos full of coffee, a sandwich and a six-pack in the cooler. Casting off from the dock, I pulled the starter cord a couple of times until the outboard broke into smoky life; then I made a slow test circle in the dark water and headed up the lake toward the north.

I turned to watch the house disappearing among the trees. From this distance, it looked cosy and welcoming. From this distance, I could think with pleasure of returning to it later in the day, to a hot shower and a scotch, but once away from the dock, the soft echoing silence of water and mountains enveloped and soothed me, emptying my mind.

The lake was very familiar to me—every house and dock along its shores, every backwater where the salmon lurked in the season, every branch where the eagles watched, each shingled beach where the raccoons came to fish, the deer to drink. I knew the shape of the mountains even when they were hidden in mist, knew how the thermals rode down the slopes, which spots on the lake lifted a sailboat, which became dead holes. Today, the lake was mine alone. For a moment, it was like being a child again, pretending I was an Indian alone with his native land before the white man came to despoil it.

It took more than an hour to reach the north end of the lake. At that point, a river emptied into the lake, with a channel deep enough for a boat and a tiny scrub-covered island to beach it. From the island, I could fish the river where it ran deep under the lea of the hillside, where the steelhead paused on their way upstream. As I headed the boat into the river mouth, the clouds rolled up from the south, obliterating the sun and improving the chances of snaring one of the secretive fish.

But when I reached the island, I was disappointed to find another dinghy pulled up on the flat rocks among the drift-wood; like any fisherman, I wanted the place to myself. I scanned the river, along the banks on either side, but couldn't see the owner of the boat. He must have waded upstream, around the bend of the river where the water grew shallow, and as this was the only spot to get ashore easily, I headed my dinghy next to the other one and switched off the engine. An immense silence enveloped me. Gradually, my ears adjusted to the stillness of the moun-tains, to the soft lapping of water around the rocks, the harsh call of a heron somewhere among the dark trees, a whisper of wind high in the conifers. Already renewed and invigorated, I took a few mouthfuls of hot sweet coffee, rigged the line, pulled on my waders, and stepped off the rocks, until the cold water was above my knees, then cast the line.

I aimed for a spot about twenty feet away where the alders leaned into the river and the water eddied sluggishly, but the line didn't quite make it. I was out of practice. Reeling in, I tried again. It took several attempts before I got it just right, the line singing and arcing, the reel spinning, the lure splashing gently into the black oily water at exactly the right point. Wading among the rocks, I let the line out a few more feet, waited, reeled in, started again, then again, and again. A wonderfully absorbing, brainless occupation: The rhythm of the cast, the exact turn of the wrist, the arcing flight of the brilliantly colored fly in the soft gray air, the movement of the river, the cadence of the water—were a hypnotic end in themselves. The purpose of the exercise, the catching of a fish, became meaningless.

Time passed.

How much time passed, I wasn't sure, until my trance was disturbed by the sound of a human voice, near to me.

"Hi there, buddy! Any luck?"

I'd long forgotten about the other fisherman. A few yards away, from the river end of the island, a big ruddy-faced man in a down parka, green waders to his thighs, and a khaki cap festooned with lures came splashing through the shallows toward me. Two good-sized steelhead swung from his hand and he grinned triumphantly, teeth large and white. "Tombstone teeth," we called them when I was a boy.

"Any luck?" he asked again as he stood watching my line stretching across the river.

"Nothing so far." I walked backward into shallower water, reeled in, and for the first time became aware how chilled I was.

The stranger beamed under the brim of his gaudy fisherman's hat. "It's a great life, though, isn't it? Christ, we're lucky to live in such great country, aren't we? Just step out of your back door and in a few minutes, you're miles from the damn telephone. Don't have to drive for hours, don't have to jostle with the crowds. As an extra bonus, you can catch some damn fish, too." He held his catch up to be admired.

"Where d'you get them?" I asked, to be polite.

"Hundred yards or so upstream, round the bend. There's an eddy like that one you're trying, but more sheltered. I usually get something there if I'm out early enough."

"Yeah, I'm late. And out of practice." I examined the fly I was using. "Not one damn nibble so far." Propping the rod against a log, I blew into my hands and slapped my arms around my body. "Bit chilly, isn't it?"

He grinned again. "Only when you don't catch anything."

"There's some coffee in my boat," I said. "Want some?"

"Coffee won't cut it." He reached inside his parka and flourished a small silver flask. "Brandy. That'll warm your gills," and he offered it to me.

I took a grateful swig. The liquor slid down my throat and made me cough, warmed my stomach and lungs. Wiping the back of my hand across my mouth, I returned the flask to him and, in turn, he took a swallow. It was sort of friendly, standing knee-deep in cold rushing water, miles from anywhere, not another soul in sight, sharing a dram with a stranger. He waded closer and looked at my line.

"I'd say that lure's too heavy. The lighter ones work better along this particular stretch of water." He shoved the flask back in his pocket and took off the khaki cap, examining the array of flies. His bared head had smooth, thick white hair. "Here, try this," and he handed me a small shiny green arrangement, beautifully fashioned.

I turned the lure in my cold fingers, admiring the way the fine strands of fur and feathers caught the dull light of the day. "It's a work of art. Where do you find pieces like these?"

"Don't find 'em. Make 'em myself. Nice change from my normal line of business." He laughed. "Well, maybe not such a change. But with flies, you can throw away the ones that don't pan out, start again. Bit more difficult to do that with the failures in my everyday work.''

It was the sort of remark calculated to make me ask what his line of business was, and so I did.

''I'm a surgeon,'' he said, and as though we weren't standing in a river miles from civilization, he stuck out his hand. ''Name is Woods. Carl Woods.''

I had taken the proffered hand automatically. It was surprisingly warm and firm and the fingers clasped mine tightly. I felt as though I'd been burned.

It was unbelievable that chance had put us together in the immensity of the Cascades. I dropped his hand, too quickly, and he looked at me more closely. ''You from around here? Your face is familiar somehow.''

Stepping back two more feet onto the rocks, I stared around at the black rushing water, at the mist-wreathed trees, at the gleaming fish hanging from his left hand—anywhere but at his face. There was a chance, I supposed, that he wouldn't know my name. At last, I said reluctantly, ''I live in Springwell. Noah Richards.''

''Noah Richards?'' He screwed up his eyes. They were a light hazy blue, the eyebrows oddly black above them. ''Now where have I heard that name before?''

I could have changed the subject. I could have talked of the fishing, the weather, the state of the nation, the Seahawks, anything. But the avoidance of truth is as much a lie as a deliberate untruth. Foolish as it might seem out there in the wilderness, it was only ethical to tell him who I was, before I engaged him in another word of conversation. He had shared his drink with me. I had to share the truth with him.

''You've probably heard it before, Dr. Woods,'' I said deliberately, ''because I'm about to file a malpractice suit against you. In the matter of the death of Jordan Ambrose.''

It didn't register at first, as though he hadn't heard what I'd said, as though he was still trying to place my name.

Then he sucked in his breath and dropped the fish from his hand. They floated for a moment on the water around his feet and he stared down, immobilized, watching as they circled sluggishly on the surface. We both stared at them, and when they began to drift into the body of the river, I reached out, grabbed hold of the line, and tried to hand them back to him. He shook his head wordlessly. His face had gone a sickly pasty color under the cap and his body sagged as though all the blood had run out of it. His fingers clutched at the front of his parka.

Alarmed, I said, "Are you all right?" and took hold of his arm. The truth could perhaps have waited for a better place and time.

The icy river curled around our knees.

Pushing my hand away roughly, he started back to dry land, stumbling on the slippery rocks, reached a bleached log, and lowered himself carefully and painfully, as if he'd been in a fight. I followed him out of the water and bent down, peering into his face.

"Are you all right?" I asked again, and I knew he wasn't.

He shook his head, a barely perceptible movement, closed his eyes, and fumbled inside his jacket with a shaking hand. I expected the brandy flask, but he pulled out a small pillbox, his chest heaving as he pried it open and carefully slipped one of the capsules into his mouth. He muttered, "Angina." He didn't open his eyes and the color didn't come back to his face.

Frozen with dread, I hovered over him helplessly. It had all happened so quickly, his name, his reaction, the specter of a heart attack. The sickening thought that this was the way my father had succumbed. I couldn't think, couldn't act.

"What should I do?" I pleaded. If I could get him into the dinghy, I could find some help. It would take at least half an hour to reach a dock on the lake and a telephone. My father hadn't had that sort of time.

Making an odd fluttering gesture with his hands, he waved me away. I stepped back and wished to God I knew CPR. I expected him to keel to the ground at any second.

But he didn't. After long agonizing minutes, he opened his eyes, the pupils tiny dark spots in the pale irises. "Takes a moment to work." The pastiness was leaving his face, but a nasty blue tinge still clung around his lips.

"I'm sorry," I said inadequately. "I didn't intend to give you such a shock."

He felt in his jacket once more and this time brought out the brandy flask. Tipping it back, he coughed, closed his eyes again. I waited, hovering and guilty. I'd damn near killed him out here in the middle of nowhere with my insane notion of ethics. What price ethics if they risk someone else's life? I stared hopelessly at the fast-flowing river, the steep hills, the distance of human contact.

"If you can make it to the boat, I'll get you to dry land. You can't go on your own."

He flapped a hand at me. "Just leave me be for a minute, will you?"

Lowering myself onto another driftwood log a few feet away, I watched him. The weight of the mountains closed in on us.

After awhile, he said. "What did you say your name was?"

"Richards. Noah Richards."

"Any relation to Jonathan Richards?"

"He was my father."

"Jonathan Richard's son! Who'd have believed it?"

"Please," I said. "Don't try to talk."

He slumped on the log, sagging, legs stretched out straight, waders to his thighs, holding the silver flask in his hands, the hands that had proved so inept on Jordan Ambrose. They were thick-knuckled, the fingers wide and stubby, not at all delicate, not like Sweigert's, and I had a sudden sickening image of them inside a little boy's belly, cutting savagely. He took another swig of brandy and some of the color came back to his face.

"It's always a shock, that word—*malpractice*. Strikes the fear of God into a surgeon. You can't understand what effect it has."

I'd seen the effect it had on him. "When you're ready, we must get you home."

"That kid. Tried to do my best for him. Guess my best just wasn't good enough."

"Don't talk about it now."

"Shouldn't have tried an anastomosis, you see. Should just have cut out the dead bowel and made an ileostomy. You lie awake at night and think about these things."

"Please, Dr. Woods. We'll work it out somehow."

"How can it work out? It's too late for it to work out now. Surgeons have got to get it right the first time."

I suddenly found myself asking a question, even though I knew I shouldn't ask him anything. "Why did you wait so long to do something for that boy?"

Sighing, he said without rancor, "What in God's name do lawyers know about anything? About getting out of bed in the middle of the night? About making a diagnosis? About weighing the risks? About trying to save a sick kid? What makes lawyers think they know a damned thing about anything worth a damn?"

It was ridiculous to be annoyed, but I was. "I'd just like to know where the hell you all were while he was getting so sick?"

He closed his eyes again and breathed in small shallow breaths, as though deeper breaths would hurt. In slow motion, he unzipped his parka and rubbed at his sternum, his hand folded into a fist, his mouth twisted. Everything about him seemed slowed down to a minimal effort of living.

"Listen," I said, "we've got to get you out of here.

We'll take my dinghy to the first place we can find and then we'll call an ambulance. Can you make it?''

"Lawyers. Don't even know about angina. Let me rest a few minutes. It'll pass. It always does.''

After awhile, he said, "Your father was going to sue me once. You know about that?''

"Yes. I read the file.''

"I cut the bile duct. Easy to do, you know. Do a couple hundred operations and something will go wrong. I thought your father was my friend until then. We played bridge together. Never thought a friend would bring a suit against another friend. Makes you wonder about life. It could have finished me in Springwell.''

"But it didn't, did it?''

He looked at me. "Sometimes wish I'd had a paper-pushing job like yours. Your mistakes can be dealt with by an eraser, can't they? Or a computer. Press the escape button and that's it. Must be nice.''

"Dr. Woods, I don't think you should talk just now.''

His eyes wandered away from me to the river. "I was sorry about that kid. Don't think I'm not sorry. Had to do something in such a hurry, only did it to help out. Thought I could save him, didn't recognize how sick he was. Not used to kids, that's the truth. Clarke should've told me earlier he needed surgery, but Clarke's an idiot. Always was. I should've known better, I guess.''

The hazy blue eyes grew more opaque, dimmer. "I won't fight it, you know. I'll settle. I'll retire now. Time really. Had a good run, saved a few lives. Got a few grateful patients. What more can a man ask for?''

"Dr. Woods, we should go now.''

The river lapped around our feet and a wind was rising among the trees. He sat in a long silence, then said, "Why not? Not much point sitting here waiting for the stars to come out, is there?''

I put a hand under his elbow and he got slowly to his feet, like an old man. "What did you say your name was?"

"Noah. Noah Richards."

"Ah, yes. Richards. Knew I'd heard it before."

He leaned heavily on me and somehow we made it across the shingle and the impeding logs to where the dinghies lay. It seemed eons ago since I'd pulled my boat up beside his. "I'll come back for yours," I promised, and hauled it farther up the rocks. "It'll be okay for the time being." He didn't seem to care.

I floated the dinghy a couple of feet out into the river, held it, and then helped him over the gunwale. He slumped on the wooden thwart, weighing the small craft down so the bottom scraped on the riverbed when I climbed in. But the outboard started the first time, like a miracle, and I headed thankfully out of the river, back to civilization.

Revving up the engine, I watched him, head sunk between the wide shoulders, hands dangling between his knees. I thought how I'd quite liked him and I wished he hadn't been where he was, that he wasn't who he was, that I hadn't chosen that place and this day to go fishing. It would have been better if we hadn't met. It didn't do to feel responsible for an adversary.

We didn't speak on the return journey except that, just as we were nosing into the first dock we came to, he said, "We forgot the fish. What the hell. I'll never live to eat them."

His words filled me with alarm.

FOURTEEN

THE CLOUDS that had rolled in from the south were dumping rain on us by the time we reached the dock. Most of the houses at this far north end of the lake were only summer residences, but at this one, thank God, a thin column of smoke wreathed from a crooked metal chimney, and when I hollered loudly, a disheveled pair of youths ambled without haste down to the dock. Then they saw how I needed help and their strong young arms took Dr. Woods's weight; together, we hauled him out of the dinghy, up the dock, and into the shelter of the cabin. I couldn't possibly have done it without them. The teenagers looked hungover and unhealthy. They were alone for the weekend, fishing, they said, but by the number of beer cans strewn around, I guessed they hadn't done much fishing, but in spite of their obvious malaise, they were helpful and kind, their bleary eyes concerned.

We lowered Dr. Woods onto the sofa. I eased off his sodden jacket and khaki cap, the gaily colored flies around the brim incongruous and pathetic now; then I rang 911 for an ambulance and prayed it wouldn't be long in coming.

In the warmth of the cabin, with his head resting against the cushions, his breathing became easier, the thick flesh of his face gradually losing the ominous tinge of blue that had so alarmed me. But he still looked like a very sick man.

The boys and I hovered around him anxiously.

"Do me a favor?" he muttered. I bent near to him. "Call my wife? She worries about me."

One of the boys handed me a phone book and I riffled through the pages, searching for his home number, gritting my teeth as I dialed. Who wants to be the bearer of bad news?

A high-pitched voice answered, somehow expectant, as though she heard only good news on the telephone.

"Mrs. Woods? I met your husband when I was fishing today and…"

She must have had an instinct for trouble. "Carl? Something's happened to Carl?"

"It's all right," I said quickly, although I wasn't too sure about that. "But he does seem to have had some sort of attack."

"His heart? He's had another heart attack?"

"He said it's angina."

"I knew it! I knew he shouldn't go out fishing in this weather. I told him, 'Carl, it's stupid to go struggling in the river in November with your heart. For what? Some stupid fish? It's worth risking your life for some stupid fish, getting up at crack of dawn…'"

"Mrs. Woods, please listen. We've sent for an ambulance and it'll be here soon. They'll take him to the emergency room at St. Mary's. Shouldn't you call his doctor?"

"His doctor's in Seattle. Where are you?"

"Up at the top end of the lake. The ambulance will take him to St. Mary's. It's the nearest hospital. Why don't you get a doctor to meet him there."

"Oh, I will, I will. Right now. Who did you say you were?"

"It's not important." I heard the blessed wail of sirens along the road. "The ambulance is coming now. He'll be at the hospital before too long." The sirens grew louder.

"He's going to be all right?" The fright in her voice hurt my ears.

"I'm not a doctor," I said. Thank the Lord, I thought. There was one final excruciating blast from outside and doors began slamming. "I've got to go now, Mrs. Woods."

Two paramedics, uniformed and reassuring, pounded

into the cabin with boxes of equipment and crackling two-way radios. In a few slick minutes, they had stripped off his shirt and hooked up blood pressure cuffs and monitors. The teenagers and I flattened ourselves against the walls in useless spectator roles, trying not to be in the way. Dr. Woods seemed to have slipped into a state of semiconciousness, barely responding when the paramedics spoke to him. As they worked, they asked me what had happened and I told them—apart from the conversation that had precipitated it all. I didn't think that was necessary.

The radio crackled instructions, the medical jargon flew backward and forward in the room, and at last the patient and the equipment were loaded onto a stretcher. The medics took names and addresses and the kids and I followed as he was wheeled into the back of the ambulance, its flashing lights brilliant in the rain.

"Is he going to make it?" the boys asked doubtfully.

One of the medics clambered into the back with the stretcher and clanged the door shut; the other man jumped into the driver's seat. "He'd most likely be dead by now if he'd been left out there in the river," he said. Engaging the gears, he leaned out the window. "It was lucky he met up with you, sir."

"Very lucky," I said.

The ambulance wailed away into the distance and the day became unnaturally quiet. The teenagers looked at each other, at me.

"Man, I need a beer," one of them said, and we went back inside the cabin to wait out the rain.

The next day was Sunday. I was lying with my feet up on the sofa, watching the Seahawks on the box, another beer in my hand, wondering how Carl Woods was, knowing I should call the hospital but putting it off, when I heard the front doorbell ring. For a moment, I failed to recognize the unfamiliar chiming sound echoing through the house. By the time I identified it, got to my feet, and opened the resistant door, my visitor was retreating off the porch. She was a dainty woman, her hair frosted in a soft blue suit and high heels, dressed for church—someone I'd never seen before. She turned, neatly gloved hands clasped to her breast, and smiled uncertainly. "Mr. Richards?"

The voice was instantly recognizable.

"Mrs. Woods?"

"How did you guess? How clever of you."

Her makeup had been carefully applied, but around her eyes the flesh was swollen and blurred, as though she'd been crying or hadn't slept well. Anxiety exuded from every inch of her neat round body.

"I'm on my way to the hospital, but I had to stop by to say thank you for helping my husband. They told me at the hospital who'd called the ambulance and they told me how you'd brought him out of the river, and so I came around to thank you. Who knows what would have happened if you hadn't been there."

The words tripped over one another as they had on the phone. Staring at her across the wide porch, I wanted to say, "Jesus Christ, lady, if I hadn't been there yesterday, he'd be just fine today." Instead, I said, "How is he?"

Her gloved hands flew apart in a fluttering, helpless gesture. The sum of her was fluttery and helpless.

"Oh, I don't know. As well as can be expected, they say. Though what that means, I'm not too sure. He's in intensive care. They say his condition is stable."

"That's good, isn't it?"

She came nearer to me, treading daintily across the porch, pulled off her glove, and held out her hand. "When you called yesterday, I was so terribly flustered, I know I didn't thank you properly. You saved his life, Mr. Richards." Tears welled in the faded eyes and she tried to blink them away.

I could tell she wasn't the kind of woman who offered her hand easily to a man. It would have been churlish not to take it, but with the small hand resting in mine, I felt as though I was betraying a trust.

"I'm so grateful," she said. "We're both grateful. I'll never be able to thank you enough."

Her smile was sweet and girlish, her body gently middle-aged. I felt like a cur.

I cleared my throat. "Would you like to come in?" I hoped she wouldn't. I didn't want to prolong the interview.

"Oh, no, thank you. I'm on my way to the hospital. I went to church first. I'll tell Carl I've seen you."

I didn't know what to say to her. "His dinghy is still up there, you know. I told him I'd bring it back. I could get it today if you like."

"Oh, you don't have to do that. It won't hurt for the time being, will it? My daughter's husband can get it."

"Will he know where it is?"

"Carl can explain—when he's well enough to talk. The doctors won't let him talk yet."

So he couldn't have told her what had been said yesterday. Which was obvious, I suppose. Otherwise, she wouldn't be here now, thanking me.

She said, "I brought you some flowers. I thought no one was home, so I put them by the door."

Looking down, I saw at my feet a large flowering plant, so large, I couldn't believe I'd missed it before. It was wrapped in shiny florist's paper with a huge pink bow, straight out of a hospital gift shop.

Embarrassed, I cleared my throat again. "How kind. But it wasn't necessary, really."

The faded eyes clouded with more uncertainty. "I suppose flowers are a silly thing to bring to a man, aren't they? It's an azalea. When it's finished flowering, you can plant it in the garden. Perhaps your wife would like it?"

I bent down to pick up the plant, a riot of pink-and-white-fringed blooms. "Men like flowers, too."

"I wrote a note, in case you weren't here. I'm glad you

were, so I could meet you." She hesitated, somehow expectant; then she said, "You know, I used to know your mother, when she was on the hospital board."

Oh God, I thought. Not another one.

"Carl knew your daddy. He helped Carl over that awful malpractice stuff all those years ago. So it's fate in a way, isn't it, that you were the one who was there when he had this attack? Your mother was so proud of you. She often talked about her son the lawyer. She hoped you might become a judge someday."

"A judge?" I echoed in disbelief. What foolish ambitions lurk in the hearts of mothers.

"Yes, that's what she used to say. Of course, you'd only just started in law school then, I believe. She's been gone quite a long time, hasn't she? I didn't know you were living in Springwell. Will you ever run for judge, Mr. Richards?"

"I think it's very unlikely."

She smiled, the skin wrinkling around her kind eyes. "Mothers are always full of grand ideas for their children, aren't they? I'd vote for you if you ever did run. Well, I really should be going. Carl will be waiting for me. I'll tell him I met you."

She put one foot on the steps, looked back at me. "He'll have to retire now. A good thing, really. I won't be sorry. There'll be time to do all those things we've never been able to do before. A surgeon's life isn't easy, always on call, all those weekends and holidays. He's a big strong man, but he gets awfully tired sometimes. Never free of the responsibility for the patients, you see. It'll be a relief not to have that worry anymore."

I said nothing. What was there for me to say?

As she went down the steps, she turned again and gave me that sweet smile. "When Carl is better, we'll have you round for dinner. I hope you'll come, you and your wife."

The note with the flowers was written in a careful

rounded script on a stiff white card embossed with ESW. "To a Good Samaritan. With heartfelt thanks. Betsy Woods."

Shit. Oh shit, I thought.

FIFTEEN

I RETURNED TO THE SOFA and my beer and gazed balefully at the game on TV. I felt as inept and unproductive as the Seahawks, running the ball a few yards, fumbling, missing tackles, getting dropped for a loss. Exasperated, I pressed the pointless game into oblivion with the remote control and wished I could do the same with my conscience.

But I kept staring at the darkened set as if something could yet arise out of it to distract me. I tried not to think about Carl Woods, who seemed a decent man, or about his wife, who'd given me flowers. Eventually, resigned, I buckled down to yet another examination of Jordan Ambrose's records. God knows, I had been over them enough, but there had to be something I was missing. I spread the notes out on the dining room table and tried not to put faces on the people who leapt off the pages: Angel and Joseph, with their broken hearts and troubled marriage; Lauren Watson, with some secret terror; Carl Woods, in intensive care, nursing his own wounded heart. I tried not to put a face on Jordan Ambrose, who, I suddenly saw from the date of birth on the admission note, would have been six years old this very day.

Six years old. Not even allowed six short years.

Pushing the notes aside, I groaned with frustration. The nurses' assessment of their patient's condition was clear and unequivocal; Sweigert's opinion was clear and unequivocal. What was neither clear nor unequivocal was why in God's name the doctors had ignored those same signs and symptoms for so long. I began to think I was going to get nowhere until I filed a suit. Once the suit was filed, I could start taking depositions, start asking questions.

"Where were you, Doctor? Why didn't you come when you were called?" But I didn't want to file until I had a reasonable idea in my own mind about what might have been happening all that time at the hospital. Otherwise, I might not ask the right questions. Never ask a question to which you don't know the answer.

Why hadn't they come?

The result of not coming was all too obvious, but what wasn't obvious was why Lauren Watson should be so afraid, or why Nita Barnes should vanish. Lauren's alarm about Nita's disappearance was infecting me. If I could find this Nita and talk to her, perhaps she could lift part of the fog. Someone had to know where she was. People don't normally drop out of sight without any indication of where they've gone or why. They tell someone, employers or friends or neighbors. Tomorrow, I'd ask personnel at the hospital if she'd given notice or taken a leave of absence, left an address for pay to be forwarded. It was the natural place to start.

Restless, I roamed the house, trapped by the weekend. I wanted to do something today, not wait until tomorrow. Lauren Watson was hiding the truth about something, but her concern about the missing nurse seemed genuine enough. Nita Barnes must have friends who knew where she'd gone. All I had to do was find them. She had to have neighbors who'd know, someone other than the creep with the dog. Cursing that today was Sunday, I suddenly realized Sunday was the perfect day to find neighbors at home. They'd almost certainly be watching the Seahawks on the box. Every Sunday in the fall, 90 percent of the state was watching the Seahawks.

So for the second time in as many days, I drove to Fairview.

At the bottom of the drive to the shabby blue house, the view to the west as entrancing as ever, I saw I wouldn't need to go knocking on neighboring doors. The front door was open and a car was parked in front of the ramshackle garage; there was someone in the house itself. As I came up the driveway, the ubiquitous football commentary blared through the open door, and when I rapped hard with my knuckles, whoever was inside didn't seem to hear.

I stepped through the door.

In the living room, a woman was pushing a vacuum cleaner over the shag rug, her eyes riveted on the television set. The volume was turned way up and she obviously didn't see or hear me. Dumpy and middle-aged, in a shapeless flowered dress, permed hair fading to gray, she wasn't at all my idea of someone whose name was Juanita. I cleared my throat, and still she didn't hear. She wasn't watching what she was doing with the cleaner, just running it backward and forward in the same spot, her whole attention taken up with the stupid game.

"Excuse me," I said loudly.

Shooting a startled glance over her shoulder, the woman switched off the machine, reducing the noise level by one layer.

"Goodness, you did give me a fright! Where did you come from?"

I had to raise my voice above the TV. "I knocked on the door, but you were busy. I'm looking for Nita Barnes."

"Who?"

"Nita Barnes. This is her house, isn't it?"

"Oh, the girl who used to live here? No, of course I'm not her. I'm just here to get the place cleaned up for the next tenants." She wiped her hands down the front of the dress and thankfully lowered the volume on the set. But she kept gazing wistfully at the screen. "Not doing too good, are they? The Seahawks, I mean. I like to watch them on a Sunday, but he wanted the house done today, so well, what could I say? The money comes in handy, doesn't it?"

"You don't happen to know where she's gone, do you?"

"Who?"

"Nita Barnes."

It was obvious the missing Nita Barnes was of no interest to her. She shook the permed head vaguely. "No idea. I wouldn't know her if I saw her. All I know is that this place has to be cleaned today, so here I am. I've nearly finished. Why don't you ask Dr. Grogan? He'll be along shortly to check it out. All right for him—I bet he's watching the game in peace and quiet."

"Grogan? Coming here?" The nontreating surgeon, Carl Woods's colleague? Nita Barnes's landlord? Maybe a chance to get a clue to the puzzle? It felt like my first stroke of luck. I smiled at the woman. "Do you mind if I wait?"

"Help yourself. It's not my house. There's some coffee in the kitchen." She switched the cleaner on again and raised her voice above it. "Don't make a mess, because I've done the kitchen."

I stood looking at the view out of the windows for a moment longer, then skirted around the sofas and the vacuum cleaner and headed for the kitchen. As soon as I'd left the room, the sound on the TV set rose to its former ear-splitting level. In the tiny hallway off the living room, the door to a bedroom was open, and I made a detour into it, hoping to find some clue to the young woman who'd slept and dreamed and maybe even made love in here—though I didn't know if she was young or old or anything else about her, except that she was Hispanic and that Fairview was an unfriendly place for Hispanics. But the room held only a bare bed, an empty chest of drawers, and an empty closet. Like the bed, the room was totally stripped of any personality. I went back to the living room.

"Did she take everything with her? She didn't leave anything?"

Exasperated, the woman shouted over the machine, "I don't know. There's nothing here now. Dr. Grogan could've cleared it up, couldn't he? Wouldn't want the place cluttered with someone else's stuff, would he?"

In the bathroom, next to the bedroom, there were no towels, no toiletries, not even a roll of toilet paper; in the kitchen, everything was cleaned and shining, just a coffeepot and a telephone on the white Formica counter, a used cup in the newly scrubbed sink. I didn't want any coffee. There was nothing in the kitchen to give any hint of its former inhabitant. The empty refrigerator stood open; the white-painted cabinets held a bare minimum of impersonal white dishes. There wasn't even a calendar left pinned to the wall. There were no telltale signs of anyone ever having cooked or eaten here, of ever having existed in the whole house. It was unseemly how all evidence of someone's life could be so quickly erased.

I stood by the half-glass back door, gazing down the steps, envisioning the guy in the fatigue cap, the hand in his pocket, the menacing dog at his side. Did he still lurk out there somewhere, paranoid and threatening? Where had he come from, sneaking up so silently? There was nothing to be seen beyond the shrubbery at the top of the yard. From the back door, I couldn't even see another house, just the dilapidated garage to the side. Did he creep up on Nita Barnes in that fashion, scaring the wits out of her?

I should have done something about him. I shouldn't have stood listening politely to the bullying voice, the racial slurs. People like me should stand up to people like him. How on earth could a defenseless woman deal with him? No wonder she didn't stay around, with someone like that watching her. I should have insisted on getting his name at the very least. I should have dealt with him in some way, not tried to reason with him. I wasn't proud of the way he'd intimidated me.

Deciding to have some coffee after all, I took a clean cup out of the cupboard, stretched my hand for the pot, and knocked over a telephone book leaning upright on the counter against the wall. I replaced the book and saw it had been covering the small flat box of a telephone answering machine. The machine I'd failed to leave a message on the other day because the tape was full. The red light still blinked in it, the only thing alive in the kitchen.

I poured some coffee and contemplated the little black box. In the living room, the vacuum cleaner whirred away, the commentary loud on the TV. I pressed the rewind button, then the play button. The tape began in the middle of a rapid incomprehensible message in Spanish that I couldn't decipher. At last, a piece of Nita Barnes's life that hadn't been erased. The end of the message was followed by a succession of beeps and a mechanical voice announcing the time of day. Rewinding a bit farther, I came across a male voice speaking English. "Hi, Nita, this is Jeff." The vacuum cleaner fell abruptly silent in the near distance and I stopped the tape, flipped open the plastic lid, picked the tape off the sprockets, weighed it in my hand, and slipped it into my pocket with a tiny prickle of expectation, and with the minutest prickle of guilt. Lawyers aren't supposed to lift evidence.

The cleaning lady was now busy with a spray bottle and paper towels at the windows in the living room. I went close to her to ask, "Do you know a man who lives round here with a pit bull? Wears an army fatigue cap? Tall and thin. Probably very light hair?"

She stepped back to admire her handiwork. "Lovely view these houses have, don't they? Wouldn't mind living here myself." Then she went over to the set and turned the sound down again. "That sounds a lot like Brett Gurning. He always has a pit bull with him. Nasty dogs, aren't they? Shouldn't be allowed, I say. One of them bit a kid from my neighborhood a few years back. All over his poor little face. Had to have seventy stitches put in at the hospital. Still got the scars."

"Brett Gurning? Bony face, pale eyes?"

"Yes, that's him. He's vicious like those dogs. Done prison time, I heard. But he doesn't live round here. He lives out my way; that's how I know him. There's a whole family of Gurnings, and they're all the same. Give me the creeps, to tell the truth. But Brett's the one with the dog.''

A whole family of them? And if this Gurning didn't live around here, what was he doing watching this house?

I said, "My name's Noah Richards, by the way."

"I'm Hattie," she said. "Hattie Coppes." She examined the windows, her head to one side. "Look better, don't they?" She hadn't asked what I was doing in the house or what my business was. Much too trusting.

"So you don't live round here, Hattie? Whereabouts, then?"

"Not far from the doctor's office. You know, up behind the old Sears building. I clean his place every night for him; that's how I know him." She moved forward to rub at one last mark on the glass. "And speak of the devil, here he is now."

Looking over her shoulder, I saw a large Jeep-type vehicle with a soft top and four-wheel drive lurch up the driveway to a stop behind Hattie's little car. A thickset man with a mop of gingery hair jumped from the driver's seat, slammed the door, and strode purposefully up to the front door. His down parka hung open and under it was a red checked shirt that clashed with the color of his hair. I stepped away from the window.

"So, Hattie, how's it going?"

He filled the doorway and the small house with an impatient energy, as though he had better things to do than be here on a Sunday afternoon. He didn't look at Hattie when he spoke or wait for a reply, just swept his eyes around the room, checking details, taking inventory. And then he saw me, of course. "Hello?" he said, still addressing her, not me, as though I were some appendage of hers. "Who's this?"

"Some gentleman who wants to know where your tenant went."

Frowning, he moved into the room. His skin was pale and freckly, his eyes an indeterminate green color, with invisible lashes and eyebrows that gave his face a naked look. There was no warmth in the bare green eyes. When he spoke again, I recognized a strong Boston Irish accent. "Well, I'd like to know that, too. Have you come to pay the two months rent she owes me?"

"Sorry, no. I was hoping you might tell me where she's gone."

"If I knew that, I'd get the rent from her myself, wouldn't I? So who are you? Why do you want to know about my tenants?"

The brisk used-to-being-obeyed tone was instantly irritating. "My name is Noah Richards. I'm an attorney."

If there's one good thing about a law degree, it's that it provides instant identification, instant credibility. It put me on an equal footing with him, a fellow professional, and it showed in his eyes, in his voice. He dropped the arrogant posture.

"She in trouble with the law?" he asked almost jocularly.

"No. I just need to talk to her."

"Well, sorry, I can't help you. She did a bunk. I've no idea where's she's gone. When you find her, let me know."

"She didn't give any kind of notice? Didn't you wonder what might have happened to her?"

"Look. I just rented the house to her. I didn't have charge of her life. As long as she paid the rent, where she went and what she did was none of my business, was it?"

"And when she stopped paying?"

He shrugged. "That's the problem with renters, isn't it? You can get all sorts of references, but if they decide to skip town, there's not much one can do about it. File with a collection agency, that's about it."

"Have you filed?" I asked.

He peered at me. "Not yet, no. But don't worry, I will."

"Did she leave any of her stuff here?"

"Took everything, as far as I could tell." He brushed his hands together in a dismissive gesture. "Well, if you'll excuse me, I'm going to check around, make sure everything's in working order. Got new tenants coming in this week, thank God. Can't afford to leave property lying about empty. You nearly through, Hattie?"

"I'll be on my way any minute." As she swept through the room, gathering up a bundle of rags, a plastic pail and mop, the vacuum cleaner, her eyes wandered wistfully to the television, the subdued game still in progress, and it was obvious she'd have liked to settle down on the sofa and watch the end of it. Switching off the set, she trailed rather disconsolately out of the room.

Grogan was waiting, impatiently, for me to leave. I could tell he wasn't pleased that I wasn't moving. I hesitated, trying to decide how much to say to him. My name hadn't struck any nerve in him, which surprised me, because I'd have expected Lance Todd or Carl Woods or someone to have mentioned it in connection with an impending suit. I'd no idea who else knew a suit was in the air, but I knew that once records are sent for, alarm bells go off all over the place, especially in a hospital. The grapevine usually gives warning, even to those who aren't involved. It was because Grogan wasn't involved that I had the leeway to speak to him.

But I wanted to pick my words far more carefully than I had with Woods only the day before. That disastrous confrontation seemed a lifetime ago. And maybe, for Dr. Woods, that's exactly what it was, a lifetime.

"I wanted to ask Nita Barnes about a child called Jordan Ambrose." I waited for some reaction. None came. "The child who died on the operating table at St. Mary's a couple of months ago. Maybe you heard about it? Your colleague Carl Woods did the surgery."

He woke up to me then. At first, his face went a curious

pallid green, the freckles on his forehead and across his cheekbones standing out in dark splotches. Then a violent red flooded the pallor, suffusing his skin and eyes in crimson, and the flat, hard eyes became stony and opaque. The reaction, when it came, was dramatic. For a moment, I imagined he was going to launch himself across the room at me. But he didn't. He thrust his hands deep into the pockets of his jacket, straining down on the material, and took a couple of breaths through his mouth. The crimson washed out of his skin as quickly as it had come. "Jordan Ambrose?" he said quite casually. "The name doesn't ring a bell."

If I hadn't seen the involuntary rush of blood into his face, the casual tone of his voice would have been quite convincing. "You were asked to consult on him, I believe, Doctor, but you didn't ever go to see him. I wondered why."

He narrowed his eyes, eased his shoulders against the wall, shrugged. "I'm asked to consult on quite a few cases, you know. It isn't always possible to see everyone. And this is hardly the time or place to discuss such a matter, is it?"

"It isn't," I agreed. "But you might be interested to know that the parents will be bringing a wrongful-death suit against the hospital, the pediatrician, and Dr. Woods. Which is why I'm here looking for Miss Barnes. She was one of the nurses who took care of the child."

"And you're the attorney, I suppose?" Now he didn't try to keep the disgust out of his voice. "Do you know that even as you speak, Dr. Woods is in the ICU at St. Mary's with a coronary occlusion?"

"Yes," I said. "I heard."

He stared across the room at me and said, almost conversationally, "Fucking lawyers. Sitting on your fat backsides in your fancy offices, risking nothing, spiders waiting in a web to cash in on decent people who are trying to do their job. You're nothing but bloodsucking parasites."

There was a long cool silence. "Invective aside," I said politely, "the parents have a good case." Out of the corner of my eye, I saw Hattie in the hallway with her coat on, her mouth agape. "That child was left for three days without any treatment. If it's any consolation to you, Doctor, it seems you won't be named in the suit, because you didn't appear to treat him. I'm interested to know why that was. You were called, I understand, but apparently you didn't attempt to do any sort of job on that particular occasion. I'm planning to get a deposition from you as to why that was. Dr. Woods was certainly left holding a hot potato, wasn't he?"

The bare green eyes blazed, but his voice maintained the strangely normal level. "If you think I'm going to give some stinking attorney any help in a malpractice case against Carl Woods or any other physician, you're much mistaken. Now I suggest you leave this house before I throw you out."

"Sure. I'll be glad to leave. But you have no choice in the matter of a deposition, Dr. Grogan, so I'm certain we'll meet again. I wish I could say I was looking forward to it."

I had to pass close by him on my way out of the room, and he glared at me with unsettling distaste. He was hardly my idea of your friendly neighborhood physician. Took all sorts, I supposed. Surgeons, they say, are a different breed.

When I reached the open door, I turned. "I'm also interested in someone I believe is in your employ. Name of Brett Gurning."

The blood surged into his naked face again. "Out. I don't have to talk to you."

So for the second time in as many days, I was watched as I set off from the shabby little house with the outstanding view. I walked down the drive with as much dignity as I could muster, the purloined tape comfortably heavy in my pocket. As I got into the car, Grogan had come out of the house and was watching me the same way his friend in the cap had watched. I wondered how much they had to do with each other; what it was they had in common, apart from being repellent bullies.

SIXTEEN

I TOOK THE TAPE to the office for the simple reason that there was no answering machine at the house. Father had been old-fashioned about such mechanical devices, as he was about so many things, and I'd never bothered to get one myself—just more evidence of the inertia that had gripped me since he'd gone. I resolved to go out and buy one the very next day.

It was rather warm and cosy in the office, better than at home. The answering machine was on Bella's desk. I sat in her chair, took out the office tape, slipped in Nita Barnes's, pressed the rewind button, and watched it run backward. As I prepared to listen in on someone else's life, a sense of anticipation trickled between my shoulder blades. Playing detective was more fun than playing lawyer.

But though I learned something about Nita Barnes's life from the taped messages, they were all in all a disappointment. I'm not exactly sure what I'd been expecting—threats, blackmail, revelations? What I heard instead, in varying order, were a couple of "We will have a truck on your street" charities; three messages from Lauren Watson, which said essentially, "Nita, where are you? I'm worried"; no less than four in the unmistakable bullying Boston Irish of Grogan, all of which said basically the same thing: "Return this call immediately"; two more from the hospital: "If you are sick, please let us know" and "Miss Barnes, you have not been at work for three days, so let us know why"; a couple of male callers, "Nita, this is Jeff. How about going out for dinner Friday? Call me"; "Hi, this is Pete, remember? We had fun, didn't we? I'd like to see you again. I'll call."

These quick calls were interspersed with long messages in Spanish. I strained to understand the language, but it was all too rapid for me to make out more than a few words. The Spanish speakers seemed to be the same two people, one male, one female. The last one from the male caller ran off the end before he'd finished speaking.

If Pete and Jeff had left their numbers, I'd have tried them, but they hadn't. I was glad someone had liked her in Springwell, glad her life wasn't only dying children, paranoid punks, and an unpleasant landlord. Rewinding and listening again, I wrote down each call in the order it had come and from whom. An automated voice announced the time of each message but didn't announce the date, so I had no way of knowing which day was which. It wasn't too hard to take an educated guess. The second call from the hospital was obviously three days after she didn't turn up for duty. There was one from Lauren before that, two a little later. So I worked around those. I was interested in the calls from Grogan, why he'd made so many.

Grogan called twice before Lauren's first call, twice after. He didn't call again. Did that mean he knew where she was and why? The first call from Grogan was actually the first one on the tape.

I also had no clue whether Nita had answered any of these messages. I knew she hadn't returned Lauren's calls, because Lauren had told me so. It didn't sound as though she'd responded to the hospital, either. Did she erase her messages as she listened, or did she run the tape until it was full and then turn it over? Janet had done it that way, often going back through in case she'd missed something. Anyway, she said, she liked to hear the sound of her friends' voices. Remembering that, I smiled. So when I came to the end of the tape again, I turned it over to listen to the other side. Quite empty—which meant, surely, that Nita wiped her messages off as she went along and this thirty minutes had been recorded since she'd gone. That could mean she'd left almost immediately after Jordan Ambrose's death.

Where had she gone? And why? And had she gone voluntarily?

It was frustrating not to be able to translate the Spanish. Casting around in my mind for someone who could do it for me, someone who wouldn't be too curious about where the tape had come from or whose it was, I couldn't think of a single person in Springwell who might speak the language. Or in Seattle, come to that. It was appalling how limited my social circle had become. Not just in numbers, but also in cultural diversity, as everyone is so fond of saying these days. In L.A., I'd known plenty of people whose native language was Spanish.

God, I thought, how I miss California! Returning to the Pacific Northwest was the worst move I'd ever made. If Janet's life had been saved, the move would have been worthwhile, of course, every second of it. But it achieved nothing. *Nothing.* I'd swapped a good career, sunshine, and color for doom and gloom and rain and a case that was depressing the hell out of me. I couldn't see any good end to what I was pursuing now.

Paralyzed by doubts, I gazed at the answering machine, at the telephone. Thought of California, of the good times. On an impulse, I lifted the receiver and punched in the number in Santa Monica I used to know so well. It was months since I'd spoken to my wife's parents. *Wife*—the very word had begun to sound strange.

Janet's dad answered, his cheerful voice loud and Californian, blowing dry, warm air straight into my heart.

"Noah! How in the hell are you?" He didn't wait for me to tell him. "We haven't heard from you in ages. The sun's shining like gangbusters down here. What's it doing up there?"

All the light had gone from the outside world beyond the glass door; only the feeble glow from the neon sign across the road illuminated the dark sky. "Color it gray," I said.

"You should get away for some sunshine. I hope you're calling to say you're coming for the holiday?"

"Holiday?" I repeated stupidly. "What holiday?"

"Noah! Are you so busy you don't even remember it's Thanksgiving this week?"

Bella's calendar, a folded cardboard thing, sat by the phone. I pulled it nearer and stared at the treacherous date in disbelief.

"Good Lord! So it is."

There was a small pause; then he said, "You all right, son?"

It might have been better if he hadn't called me that. For a moment, I couldn't answer.

"I'm okay, Ben."

There was a wistful note in his voice. "I don't know why the devil you don't move back down here."

The air in the crackling dry canyon would be filled with the scent of pine trees, the hills bare and brown, the sky very blue. A wave of nostalgia broke over me. "Sometimes I don't know, either. Maybe one day. When I get my act together."

"I bet they'd be glad to have you back at Buckins and Brent."

"Doesn't do to try to retrace your footsteps," I said. I believed that.

"I don't know. That was a damn fine job you had, Noah."

"I'm not sure I'm interested in that sort of job anymore."

"No? So what interests you nowadays?"

"Ah well, that's the question, isn't it?"

I heard him sigh. Ben wasn't really the sighing type. "Beth and I think of you often, Noah. Wonder how you're doing. How you're keeping. I know it's been a tough couple of years for you."

"Don't worry," I said. "I'm working my way out of it. I've a pretty interesting case going. It's taking up a lot of my time."

"Good. That's good. You'll be all right, Noah, fine young lawyer like you. Still in that one-horse town?"

"Still in the one-horse town. Still in the one-horse practice."

"Listen, son. Take my advice. Get yourself with a decent firm; don't waste your talents. One-man law offices don't cut it these days." Another small pause. "Got a girlfriend yet?"

I liked my father-in-law. My ex-father-in-law. I knew he had my best interests at heart. "No," I said. "Not yet."

"Noah, I'll say it again. Don't waste your talent and don't waste your life. A healthy young fellow like you can't spend the rest of his life in mourning."

I think he really meant it. I knew then why I'd called. Because in spite of everything that had happened, Janet's parents liked me. Loved me, if only for Janet's sake. And right now, a little affection would be very welcome.

"Perhaps I could come for Thanksgiving." I tried not to sound pathetic. "I think I could get away. Would it be a problem? Say if it is."

"A problem? Noah, my boy, you're one of the family. Jeez, we'd love to see you again. It's been far too long. Let me know what time your flight gets in and I'll be there to meet you."

I thought about it—very briefly. A few days in Santa Monica? In the sunshine? There was nothing to keep me here. There was nothing I could do about the Ambrose case until after Thanksgiving. After Thanksgiving, I'd file. I'd made up my mind.

"Thanks, Ben," I said. "Thanks a million. I'll call you back."

I put the phone down and went on repeating, "Thank you. Thank you. Thank you." It would be painful, their house too full of memories for me, my presence a reminder for them, but we'd talk about Janet and pore through the family pictures, and the sun would shine, and Ben and I would play a round of golf, and I'd be part of a family again—for a few days at least.

I called the airlines. As I waited for someone to answer, I put Nita Barnes's tape back in my pocket. In L.A., there'd be someone to translate it for me.

SEVENTEEN

IT PROVED IMPOSSIBLE to find a seat on any flight to Los Angeles on Wednesday, the day before Thanksgiving. Even Tuesday was difficult. But Alaska had a seat available late on Monday evening. I took it.

The prospect of getting out of Springwell the very next day cheered me to no end. I locked the office, remembering the alarm, and drove home with a lighter heart, but as I entered the house, the phone was ringing and the lightness left me when I heard Mrs. Wood's uncertain voice at the other end.

"My husband," she began, and the blood ran thick in my ears, because I thought she was going to tell me he was dead. It took a moment to concentrate on what she was saying—not that he was dead but that he wanted to see me.

"I don't know what it's about, but there's something he wants to tell you. The doctors say it would help if he talked to you. Relieve his mind, they say. Will you come to the hospital? Please, Mr. Richards."

I couldn't talk to him. Sick or not, I was still going to sue him.

"I called several times this afternoon, but you weren't home. I know it's bothering him, because he asked for you again this evening. You'd be doing us a favor, Mr. Richards."

A favor? Hadn't I done them enough favors? Now was the moment to tell her about the suit, but somehow I couldn't. God knows, she had enough to worry about. "The doctors really think this is a good idea?"

"They say he'd rest more peacefully. Rest is what he needs, Mr. Richards."

I hedged. "It isn't that I don't want to talk to your husband, but..."

Of course I wanted to hear Carl Woods's side of the story, more than the snippet he'd offered my unwilling ears out on the river. But the correct way to get his story was in deposition, and I couldn't take a deposition until I'd filed suit. There was no way I should interview him in the hospital at this stage, whatever it was he wanted to tell me.

"Mrs. Woods. There's a legal difficulty about his talking to me, which I won't go into now. But if your own lawyer is present, I can do it. Lance Todd is your attorney, isn't he? Call him, explain the situation. If he agrees, I'll be happy to see your husband. If you really believe it will help."

She sounded bewildered. "Lance? Well, if that's what it takes, I'll ask him. Could you come tomorrow?"

"Three o'clock. I'm leaving town in the evening. And Mrs. Woods, if you don't mind, it might be better if you weren't present."

"Why?"

"Trust me," I said, although I knew she'd be foolish to do that.

Inevitably, the phone rang again in a few minutes. It was Lance Todd.

"What's going on, Richards?" he asked tersely.

"Your guess is as good as mine. But Mrs. Woods says he wants to talk to me. As long as you're there as well, I can't see any harm in it, can you?"

"Yes, I can see a lot of harm in it. Does she know about the suit?"

"Not unless you've told her. Maybe that isn't what he wants to talk about."

He laughed cynically. "And maybe pigs have wings." And then, reluctantly, he said, "If you let him do the talking and don't ask anything about this malpractice business, I suppose I have to agree. Only because Betsy Woods wants it. I'm not going to let him say anything about the Ambrose child. Understood?''

"Understood." It didn't appear likely I'd get anything useful out of the meeting.

On Monday morning, I had to wrestle with Jack Probert's family trust again. Jack was a nice-enough guy, but he'd made the mistake of divorcing his first wife for a much younger woman. Now he wrote and rewrote his will. First, he'd made everything over to his new wife; then he began to doubt her affections, changed his mind, and left it all to his children. Then changed his mind once more. That's the trouble with being unfaithful in the first place. How can you ever believe in anyone again? The living trust had already been rewritten three times, and now he was in the throes of yet another jealousy fit. I'd no idea whether Jack's suspicions were based on any sort of fact, and I'd begun to believe we'd never be done with it.

When we'd finished, and as he was leaving, morose and depressed, I asked casually, "Jack, you're not associated with St. Mary's by any chance, are you? On the board or anything like that?"

His mind was preoccupied with more personal matters. "St. Mary's? You mean the hospital? Why do you want to know that? What's that got to do with my estate?"

"Nothing. I was interested, that's all. Everyone I speak to these days seems connected with the hospital in one way or another."

"Not me," he said. "Can't stand hospitals."

He went on his unhappy way and I called the personnel department about Nita Barnes. A woman with the overtones of a hostile witness told me, "Miss Barnes did not give notice and we haven't heard from her since. Most irresponsible."

In answer to my question about pay, she said frostily, "Any outstanding salary would have been deposited to her bank account, as usual."

"Which bank?"

"That's private information."

I rang every bank in Springwell, hoping to find someone rash enough to confirm Nita Barnes had an active account with them. No one would.

I had another fruitless meeting with Bigelow Harrison about the wetlands issue. Once more, he stalled, and once more I put off explaining the potential conflict of interest. You can put off a hell of a lot of things in the legal world.

"You thought any more about coming in with me?" he asked.

"There're a few things I have to sort out before I can give you an answer to that, Bigs."

"I tell you, Noah, if we don't get some deal like this off the ground, there's going to be a lot more folks than me in trouble. Take the hospital. There's a rumor flying round they're about to be sued, and I know for a fact that they'll be in deep shit if that happens. St. Mary's is hanging on by its fingernails. If they don't get a larger patient base, they're gone. The board's trying to put one of those medical-management deals together. You know, patients and doctors tied to one facility in one insurance packet. Ain't easy, Noah. I don't know what this suit's about—people are tight-lipped about it—but the last thing that place needs is bad publicity."

If the Ambrose case went to court, the publicity would be very bad.

I took a tape recorder with me for my interview with Dr. Woods. It was a long while since I'd had any need of it; I had to buy new batteries and a new tape on the way. I also had to have Todd's permission to use it, and I hoped we weren't going to spend too much time wrangling over legal niceties.

I met Todd and Mrs. Woods outside the ICU, and it seemed we weren't going to have much time. "Fifteen minutes," the attending physician said severely. "His condition isn't stable, and I don't want him exhausted. I don't know what you lawyers have in mind, but my advice is just to let him talk. Don't ask too many questions. Don't get him excited or upset, or you'll have me to answer to. If I hear any problem on the monitor, I'm going to stop the interview immediately, understand?''

Obviously, this was yet another physician who didn't like lawyers. Todd looked at me accusingly and I was defensive. "I'm here at Dr. Woods request, plain and simple. Isn't that right, Mrs. Woods?''

Today, she looked tired and worn, myriad wrinkles in her face that hadn't been so evident the day before. "I just hope this makes him feel better, that's all.''

She stayed outside while Todd and I went in. The ICU unit at St. Mary's, a semicircular room divided into half a dozen glass cubicles, was much smaller than the one I'd grown too familiar with at the Cancer Center, but it was crammed with all the same formidable high-tech medical machinery, the tubes and the bottles and the clicking monitors, the sighing respirators—a terrifying array of twentieth-century healing, a factory of purgatory.

Dr. Woods lay in a white metal bed, propped up on white pillows, white sheet draped over a white gown. His face, ruddy and thickly fleshed when we'd met only two days before, had lost all the healthy glow, and now the skin was slackened and loose and almost as pale as the surroundings. Electric leads snaked from under the sheet to the monitor above his head and the green fluorescent lines zigzagged across the screen as if it were the machine that had the life in it, instead of the other way around.

But his eyes were alive enough, and as we approached the bed, he bared his large teeth in a brave smile. "Good of you to come, young Richards,'' he said politely, as if we were on a social visit. "I wanted to talk to you.''

"Yes, sir. I hope you're feeling a little better.''

He lifted one hand in a halfhearted gesture. The back of

his hand was bruised and strapped with tape, an IV running into a ropy vein.

"What's Todd doing here? I didn't ask to see him."

"Dr. Woods, your counsel should be present when you talk to me. He's here for your protection."

"Protection?" Something like laughter wheezed out of him. "He'll be useful only if he can protect me from the ravages of myocardial infarction. There's not a lawyer I know who can do anything as useful as that. Come and sit down beside me, my boy. Let me get off my chest what I want to get off my chest. That'll do my heart as much good as anything. And don't you interrupt, Lance."

Todd shifted uneasily on his feet. "I don't like this, Carl."

"Lump it then. I haven't the energy or the time to argue with you."

"I've told Richards he's not to ask you any questions about Jordan Ambrose. That would be improper. Don't volunteer any information about his treatment."

"I'll say what I like, Lance. Don't try to stop me."

I sat in a chair close by the bed, and brought out the newly primed tape recorder from my briefcase. "Do you mind if I record our conversation?"

"Do what you like. Just let me tell you what I need to tell you."

Todd opened his mouth to object, then clamped it shut. As long as I asked his client's permission to be taped, there was nothing he could object to. I switched on the machine and it made a small whirring sound, barely audible above all the other machines in the room.

I spoke the date, time, place, and people present into the recorder.

"About that kid," Dr. Woods began.

Todd made a warning sound and Woods gestured him into silence.

"Jordan Ambrose?" I said.

"Yes, Ambrose. I want to settle the suit. Understand, Todd? I don't want to contest it. The insurance company can pay up. Hell, I've been paying malpractice insurance all these years. I screwed up the surgery and that's all there is to it. His people deserve some recompense and I don't want them to have to fight for it. It won't undo the harm, but I sure as hell don't want to put them through a court case. No reason to. Got that?"

"Got it," I said, and waited for him to say more. He closed his eyes.

"All right," Todd said. "I guess you've got what you came for, counselor."

But that wasn't what I'd come for. I'd come for the rest of the truth. I already knew Carl Woods had screwed up the operation. I wanted to know why he'd waited so long to do it. I wanted to know about Grogan, and I couldn't ask him that. I couldn't ask him any leading questions. In his condition, I didn't dare ask him any questions at all. The doctor had warned me, and I didn't need anything more about Dr. Woods on my conscience. But I was disappointed.

"If there's nothing more, Dr. Woods, I'll turn off the tape recorder."

He opened his eyes. "Your father was a friend of mine," he said. "We used to play bridge together, did you know that?"

"Yes," I said. "You told me."

"I did? We fell out over that case he was going to bring against me. Westing, was it?"

"Westing," I agreed.

"I was hurt as hell that a friend would go after me, but in the end, I guess we forgave each other. Surgeons make mistakes, and I made one that time. Another one. It's a hell of a trade, surgery. You can't make the little mistakes everybody makes in any business. Your father agreed to keep it quiet if I settled. He came to me with the evidence and made me an offer, and so I settled. Nobody else knew about it. It didn't ruin me in town, as it might have done. It could have finished me. You going to keep this one quiet, young Richards?''

My father kept a suit quiet? Made an offer? Colluded with a friend to protect him? My father? I stared at the ashy-faced man in the bed, at the tape machine recording a nasty little secret. I nearly switched it off, and I saw Todd watching me, waiting for me to do just that.

"How did he keep it quiet?"

Todd said, "Apparently, your father had more sense than you, Noah. It seems he understood what harm can be done with suits like this. Reputations ruined over a small mistake. There are more important ends than bringing people down, you know. More ways of skinning a cat."

"My father would never have compromised a client's claim." I wanted to believe that, desperately.

"Noah," Todd said patiently, "there's not a person alive who hasn't cut his cloth a little. Compromise is what it's about, isn't it? Plenty of suits get settled without a fuss being made, without the whole world knowing. Happens all the time."

I was struggling with the idea of my father cutting a deal. "Well, I'm not going to keep this one quiet. This is a different matter. This is about more than malpractice. It's about something else. It's about us as a town. As people."

Carl Woods's washed blue eyes fixed on me. He moved his tongue over his lips. "I'm dry as a desert. Get me a drop of water, will you?"

I poured a small amount of water from the covered pitcher on the locker by the bed, let him sip on it. I knew how to do such little nursing tasks.

"If I make it through this," he said, "I'm retiring. I've had it with surgery, getting up at night, sweating through difficult operations. That kid's operation shouldn't have been difficult. I lost my judgment, thought I could save him.

But he was so damned ill by the time I got to him. Do you know why he was so ill?''

At last we might be getting to the nub of it. I tried to put my father out of my head. "Why?"

"Ask my associate. Grogan. He was supposed to see that kid. He takes care of any complicated kids' surgery. Guess he never saw him. I saw the boy once, that first day, and I told Clarke to get Grogan. The problem was, who was in charge? Clarke? Grogan? At the end, I went rushing in like a fool to try to save everyone's hide. But sick kids need someone who knows how they tick. They're not adults; they need special care. Grogan did a residency in pediatric surgery. He's good when he wants to be."

He paused, gestured for the water again. It wet his lips. "You know who Grogan was named for? William Wilberforce. Know who he was? An Englishman, an abolitionist. Ironic, isn't it? Grogan's Irish. Can't stand the English. Sends money to the IRA and is proud of it. As for little black kids... Never came up before, not here in Springwell. Don't get many blacks up here in Springwell."

He was mumbling now, his voice trailing away. His eyes were closed. The tape recorder whirred on and the monitor above his head beeped steadily. I looked at Todd, then leaned over and spoke into the recorder. "This conversation with Carl J. Woods, M.D., was recorded on November twenty-third at three p.m., in the presence of Lance Todd, J.D., and Noah Richards, J.D."

Switching it off, I put it in my briefcase and stood up. "Thank you, Dr. Woods."

His eyes opened. "Ask Grogan, young Richards. Perhaps you have more principles than your father."

Mrs. Woods wasn't outside the ICU when we left. I hoped I'd done her husband no harm. Todd and I walked down the corridor to the elevator in silence, pressed the bell, and waited.

"This doesn't change anything," I said. "I'm still going to file against Carl Woods."

He looked at me coldly. "You're going to sue a sick man like that?"

"I'm sorry about it. But I have to think of my clients."

"Two hundred thousand. That's my offer."

"And what about Grogan?"

"Grogan didn't treat that kid. You can't get at him."

"He's on the hospital staff. There're a few questions the hospital might have to answer."

"You want to ruin the place?" he said.

"I don't want to ruin anything, Todd. Beyond what's been ruined already."

Nothing had changed, I'd said. It sure as hell had. It had changed my way of thinking about a hell of a lot of things.

Pausing on the steps at the front entrance to the hospital, Todd was considerably less smooth and convivial. "I'm telling you, Richards, I'm not going to let you bring this place down. So perhaps everything didn't go as it should have with that kid, but there's a lot more at stake here than one kid. I've tried to talk to you reasonably, but you seem hell-bent on destroying everything in sight. For what, may I ask? For some deluded principle? Or is it just money? Is that what you want more of? Think you're going to get millions in this case? You know damn well you won't. I'm going to skin you alive, Noah Richards. Your reputation and your father's reputation won't be worth a damn in this town by the time I've finished with you."

"My father's dead," I said, and for the first time, I really believed it. "As for my reputation, well, I'd rather sleep soundly at night, thanks very much."

"Take the damn offer. Save yourself a load of grief. Don't stir muddy waters."

"Water gets that way because of dirt underneath, doesn't it? If you really have the welfare of this town at heart,

Todd, perhaps you should be interested in the muck at the bottom."

"Oh, for God's sake. I'm talking to a fool."

We parted company.

Walking toward the Saab in the parking lot, I looked back at St. Mary's, white and stark behind me. Looked down across Springwell huddled among the trees. I'd lived here half my life, and how much did I really know about it?

Then I saw, across the lot, the small figure of Lauren Watson standing by her little red Datsun. I lifted my hand to greet her, but she didn't wave back. She was wearing the same voluminous coat and her face was pale and drawn, as though the burdens of the world were on her shoulders. Putting the car keys back in my pocket, I walked over to her.

"I'm glad to see you," I said. I was. "Are you feeling better?"

She looked confused. "Better?"

"You disappeared so suddenly the other evening. I'm sorry if I upset you."

"Oh." She retreated into the coat. "That was rather silly of me. It wasn't you. I was upset about all sorts of things."

"Are you going home now?"

The merest flicker of a smile curved her mouth. "I'm off duty now, if that's what you mean."

"Maybe that's what I mean. Would you care to come and have a cup of coffee with me?"

For a moment, she seemed to consider it; then she shook her head. "I'm sorry, but I don't want to talk about that case."

"We don't have to talk about it. We could talk about something else."

She was wary. "Like what?"

"Oh, like our life histories, our signs, the weather. There's a lot of things people can talk about."

She smiled then, the flecked eyes amused, and I smiled back at her.

"It's just that I've had a rather bad day and it would be a nice change to talk to someone halfway human."

For the first time since I'd known her, which was, after all, no time at all, Lauren Watson laughed openly. "That's what I am? Only halfway human?"

It was delightful to see her laugh. The pale, almost translucent skin flushed into a rosy peach color, and her eyes, full of doubts and cares a moment before, gleamed. She had even white teeth and there was, I noted, a dimple at the corner of her mouth. I've always been a sucker for dimples. I decided one of my new ambitions might be to try to make this young woman laugh more often.

I apologized. "I guess I'm awfully out of practice at this kind of thing."

The color ran deeper in her face. "You can't be more out of practice than I am."

"Good." I was encouraged. "Then we can practice together. Where shall we start?"

My hopes began to fade as she pulled back the sleeve of the coat to look at her watch. "I really don't have much time. I have to be somewhere in an hour."

"An hour's plenty. As a matter of fact, I've got to catch a plane this evening." I'd almost forgotten.

"You're leaving town? Lucky you."

"Los Angeles. Let's go somewhere and I'll tell you about it. I promise to bring you back here in an hour."

The trouble was, there was nowhere to go in Springwell. The only place I could think of, apart from the Dairy Queen and McDonald's, was Joe's, and Joe's was probably not the right place for someone who'd already told me she didn't like liquor. Seattle was full of coffee bars, and in Los Angeles there were open-air cafés, but what was there in Springwell?

Lauren smiled again. "My grandmother always told me

never to get into cars with strangers. There's a café just around the corner. We can walk to it.''

So we walked down the hill in the direction of the town; it was pleasant to be strolling along a street with a pretty girl beside me. She introduced me to a sweet-smelling bakery, the sort of place I didn't think existed in Springwell, with the ubiquitous espresso machines that were springing up all over the state and tiny metal tables and chairs that weren't made for men to sit at. But I didn't mind. We had to sit so close, our knees brushed occasionally, and it gave me an excuse to examine the hazel eyes only a few inches away. I didn't care that she didn't want to talk about the case. It was a relief not to have to talk about it.

After we'd ordered coffee and cookies, Lauren said, "You were going to tell me why you're going to Los Angeles."

"Oh, yes. To spend Thanksgiving with my wife's parents."

There was a tiny pause. Leaning away from the intimacy of the table, she raised her eyebrows minimally. "Your wife?"

It wasn't easy to say it, even now. "She died two years ago."

Her eyes widened. "Died?"

"Leukemia. They tried a bone-marrow transplant, at the Hutch. It didn't work."

"I'm so sorry," she said, then was silent for a moment. "Do you have children?"

"No. We weren't in any hurry to have a family. I guess we waited too long." Suddenly, I wanted to tell her what no one else knew. "As a matter of fact, that's what took Janet to the doctor. She thought she might be pregnant because she was getting sick all the time and feeling lousy. She was never sick. So they did a few tests and then they told her. Can you imagine how that was? Finding out—not that she was going to have a baby but that she was going to die?''

Lauren looked closely into my face for a brief few seconds and the flecked eyes filled with empathy. A small painful noise came from her throat. ''Nobody understands, do they? But I do. I understand. I had a husband. He was twenty-nine years old and he was drowned on one of those damned crab boats. The kind that are always turning over. In Alaska. Eighteen months ago. They never found any of them.''

''My God! How terrible.''

''I woke every morning for weeks thinking that day they might find him safe somewhere. He could have had a survival suit on. He could have been washed up on an island. Every day, I hoped that—one day, the next, someday. It was as though he were getting lost over and over again.''

Her face was full of remembered anguish. I reached out and caught hold of her hand.

''Eighteen months ago? Is that why you left Harborview?''

''I didn't have the energy for it anymore. You've got to give so much of yourself in places like that. I didn't have anything left to give. My sister lives up here and I needed to be near someone who understood. For convalescence, you might say.''

I grasped her hand tightly and she hung on to mine. It was as though we were survivors of the same wreck, clinging to each other for dear life. The aching tightness in my chest that I'd begun to believe would always be there, that I'd begun to accept as normal, started to lighten, as though an enormous weight was being lifted from me. I thought there might never be any necessity to explain anything ever again. I'd found someone who'd always understand.

We sat in silence, without need for words.

At last I said, ''Lauren, when I get back from L.A., will you come out for dinner or something?''

The dimple reappeared in her cheek. "Or something?"

"Do you by any chance like opera?"

"Opera?" She made a funny little face. "I don't know anything about it."

"You don't? You'll love it. I promise."

EIGHTEEN

How QUICKLY perceptions can change. Springwell no longer seemed to me a dreary and dark place; it took on a sheen, a warm bucolic feel, the towering conifers not so much oppressive as rich and softly green. I was sorry to be leaving. Hurrying back to the office, I cleared my desk, wished Bella a happy Thanksgiving, drove home, threw a few things in a case, and arrived at SeaTac only just in time to get the flight. But as the plane reached above the lowering clouds and I saw the stars for the first time in weeks, there was still a sense of escape.

At LAX, Ben waited at the top of the ramp. He threw his arms wide and wrapped me in a bear hug, thumping my shoulders with his large hands. "Dear God, Noah! It's been too long. Don't leave it so long again."

My own father had never hugged me like that. It was good to be back.

But when Beth met us at the door of the house in the canyon, my heart slid sideways at the sight of her. Somehow I'd already forgotten how like her daughter she was, the same short blond hair and compact body, the same defiant tilt to her chin. Beth put her face up for a kiss, blinked tearfully, and clung to me for a moment; then we sat up past midnight while they filled me in on Janet's sisters, also expected for Thanksgiving, on Ben's latest hassles with the building department and the general state of his contracting business. He promised we'd play golf the next afternoon. It wasn't, after all, necessary to speak of Janet. Her presence hung like a gentle shadow in the airy white house, her photograph on the piano, her eyes the same color as her mother's, smiling ruefully across the room, forever part of our lives.

I slept better that night than I had for months, and in the morning the sunshine struck bright and blessed through the open window.

And in the morning, I realized my translator for the tape was right here in the house. As I went downstairs, late for breakfast, Beth was talking on the phone in rapid, fluent Spanish. Had I forgotten she spoke Spanish? Was that one reason I'd come, subconsciously? The subconscious mind plays strangely devious games.

Over coffee and toast, I told her something about the Ambrose case. Not all of it, not about the child dying. It wasn't fair to speak of that. Beth and Ben seemed whole, put back together, their mourning done, as far as mourning can ever be done, and I'd no wish to see pain again in those eyes so like Janet's. So I told her the merest details, that perhaps there was a clue to a missing witness on the message tape. "A mystery?" she said. Her eyes glowed. "I love mysteries."

I put the tape in their machine and the voices spilled out into the sunny room, transported from a different world. Beth hung over my shoulder, and at the end of the first Spanish bit, I switched off. "Well?"

"That's not Mexican Spanish. It's from somewhere else, some other country. It's purer, more Castillian."

"Maybe that's why I can't get it. Any Spanish I know is strictly gutter level. So, what does he say?"

I played the tape again and Beth made a simultaneous translation. "'You are always welcome in our house, Juanita. You must not stay where there is trouble. Your father was like my own father to me. I honor his memory. He would expect me to take care of you. We are strangers in a dangerous country and there is much trouble waiting for us.'"

Writing the words down, I gazed at them. "What do you make of that?"

"'Strangers in a dangerous country?...Your father was like my own father to me?' A poet, I'd say. A revolutionary poet."

I hadn't expected to find a poet. "Poets are a bit thin on the ground where I live."

"But then he probably doesn't live where you do, does he?"

Beth didn't approve of the great Northwest. To her, it was a dark and sorrowful place where people went to die.

I located the woman's voice, soft and murmuring, and Beth translated again. "'Don't worry about money. We have money. We can find a job for you, no problem. Our friend at the County Hospital here in L.A. can always find jobs for people like us. We will speak to her. Don't worry.'"

"L.A.? Los Angeles?" We stared at each other. "Beth! Could she be here? Right on the doorstep? I can't believe it!"

Beth laughed with me in triumph and translated more of the one-sided conversation.

"'If we haven't heard from you by Wednesday, we will be worried. If you've started already, you will be here very soon. But we don't know if you are getting these messages, Juanita. Please call. Please.'"

Had she heard the messages? Or when this was playing, was she somewhere she would never hear any messages again?

The last speaker, running off the end, was the poet once more, his voice mellifluous. "'Juanita, we didn't hear from you. Who are these people that they threaten you? What is this place where you live? I will come up there to find you unless we hear soon. We are waiting for you every day and it is already—'" There the tape ran out.

Beth frowned with concern. "They were so worried about her. Are you worried, Noah?"

"Yes."

" 'Tu padre es como mi propio padre. Yo honra su memoria.' I like the ring of it—'Your father is like my own father to me. I honor his memory.' They sound like proud people. Why don't you call the hospital, Noah?"

Getting through to the personnel department proved difficult. Three times I was put on hold and then cut off; eventually, I gave up on the telephone. At lunchtime, Ben agreed that looking for a missing witness was more important than playing golf; we could always play golf. He lent me his car and by one o'clock I was on the freeway and headed toward the hospital, where I could inquire in person. The California traffic swirled and merged and spun off in an idle, dreamy progression, as if freeways and automobiles were natural occurrences, an essential force. The mountains, as usual, were obscured by smog. When I lived here, I complained about the traffic, the sprawl, the water shortages, the air quality; now, in spite of the smog, the city seemed sunny and vibrant, almost exotic, fruit still hanging on the orange trees, the oleander in flower along the medians, the majestic palm trees soaring high into the blue skies.

The huge, sprawling County Hospital in East L.A. was far removed from exotic or majestic. It had a nasty reputation for blood and hysteria, for a constant scream of ambulances delivering victims of urban mayhem at its doors, and my heart quailed at the thought of it. I reminded myself that Lauren had worked at a place much like this, and I was ashamed of my own squeamishness. But Seattle is not L.A. There was no parking spot closer than three blocks away, in a blighted lot among many other blighted lots, and it was threatening just to try to get to the main entrance. At the entrance, I was challenged to state my business, to prove it with my card and my driver's license, and it took a while before I was allowed inside. Squaring my shoulders, I went in search of the personnel department, eventually locating it in a maze of corridors and clanking overhead pipes, a tiny space, stuffy and oppressive, cream-painted, institutional.

A languid black woman sat behind a cluttered metal desk and regarded me with equal suspicion and dislike. "Yeah?"

"I'm looking for a nurse. I'm not sure she even works here. Could you check your files?"

"Who wants to know?"

I handed over the obligatory card and the woman read it with slow deliberation. "Name?"

"Mine or hers?"

Obviously not one to tolerate fools, she snapped, "Hers, of course. I can read yours here, can't I?"

"Her name is Juanita Barnes."

"Middle initial?"

"D," I said.

"Social Security number?"

"Sorry, I don't know that."

The phone rang and the woman picked it up, and turned her back on me. "Personnel," she said in an unfriendly tone. When she eventually put down the phone, she drummed her fingers on the desk. "We got a lot of people working in this hospital. You'll have to come back."

"Please. I've come down from Seattle specially to find her. If you could just look? Please, ma'am."

I smiled at her, but she didn't smile back, just looked at me the way Angel did, with hostility and challenge, as though white folks deliberately set out to make life difficult—which was probably true.

"You'd be doing me a favor," I said humbly.

"I'll have to ask my boss," she said.

"Whatever it takes."

Unwillingly, she rose slowly from the desk and disappeared into further depths of the labyrinth. The phone buzzed constantly and no one answered. I read all the notices thumb-tacked to the bulletin boards, about AIDS testing and illegal immigrants and green cards and licenses and positions available, read them again. At last, the woman returned, unhurried, picked up the phone, which was ringing again, and pushed a piece of paper at me. On it was written, by hand: "Juanita Barnes, R.N. Emergency Room—7 to 3:30 shift."

I felt like a genius. "She *does* work here, then? In the emergency room?"

"That's what it says, doesn't it?"

I retreated.

Now I had to face the emergency room.

It took another age to work my way back through the building. Elevators disgorged me into fresh mazes and into long corridors too bright under fluorescent lights, too crowded by wheelchairs and patients on carts and janitors pushing buckets and mops, and by hurrying, distracted people with life and death on their minds. There was a constant cacophony of overhead paging and a pervasive aroma of panic barely under control, of disinfectant and unwashed bodies. Dread weakened my resolve. Yet once I found the entrance to the emergency room and stepped gingerly through the automatic doors, it appeared quiet and calm enough, no trails of blood, no screams, no stretchers thundering by with bodies and hysterical relatives in tow. On the long wooden benches in the middle of the tiled floor, a group of black youths in knitted caps jabbed one another in the ribs and laughed defiantly and loudly, as if afraid of something; an ancient Asian woman in a blue padded jacket sat alone, so tiny, her feet didn't reach the ground, infinite resignation in her prunelike face. The emergency room seemed to be in a lull. I hoped it lasted.

A young girl in green scrubs came out of a curtained cubicle, knelt down, and spoke in a low whisper to the old lady, who got up obediently and trotted down the hallway with her, stooped and bent, much, much shorter than her escort and about a hundred years older. They disappeared together behind the curtain. A very young doctor in a white coat slouched out of another room and used the telephone at the empty reception desk. A cart with a sobbing passenger was wheeled out of another cubicle, followed by a man carrying a brown paper grocery bag, as though he'd been interrupted in the middle of shopping for dinner. It was like watching a movie with the sound turned down. The overhead lights flickered and hummed with a separate life of their own, and except for the teenagers horsing around on the benches, everything seemed under control. At any moment, I expected the doors to burst open to admit the torn and bloodied victim of a gun battle, a mortally afflicted heart attack patient, a corpse on a stretcher. All my ideas about emergency rooms came from TV.

No one took any notice of me or asked what I was doing there, if I needed assistance, if I was sick. There was no one at the reception desk to help me.

After a long pause, as though the whole place had been holding its breath, a small flurry of activity erupted. Green-gowned nurses, necks draped with masks and stethoscopes, crossed and recrossed in front of the benches and crowded around the reception desk. The clock above the desk read 3:15—time for the shift change.

I approached the desk. The three women filling in paperwork ignored me, intent on more important matters, and when I cleared my throat, they appeared displeased at the interruption.

"I'm looking for someone who works here. Nita Barnes."

Like a charm, the eyes of two of them turned to the third.

"Nita Barnes?" I couldn't keep the triumph out of my voice. "You can't know how relieved I am to have found you."

I *was* relieved. I'd been afraid, until that moment, that some harm might have befallen her. The man at her house had made me feel that way, the sense of menace that lurked in him.

She straightened up, tall and thin and not quite as young as I'd imagined, but with smooth skin the color of coffee cream, large brown eyes with long spiky lashes that gave her the look of a startled deer; without the ugly paper cap covering her hair, she could have been almost beautiful. Another face come to life from the pages of records.

Glaring at me, she tapped her pen against the counter in an irritable nervous clatter. "And who are you?"

I slid a card onto the countertop and all three of them peered at it. "Noah Richards," I said. "Attorney for the plaintiffs in the case of *Ambrose* versus *St. Mary's Hospital*."

She drew in a sharp breath. One of the other nurses said immediately, "Don't say anything, Nita. Never speak to an attorney."

"I have to ask you about Jordan Ambrose, Miss Barnes. You remember little Jordan Ambrose at St. Mary's, don't you? It won't do you any good to refuse to talk now, because I can always serve you with a subpoena."

"I don't want to talk to you. I don't know anything."

The slight Spanish accent, distinctive on the answering machine, was fainter in person and disguised by antagonism.

"I think you know a good deal about Jordan Ambrose, Miss Barnes—about the doctors, about his treatment."

"What treatment?" she said scornfully.

"That's exactly what I need to ask you. I'd also like to talk to you about Dr. Woods and Dr. Grogan."

"Grogan?" The arching eyebrows straightened into a narrow black line. "That son of a bitch?"

The other nurses looked anxious. "Nita!"

"Don't worry," she said. "I can handle this."

I imagined she could handle most things.

Staring at me fiercely, she said, "Are you suing Grogan?" I thought I detected some kind of hope in her voice.

"The hospital. Dr. Woods and Dr. Clarke. I'm the attorney for the plaintiffs."

"What about Grogan?"

"Grogan didn't treat the boy."

"I know," she said. "The kid's parents are suing?"

"Yes, the parents."

She twisted the pen in thin fingers. "I don't want to get mixed up in anything."

"But you're mixed up in it already, aren't you? Your notes are in the hospital chart. Have you forgotten how angry you were?"

She bent her head. "No, I haven't forgotten."

I waited. The other nurses waited, too, looking from her to me and back to her. She hesitated, the fine eyebrows drawn into a frown, the brown eyes uncertain. One of the nurses repeated, "Don't talk to him, Nita. You'll only get yourself in trouble."

She made a bitter little noise deep in her throat. "Trouble? You don't know what trouble is," and she threw the pen down on the desk. "Okay, all right. I'm off duty now. We can talk in the cafeteria if you like."

"The cafeteria? Isn't there anywhere else we can go?"

"Around here? You got to be kidding."

So we went to the hospital cafeteria. I didn't want to risk losing her now I'd so miraculously found her and so I didn't confess my unreasonable dislike of hospital cafeterias, the smell of the food, the clattering trays, the taste of the coffee, forever associated with endless hours of waiting and hopelessness. I followed on her heels as she rushed along more confusing corridors, as though she was trying to leave me behind.

I bought her a Coke and a sandwich at the counter and chose a table in the corner, out of the way of the traffic pattern. She took off the ugly paper cap and her hair was raven black, glossy and thick. She ate ravenously, as though she hadn't eaten for days.

Between mouthfuls, she said, "Maybe I'm glad to talk about it finally. I've thought about that poor kid a lot. It wasn't right, you know."

"We worried about you disappearing like that."

"We? Who, for instance?"

"Lauren Watson, for one."

"Oh Lauren! Yes, well, Lauren might. I guess I should've called her. I had to get out of there. Away from St. Mary's, out of Springwell. I hated the place after that child died. I hated it before, if you want to know." She fixed the shiny brown eyes on me. "How did you track me down here?"

"From your telephone message tape. I found it at your house."

"The house in Fairview?"

"I filched it from under your landlord's nose."

"Grogan?" Her lip curled. "Then I forgive you."

"Tell me about him."

"What's there to tell? He's a fucking fascist pig. You know how people like him treat people like me? Hispanics? Like shit, that's how. Like lowlife." The brown eyes glittered and hardened.

"But he rented the house to you."

"Oh yeah. And guess what he thought he deserved for that kind gesture? He must believe he's some sort of gift to women. Just because he's a doctor. Think they're God, some of them. As though I'd have let him touch me. That horrible ginger hair…" She shuddered. "I threatened to call the police if he came around one more time. That would've done his reputation at the hospital a lot of good, wouldn't it? Wish I had." She pushed the plate aside, drained the glass of Coke. "You know, he got some creep to keep an eye on me, always watching, always lurking around with his ugly dog.''

"Gurning," I said.

The eyes grew bigger. "Yeah, Gurning. How come you know about him?''

I told her how he'd been at the house. "What's he to do with Grogan?''

Hissing, she brought the creamy face closer. "Birds of a feather, that's what they are. Grogan said the neighborhood needed a watchman to make sure everything was okay. The neighborhood was perfectly okay until that creep started coming around. Thought he'd get rid of me that way. And he succeeded, didn't he?'' She smiled bitterly. "I stuck it out as long as I did because I didn't have anyplace else to go. Then I got into a fucking awful fight with Grogan about that kid, and suddenly it was as if I'd gone too far, you know. I didn't feel safe anymore. I didn't know what they'd do.''

"You had a fight with Grogan? I thought it was with the other doctor, Clarke. The morning Jordan was taken to the operating room.''

"Oh, well, Clarke, too. When I went off duty that morning, Grogan was coming into the hospital. I was so mad about the whole rotten mess, I told him I'd report him to the medical society, or someone. I didn't really know who I was going to report him to. The hospital at least. For never going to see that poor little kid.''

The brown eyes sparked defiance, but there was also a hint of fear in them. "He threatened me right back. I went back to the house and thought about it, and when he called, I didn't pick up the phone. Who knows what a shit like that will do?''

"What did you think he'd do?''

Her fingers laced together tightly. "You don't know what it's like to have a creep like Gurning watching you all the time. Come out of the house and there he is. Go in after dark and you don't know if he's standing around a corner. They're not normal, people like him. They don't have normal ideas. But they're alive and well in Springwell, aren't they? Places like Springwell and Fairview, they're breeding grounds for the sort of shit they believe in.''

''What sort of shit?''

''Shit stuff like Aryan Nation, the Brotherhood, you know, that sort of thing. The militia. We all know about them now, don't we?''

I stared at her, disbelieving. Yes, I knew about organizations like that, but I wasn't prepared to believe they existed where I lived. ''Come on!'' I protested. ''I've lived half my life in Springwell. There's nothing like that there.''

She reacted angrily. ''You think jerks like Gurning aren't perfect examples of that mentality?''

I thought of Gurning. Paranoid, menacing, the unnerving sense of being barely under control. The odd ramrod stance, the camouflage cap, the gun he claimed was in his pocket. ''Okay,'' I agreed reluctantly. ''Gurning's a perfect example. But he's not like most people in Springwell. Most people in Springwell are perfectly ordinary and decent.''

''You think so? Then how come bastards like him can operate there? Can go around terrifying people? People like me? Like Lauren Watson?''

''Lauren?'' I felt a sudden alarm, a throb in my gut. ''What do they have to do with her?''

''Her damn fool sister married one of them. Not Brett, a brother or something. Lauren's scared shitless for her sister and her kids. There isn't anyone else to look out for them, you know. I told her to get out of there, take her sister with her, just get the hell away from them.''

Lauren? Mixed up with nuts like Gurning? I had the lurching memory of her eyes filled with fear that afternoon in my office.

I tried to put it together. ''But what's it got to do with Jordan Ambrose?''

Nita Barnes looked at me as if I was stupid. I probably was. "That's what I'm trying to tell you. Grogan, the Gurnings, God knows who else. White supremacist types. They hate blacks, Jews, Hispanics, anyone who's not like them. Why do you think that kid moldered on so long? Because that shit Grogan wouldn't go near him. Because he was black."

It wasn't the first time I'd heard the suggestion, but I still couldn't believe it. "You're trying to tell me he refused to see a sick child just because he was black? How do you know that?"

The color was high on her cheekbones, the brown eyes hot. "Because he said so."

"To you?"

She nodded. "I'll tell you what happened—from the first night Jordy was in the hospital. God, what a sweet kid. Just lay there like a lamb, saying his belly hurt, crying now and then, asking for his mom. About eleven, he got much worse, so I called Clarke. Woke him up. He said it was only gastroenteritis and to watch him. So I did, very carefully. When the kid's blood pressure started going down and his belly was so hard, I called Clarke again. He said he'd send him for an X ray in the morning and that he'd asked Grogan to see him. 'Now?' I said. 'No,' he said, 'in the morning.' But when I came back the next night, no one had been. Nothing had been done except for the X ray. Nothing. And he was so much worse. The nurse on the afternoon shift said they'd expected Grogan but that he hadn't come. I called Clarke again. I called him four times that night. The child was in shock. I couldn't stand it any longer, so in the end I called Grogan myself. It's not my place to call a surgeon, but I didn't care. He told me to mind my own business, that he wasn't going to get out of bed at four a.m. or any other time to see any damned black kid. He said, 'I'm a surgeon, not a veterinarian.'" She stumbled over the words and looked sick at the sound of them.

"He said that? You're sure?"

Her eyes flashed. "Of course I'm sure. You think I'd invent something like that?"

I had him. I had someone to swear Grogan refused to see a patient because of his color. I might not be able to get him on malpractice grounds, but surely there were some grounds. Denying Jordan Ambrose his civil rights? Dereliction of duty? Something. I would crucify him. And St. Mary's, for having anyone like that on the staff. I felt a great surge of vengeful elation. I had him.

"A sworn statement from you, Nita, and Grogan is dead meat."

For a few seconds, she stared at me, eyes huge; then she lowered her eyes and pressed her head into her hands. The parting in the glossy black hair was white and straight and somehow vulnerable. "I can't."

"What do you mean, you can't?"

She shook her head, didn't look at me. "I can't risk it."

"Risk? All you have to do is repeat what you've just told me now."

"There'll be a court case, won't there?"

"I doubt it. After they hear what you say, they'll settle."

"They'll believe what I say for sure, won't they?" She still didn't look at me.

I said slowly, "Why shouldn't you be believed, Nita?"

She raised her head, eyes flashing. "It's the truth, Mr. Attorney. But I'm not telling it to any court, because...because..." Her eyes flicked around the room. "The girls were right. I should've had more sense than to talk to a lawyer."

My heart sank a little. "If there's a problem, you'd better tell me now. Before we get into something we can't get out of."

She put her head in her hands again. "I'm illegal."

It took a moment to register. "You mean you don't have a green card?"

For someone who'd lived in Los Angeles for so long, a city full of people with no green cards, I was pretty slow on the uptake. In a deposition, someone would surely ask that question. I thought about an allegation against a member of the medical profession from an illegal alien. It didn't alter the truth, of course, but a defense lawyer would make mincemeat out of it. Grogan's word against hers. Who'd take the word of an illegal?

"That was one of the things Grogan threatened. Said he'd get me sent back. I can't go back."

"Back where?"

And because I, too, have preconceptions, her answer surprised me.

"Chile."

"Chile?"

Her voice had an edge. "You think I'm just another wetback from across the border, don't you? Well, it's a bit more complicated. I met someone in the Peace Corps, in Santiago. It got difficult in Pinochet's time; he had to leave, and I left with him. Times were difficult for me, as well."

"You're saying you're a political refugee?"

She shrugged carelessly. "Undesirable, more like it. If I'd left in Allende's time, the United States would have welcomed me with open arms. Unfortunately, Pinochet wasn't a Communist."

"This peace corps guy? Did you marry him? Is that where Barnes comes from?"

She smiled slightly and didn't fully answer the question. "It gets me into places Sanchez wouldn't have."

I remembered the notice board in the personnel office. "Don't you need a green card to work here?"

Her smile was condescending now. "Let's say I got documentation. It might not stand up in court, but it does for somewhere desperate for staff."

"You didn't marry him, did you, Nita? If you'd married him, you wouldn't have had trouble with a green card."

She swirled the remains of the Coke around her glass, gazed at it. "It was stupid not to, wasn't it? But I had high principles in those days."

"Why can't you go back to Chile now? It's safe now, isn't it?"

"Maybe I don't want to. Maybe I like it here now. As long as it's not Springwell." She looked at me defiantly. "So, Mr. Attorney, what are you going to do about it?"

"Get you an immigration lawyer."

"Are you volunteering?"

"It's not my field. But I could find someone who'd help."

"Just so I can testify in your case?"

"Don't you want to get Grogan?"

She thought about it for a moment. "Yes, I want to get Grogan. I'd like to see him crucified."

"That makes two of us."

NINETEEN

LATER THAT NIGHT, Ben and I sat drinking scotch in the living room of the house in Santa Monica. I told him about the Ambroses and Grogan and the South American nurse who saw racism and fascism on every street corner. I expected Ben, the pragmatist, his political views far to the right of mine, to pour cold water on the alarmist theories. He didn't.

He said, "She's right. Hatred and intolerance are everywhere, and getting worse. Not just the old hatreds, Jews and Arabs, Catholic and Protestants. Now it's Californians and Hispanics, English and Pakistanis, French and Algerians, Germans and Turks. The list grows longer every day and there'll be more as people move around the world looking for the good life. A shrinking job market, a growing population, and a distrust of different people with different ethics. It may be regrettable, Noah, but it seems to me an unhappy fact of human nature. It'll be a long time before we humans learn to exist side by side in racial and social harmony. Much longer than you or I've got."

It wasn't anything I didn't know already, but it depressed the hell out of me. We drank our scotch, wrangled over the eternal California topics of immigration and crime, taxes and property values, and at close to midnight, the phone rang. We froze in our seats, staring at it. Telephones are not supposed to ring at midnight. Ben's face went rigid, and I had an instant unhappy memory of late-night calls from the hospital. Snatching at the receiver, he listened for a second, then handed it to me like a hot potato.

It was Bella, agitated, apologetic, her words running together, spluttering and gulping.

"Oh, Mr. Noah! I'm so sorry to call you so late at night down there in California, but the most dreadful thing has happened—to the office. I hardly know how to tell you. The office...it's...it's been burned down."

For a moment, I couldn't quite grasp what she'd said. "Burned? The office?" It didn't sink in properly. "What do you mean, '*been* burned down'? You're telling me it was set on fire? Deliberately?"

Her voice rose in a wail. "Oh, I don't know, Mr. Noah, really I don't. But that's what the firemen seem to think. The alarm went off and they went to it and then they called me at home when they couldn't get you, and I had to go down and talk to them. They say it looks like arson. Who would do such a terrible thing? All the records, all your father's files—all gone."

"Gone? Everything?"

"The front office and the file room. Mr. Richard's...your room, it's sort of still there, but it's ruined. Soaked with water. It's awful, awful."

"Shit, Bella." I couldn't believe it. "But no one was hurt?"

"No, no. It was late at night. About nine o'clock. But what if it had happened earlier? I could have been there, Mr. Noah. I'm terrified of fire."

I heard the hysteria in her voice and I made unrealistic soothing noises, got a number from her for the fire department, said I'd call her in the morning. "I'll get back as soon as possible, Bella. Go to bed now. Try to sleep. I'll take care of things, I promise. Don't worry."

Dropping the phone, I stared at Ben and he stared back at me in disbelief.

"What the devil's going on up there, Noah? Are you talking arson?"

"That's what Bella says."

I called the fire department. The phone rang and rang before someone answered perfunctorily. "Yes, there was an incident at that address. No, we don't have more information tonight. This number is for emergencies only. Call in the morning.''

Ben paced the room, rattling the change in his pockets. I was numbed and slow in my reactions, some odd sensation seeping through my body, something strangely akin to relief.

"Burned!" I said. "Everything. All those records and files and years and years of documents. Who knows, I might have to start all over again. Something different, somewhere new.''

"What about your case?''

"Ah, yes, the Ambrose case. You imagine someone else was thinking of that, too?''

Ben was never slow on the uptake. "Your office was torched to derail the case? This white hate stuff?''

"God knows. Who knows anything anymore?''

"You can reconstruct it, I suppose? The case, I mean?''

I shrugged. "If I want to.''

He looked at me sharply. "You wouldn't be frightened off just like that, would you?''

Sighing, I said, "No, I suppose not. But it's ruined Thanksgiving, hasn't it?''

I couldn't remain in sunny California, eating turkey, while my practice lay literally in shambles. I couldn't let anyone believe they'd dealt the Ambrose case a fatal blow. Because that's what it had to be, of course. An office doesn't just burn down out of the blue. There'd been too many incidents of arson around the Northwest in the past couple of years. It was getting to be a common crime, but somebody had to be awfully stupid to believe the destruction of a few papers would make a case go away, that intimidating one attorney could change the course of justice.

The prospect of returning to such a mess didn't fill me with any sense of mission. I couldn't even work myself up about my father's past being burned to the ground. All I could think of, shamefully, was that here was a perfect excuse to get out from under—an excuse I couldn't use, of course.

The next day, it proved to be as difficult to get a flight going north the day before Thanksgiving as it had been to get one coming south—which surprised me. Who could possibly want to leave California sunshine for Northwest gray? I put myself on standby and got a seat on a flight at seven in the evening, which meant I wouldn't be in Springwell before ten or eleven—much too late to do anything constructive. As I waited at the airport, I thought about the elusive Nita Barnes and hoped to hell she didn't vanish again before I could get her story in some usable form. In the crowded plane, daunted by the idea of my empty house and my empty bed, I was tempted to use the air phone and beg a bed from Daphne and Chauncey for the night. I even got out my credit card, then decided, what the hell, a few more hours on my own wasn't going to kill me. I had a better idea. Maybe the house wouldn't have to be so empty; maybe returning to Springwell wouldn't be so bad after all. I dialed Lauren's number. An inevitable machine answered. I almost didn't leave a message, but speaking to her machine was better than nothing. "Lauren, this is Noah Richards. Wednesday evening, about seven-thirty. Thanksgiving in L.A. is canceled due to unforeseen circumstances. I'll be in Springwell about eleven or so tonight. Maybe we can get together over the holiday. I'll try you in the morning."

Inevitably, it was raining as I drove away from SeaTac. The euphoria of California, of finding my missing witness, of seeing Lauren again soon drained away from me. The headlights reflected the sheeting rain, the wet waste of freeway. From the other side of the meridian, the lights of oncoming vehicles flicked in my eyes and the wretched questions of the Ambrose case scratched at my brain. But as I got closer to Springwell, the righteous anger that had

consumed me at the start of it all returned to warm my
bones and put its own fire in my belly. Hell, if they thought
they could scare me off, they had another thing coming.
Whoever they were, they'd picked on someone other than
a defenseless woman like Nita Barnes. No one was going
to torch my office and get away with it.

I stopped at the office on the way through town. The
remains of it. It was an immensely dismal sight, a scene of
destruction dimly and inappropriately illuminated by the
pink neon sign of the supermarket across the road. Rain
fell steadily into a gaping hole where the front part of the
building had been and where now nothing but a mess of
twisted metal and broken glass was left. At the rear of the
building, a huge blue tarpaulin drooped over my room.
When I got out of the car, the stench of charred wood and
dirty water was powerful. I stepped over the yellow plastic
streamers looped around the parking space and glass
crunched under my feet, stuck to the sole of my shoe. When
I bent down to remove it, I found a shard of the gold lettering that had once adorned the front door.

Richards and Richards was gone.

I got back in the car and drove home.

But as I approached the house, dark and silent among
the trees, that earlier reluctance about being alone there
grew into an acute uneasy dread. Slowing to a halt a few
yards down the road, I switched off the headlights and the
engine and peered through the windshield into the black
night. Above my head, the rain dripped off low overhang-
ing branches onto the car roof in an irregular, ominous beat,
an insistent sound, like the subdued alarm of a snare drum,
like movie music portending danger. Nothing moved. The
thick conifers crowded around and no one and nothing else
was to be seen. But somehow I was certain someone was
out there—somewhere—waiting for me. The feeling was
so palpable and unpleasant that the hairs at the nape of my
neck prickled. I shot a quick compulsive look over my

shoulder at the empty road behind me, then whipped around to stare into the darkness again. Still nothing. Only the house waiting among the trees. Only someone familiar with the house would even know it was there.

I found myself wishing, for the first time in my life, that I carried a gun with me. The idea was repulsive, against all my beliefs and principles, and it infuriated me. I shouldn't have to want a gun. I'd done nothing to merit fear. It was the sight of the office, of course, that had alarmed me. Anyone who did that might do anything. Suddenly, I had the sickening recollection of my business card in the hand of that lunatic Gurning. I'd given it to him myself. Told him to keep it. Not only with the office address on it but my home number, as well. He could have found out exactly where I lived. My office was burned down and he knew where my home was. I understood then why I sensed danger.

Switching the engine on again, but not the lights, I put the car in first gear, eased it forward, slid slowly past the house. Dark as pitch, nothing to see. Twenty five yards farther up the road, I did a U-turn where the road widened and almost ran into another vehicle tucked under the trees, practically invisible. I recognized it immediately—a red Datsun, Lauren's car.

I stared at it, uncomprehending. What was her car doing here at close to midnight? Getting out, I peered through the windows and tried the handles. Locked. Rain splattered on my head and the night was dark and threatening as I stood in the road and tried to think clearly. She had parked near my house, so it was logical that she'd gone to my house. Gone to wait for me because I'd called her from the plane?

For a moment, the thought seduced me. But some sense told me it was an incorrect assumption. If Lauren had gone to wait for me, she would have parked in the driveway, not here, not hidden from view like this. Why should she hide her car from me? I had this overwhelming feel of danger and knew it wasn't Lauren who was dangerous. Could the danger be hers? Not mine after all? "Scared shitless," Nita Barnes had put it so inelegantly. Scared of Gurnings.

Without any clear plan in my head, I found myself creeping back along the road toward the house, my footsteps light and silent on the tarmac, sneaking like a thief toward my own home.

Alongside the house, the driveway ran up to the garage; a path angled off to the porch and to the front door, used only by strangers. I always went in through the side door and never locked it. I'd been gone for several days and couldn't remember locking the damn door. Had I locked it? Had I left in such a hurry I hadn't given it a second thought? Anyone could walk in. And if it was Lauren who'd walked in, there would be lights on in the house. It wouldn't be so dark and silent and threatening.

Instead of going up the driveway, in view of anyone who might be watching, I clambered through the shrubbery, my feet slipping on the wet leafy bank. Under the protective cover of the tall old rhododendrons, I stared up at the house looming above me. Still nothing, except this irrational feel of menace.

I don't know why I was so sure Gurning was in there, waiting for me. I remembered his hand in the parka, the evil dog at his feet, the boots the man wore. In my parents' house? Damn him to hell. But worse than that, much worse, was the fear that Lauren was in the house with him. In there with her soft skin and flecked eyes, with her fragility and fear. With Gurning. Dear God!

If only I'd had a gun in the car. If only the phone in the car worked. I could have called the police if only I had a phone. They'd find Gurning if he was there. Find Lauren if she was there. I cursed my endless procrastination about the car phone. I'd have to drive off to get the police. It would take half an hour to get them back here.

I couldn't leave without making sure about Lauren.

It was my house. I knew my way around it. I stood in the darkness and pictured each door and window, how secure they were, which ones were locked and which weren't. Only the side door was ever used; all the others remained bolted and shut tight. Maybe he was waiting by the side door. I went through the house in my mind, door by door, window by window the ground floor, the inaccessible upper floor, the basement. The basement! The outside basement door was locked and bolted from inside, as stiff and rusty as the front door, but above my father's workbench was a window with a broken catch that I'd never got around to fixing.

I circled the house among the dripping shrubs and trees.

It wasn't easy to get through the tiny window, not easy to squeeze inside and drop to the bench far below without making a sound. My father's obsessive neatness made silence even more difficult, his tools in their allotted spots on the Peg-Board beneath the window rattling as I slid over them. But he'd secured them well and they didn't come loose. Balancing on the bench, I listened for sounds from above. Nothing. Was anyone really there?

It was blindingly dark in the basement. Groping along the Peg-Board until my fingers identified a large wrench, I picked at the fastening wires, cradled the comforting heft of it in my fist, a weapon against the unknown, then dropped to the floor and inched away from the workbench step by slow step, across the cement floor, past the wheezing, burping furnace, until the first of the basement stairs hit against my toes. I started up the wooden steps, each tread creaking under my weight, my hands feeling along the walls on either side. At the top, my hands met the door. I turned the knob very carefully, pushed against it, then pushed again.

The door was locked.

Very smart. I left the back door open but kept the one from inside the house locked. But there was no bolt on this door and the lock wasn't complicated, just a simple knob turned from the other side, no key or anything. Something flexible would surely slide in between and spring the catch.

My eyes hadn't adjusted to the light because there was absolutely no light to adjust to. The basement was pitch-black, even the entry window, invisible in the nightmare blindness. Fumbling in my pocket for my wallet and a credit card, I tried sliding it into the crack of the door, but the card was too short to reach round the angle. If I could turn on a light to search among the tools, I knew I'd find something suitable. Standing motionless, I wondered whether anyone inside the house would see a light, wondered whether anyone was really in the house. I remembered the flashlight in the car; I hadn't had enough foresight to bring it with me.

Pressing my ear against the door, I still couldn't hear a thing. The door was thick and sturdy, the joists and the flooring constructed at the turn of the century with the best timber, the best workmanship, to keep sound out, but even as I tried to hear something, anything, I grew aware of a faint, vaguely familiar odor drifting through the cracks. Bringing my face closer to the jamb, belated recognition of what it was hit me, sent shock waves through my body. Acrid, rank, and ominous, it was the same dirty smell as in the remains of the office. Fire! On the other side of the door, something was burning!

Scrabbling along the wall for the light switch, the appalling memory of the twisted metal and broken glass and the ugly stumps of the office walls filled me with alarm and dread. I found the switch and snapped it urgently, not caring anymore. But no light came on. I raced down the stairs, stumbling over the unseen floor, which came too abruptly, then crashed across to the workbench and grabbed at the shapes on the Peg-Board, cursing the dark, desperate to get through that door. My fingers identified and discarded wrenches and drills, planes, sanders, the neglected

tools of an amateur carpenter. I pulled the drawers open,
felt blindly among the jars of screws and nails, bolts and
nuts. There was nothing to spring a catch with. I had to
stand still and take a breath, think. No use crashing about
in the dark in the huge basement. Wasn't it better to try to
get out by the outside door, across there somewhere in the
dark, and enter the house by the side door? Had any ele-
ment of surprise been lost by the noise I was making now?

Trying to keep calm, instead I imagined fire racing across
the living room floor above my head, eating through the
carpets, the furniture, licking over the drapes, everything,
anyone who was up there. Lauren.

Jesus! My fingers felt a hatchet and grabbed at it, thinking to break down the door, then I thought the stiff plastic-
covered wire that held it in place might do the lock-opening
trick. Tugging to free the wire and the hatchet from the
holes in the Peg-Board, at last I had them both loose. I
headed back to the stairs, hit my shins on unknown objects,
turned myself around so I didn't know which way I was
facing, spun about the space, listening for the furnace, then
realized there was no sound coming from it anymore. No
light from the switch, no sound from the furnace. Had the
electricity failed? Had it been cut off? What the hell was
happening above my head?

The darkness was so profound, it weighed on me like a
physical presence, a black web entangling my head and my
eyes. The silence, too, was unnatural and sinister. Then the
furnace in the corner gave a sudden burp, a sigh, a metallic
groaning, and I was able to orientate myself again, move
cautiously across the concrete floor and find the stairwell
to the door. I poked the plastic covered wire through the
joint between the door and the jamb, praying no one was
on the other side waiting for me.

Miraculously, the wire worked, the knob turning like
magic in my hand. I cracked the door stealthily and silently,
and immediately the smell of smoke was stronger. But no

one was behind the door and there were no flames, thank God, to light the way. I was in the hallway between the kitchen and the living room and after the pitchy black of the basement, I could almost see. And I knew my way around. I swung the ax in my hand, ready for murder.

I listened. Nothing. Only the ominous smell of smoke. Sliding through the door, I inched my way across the floor and stumbled against an object where there shouldn't have been one. When I put my hand out, it felt like broken wood, and then I could see, very dimly, that it was a chair, upside down. My fingers felt jagged edges of material, feathers spilling out of the innards of the cushions, and as my eyes grew more accustomed to the dark, I saw a table lying next to the chair, also on its side—the narrow table that should have been over there under the mirror. Groping my way to the end of the hallway, my feet knocked against the brass lamp that normally stood on the table and now lay on the floor. There was the unpleasant crunch of broken glass under my feet, just as there had been at the office.

Someone had been trashing the house.

Freezing in place, I could only hope that those who'd done the trashing weren't still in the house. If they were still there, I had no idea where they might be. Watching me right now, maybe. Waiting for me to make another move. Instinctively, I sank down the wall to make myself less of a target, but nearer the floor, the smoke was worse. It made my eyes sting, made breathing difficult, rolling across the floor in a choking, creeping mass. It was impossible to see the beginning or end of it, where it came from. But I had to find where it came from; otherwise, the house would end up like the office.

And Lauren? Where was Lauren?

I stood up, took a deep breath, and ploughed my way across the hallway. In the kitchen there was a flashlight, in the cupboard by the back door. To hell with anyone waiting for me. I had to have some light. I had to find her if she was in the house.

Opening the door to the kitchen, smoke billowed out to meet me, thick, acrid, and suffocating, as though I had reached the source of it. Holding my breath, I raced across the room, my thighs jamming painfully against the edge of the table, the soles of my shoes slipping and scratching on what felt like more broken glass on the floor. I couldn't stop to think about it, could only think now about getting fresh air into my lungs. I reached the back door, threw it wide open, and took deep life-restoring breaths, then closed it just as quickly, because the air blowing in could ignite whatever had merely been smoldering before. With a light, I could find the source of the smoke and do something about it before I choked to death.

The flashlight was where it should be, thank God, plugged into an outlet so it was constantly charged, and when I pressed the button, a strong beam of blessed light sprang over the swirling clouds. I aimed the beam at the floor, littered with shards of broken dishes and glasses, and could at last see what I had to deal with—a smoldering heap of something on the floor near the stove. Leaping to attack it with water from the faucet, which sent more choking fumes into the laden air, I kicked the heap apart and saw it was a pile of rags and pieces of plastic. As the heap scattered, I realized much of it was old vinyl tiles, torn out of the floor, and the rags were not rags, but towels and tablecloths, even the fringed checked curtains from the kitchen windows, a piece of carpeting with rubberized backing which was giving off the worse of the noxious fumes. When the pile was safely dispersed and there was no more sign of active burning, I opened the back door again, sucked in deep, grateful breaths of fresh air. The smoke rushed out of the door, thinning until the flashlight was able to reveal the devastation; cupboards and drawers had been emptied onto the floor; smashed crockery and glass, pots and pans were strewn everywhere. Senseless, ugly vandalism.

I threw the beam of the flashlight higher. It created a tunnel of light and shadows, wavering across the dark kitchen, through the curling, disappearing smoke, over the upturned chairs, the shattered china, along the pine table. Then my breathing came to an abrupt, labored stop.

Slumped in a chair at the far end of the kitchen table, collapsed forward so her head rested on the surface of it, the blond hair spread in a fan around her face, was Lauren. Small, silent, unmoving. In the midst of all that deadly smoke! She had been lying there all the time. Dear God!

She lay so still, it terrified me. I touched her, frantically and fearfully, but her body, when I put my hands on it, was warm, and when I lowered my face close to hers, I could hear shallow, grunting gasps for life. Scooping her up, I ran out of the house with her, her weight nothing in my arms.

On the wet grass, a safe distance from the house and a safe distance, I hoped, from the source of the destruction, I knelt beside her. The flecked eyes were hidden behind frail lids; the soft hair trailed across her face. Her lungs had to be full of that deadly smoke, and I tried to breathe into them for her. When I put my mouth over her slack one, I could taste whisky. At first, I imagined it was my own breath, then I realized she reeked of whisky. It was as though she'd been sitting in the kitchen of my house drinking scotch—a lot of it. Someone who said she never touched hard liquor.

I kept breathing into her and prayed as I breathed.

TWENTY

THERE CAME the sound of a car in the driveway, a door slamming, feet on the gravel. Instinctively, afraid someone had returned to survey his work, I covered Lauren's body with mine. Then I saw it was Chauncey, hair gleaming in the beams of the headlights, dread in his face.

"Here," I yelled. "Over here."

He came running. "Noah! I thought you were in California. What the hell happened?" He saw Lauren and said again, "What the hell?"

"Help her," I begged.

Dropping to his knees, he pushed me aside, felt for her pulse, lifted her eyelid. The eye beneath was blank and unseeing. He took over the breathing from me, expertly.

From around the lake came a cacophony of blaring horns and wailing sirens. The machines roared and flashed into the driveway, disgorged a horde of firefighters in yellow slickers, running, shouting, dragging hoses; with them came the paramedics, thrusting Chauncey aside in turn. I watched them work on Lauren as I'd watched them work on Carl Woods, the oxygen mask, the IV drip, the static of the two-way radios, and I was sick with remorse. Another victim of the Ambrose case I'd put in the way of harm.

Chauncey yanked me aside by the elbow, "What the devil is going on, Noah? First your office, now your house. And this girl? Isn't she one of our nurses?"

"How did you get here?" I asked. "How did you know?"

"The dogs. We took them out for a last run and they could smell the smoke. They howled at it. And when we looked, we could see a cloud of it pouring out of the house.''

"Thank God for dogs.''

I saw the medics lifting Lauren's limp body onto a stretcher.

I said, "Don't take her to St. Mary's.''

"It's the nearest hospital, sir.''

"No,'' I insisted, shaking loose from Chauncey. "Not St. Mary's.''

"For God's sake, Noah. She needs help. Quickly.''

I couldn't let them take her there and I couldn't stop them. So I went with her, to watch over her.

From the back of the ambulance, I saw the firemen folding up the hoses, packing away the equipment. The house had survived, but I wasn't sure Lauren would. I thought of the god-awful mess that was inside the house and of who might have done it, who had left Lauren in such deadly danger. I clutched her hand.

Chauncey followed the ambulance, thank God. Surely he was one person I could trust. I stood by helplessly in the emergency room as he helped put a tube in her throat to get oxygen into her as they set up a ventilator to help her breathe and pumped out her stomach. There was nothing I could do, of course, only pray they were all on her side. It was a nightmare revisited. I wanted to be anywhere else in the world except in another hospital beside another fragile blond woman fighting for her life.

Once she was hooked up to the breathing machine, Chauncey told me she was out of immediate danger. "You got to her just in time. That damned smoke was killing her. But there's more going on. She's stuporous from something. Has she been taking drugs, tranquilizers, that sort of thing?''

I knew very little about Lauren Watson, but I'd have sworn she didn't take drugs. I knew she wasn't a drinker, but we could all smell drink on her.

"It's more than the alcohol," Chauncey said. "If she mixed something with it, it could be a deadly combination. We'll have to run tests to find out what the drug is."

"You'll take charge of her, won't you?"

"Sure, if you want me to. At least until her relatives get here. I'll have to call in some help. A lung specialist, that sort of thing."

"Is she going to make it, Chauncey?"

He put an arm around my shoulders. "She'll live. But will she come out of the coma? I don't know, Noah. The next twenty-four hours will tell. We'll do our best for her."

"I'm staying with her."

"There's nothing you can do. Come back to our place. Get some rest."

There wasn't enough of the night left to worry about. "I'm staying."

I knew there was nothing I could do except watch, keep vigil. I was good at that.

"You're not responsible," Chauncey said, but I didn't believe that.

Eventually, they moved her to the ICU. I followed the gurney into the elevator, into the ward where only two days before I had talked to Carl Woods. While they repositioned the monitors and lines around Lauren, I looked through the glass partitions to his bed. It was empty.

"Dr. Woods?" I asked, and guessed the answer.

Chauncey put his arm around my shoulder again. "He had another infarct yesterday, a massive one. There was nothing anyone could do."

"Jesus!"

"That's not quite all, Noah. You may as well know the rest. It wasn't only your office that burned last night. Some fools burned a cross in front of your clients' home. You know, the Ambroses."

I sank into a chair by the door to Lauren's cubicle, put my head in my hands. I had nightmarish visions of white-sheeted figures leaping around the Ambrose house, flames filling the night skies over Springwell, some sort of cataclysm unfolding: an apocalypse I'd set into motion, destroying everything in its path.

Stooping beside me, Chauncey peered into my face. "The Ambroses weren't hurt, Noah. At least not physically. But a cross burning! Like the days of the Klan. Can you imagine how that must make them feel?"

I could imagine.

"I never thought there'd be that kind of madness in Springwell. I thought this was a good place to live. I was wrong, Noah. And you were right."

I was drained, exhausted, too many terrible events piling up. Wearily, I said, "Who wants to be right about something like that?"

We went in to stand by Lauren's bed. The weight of her head hardly dented the pillow. A tube was taped into her soft mouth and her breasts rose and fell in rhythm with the machine. In spite of the ugly machinery, she looked tranquil and peaceful, the fine skin fresh and healthy, the fair hair shining. A princess asleep.

Chauncey tried to reassure me. "She's young and healthy. She should make it."

"Drugs and alcohol?" I said bleakly. "She could be a vegetable."

"Don't look on the black side of things."

It was all right for him. He didn't have her life on his conscience.

"Come home with me," he urged. "You look beat."

"I want a guard on her. Someone tried to kill her, Chauncey. They trashed my house and set another fire and left her inside with it. My office was no accident. And burning a cross at the Ambroses' house was sure as hell no accident."

He looked at the comatose figure on the bed, at me.

"Trashed your house? Why would anyone do that? Why would anyone want to kill someone like her?"

"But somebody did, didn't they? I don't want anyone near her, especially her relatives. And until I can arrange for someone to watch her, I'm staying here."

"We can't keep her relatives away," he said. "She's safe enough here, Noah. This is a hospital, for God's sake."

"I know. Hospitals are dangerous places, Chauncey."

His eyes were that cool slate color again, exasperated and baffled. "You're telling me someone would try to harm her, here in the hospital? Who, for God's sake?"

But I shook my head. I couldn't trust even Chauncey. I couldn't trust anyone in Springwell anymore.

"You're not a relative," he said. "I could order you out, you know."

"Please don't try."

Silent for a moment, he watched the sucking ventilator, the string of IV tubes. Then he said, "Oh, what the hell. You stay, I'll stay. She's my patient, after all. You don't have any idea what should happen in a hospital." He pulled up a chair on the other side of the bed. "You sit there; I'll sit here. And don't touch anything."

I didn't protest. In spite of that sudden unreasonable doubt, I was absurdly thankful to have him with me. He'd stayed with me before, comforted me before when I'd needed it. Every bone in my body ached. My head ached. My heart ached. I collapsed gratefully into the chair and watched the hospital room descend into deeper somnolent night. Nurses came and went. The doctor from the emergency room came to see Lauren; the lung specialist arrived and a neurologist. I looked on as Chauncey consulted with them, waited as they checked her vital signs and replaced the drips and took readings from the monitors. It was all too painfully familiar.

After awhile, because I needed to think of problems other

than Lauren's, which I could do nothing about, I remembered something Dr. Woods had said.

"You sent for those specialists, didn't you, Chauncey? But you're still in charge, aren't you?"

"Yeah. Why?"

"Who was in charge of Jordan Ambrose?"

From across the bed, I could see the exasperation in his eyes. "For heaven's sake, Noah. Can't you leave that alone for tonight?"

"Was it Clarke or was it the surgeon?"

He frowned, sighed. "I don't know. That's a kind of informal agreement. If you call a surgeon in for a consultation, then you stay in charge yourself. If you deliberately hand your patient over, then he's in charge. I could ask the lung guy to be responsible for Lauren and then he'd look after her. But I haven't handed her over."

"If Clarke called in a surgeon, could he have assumed the surgeon would take care of Jordan?"

The dimmed lights outlined the sharp angles of Chauncey's cheekbones, the shape of his head. I heard him sigh once more, forbearingly. "It depends on the diagnosis. Appendicitis, for instance, an obvious surgical problem. If the diagnosis is less straightforward, then several people can be involved. It is possible, sometimes, for patients to slip between attending physicians, each one assuming the other is giving the orders. But don't worry. Lauren's not going to slip between anyone."

"No one ever made a diagnosis in Jordan Ambrose's case, did they?"

"I only read those notes once. I don't remember the details."

"The problem was," Dr. Woods had said, "who was in charge." Who *was* in charge of Jordan Ambrose? It was a simple question to ask in deposition—if we all survived long enough to take depositions.

Though I struggled not to, I slept now and then in the

chair. I dreamed of a courtroom, of Angel and Daphne and an angry Nita Barnes in a jury box, of a tiny judge in a flapping black robe, barely visible behind the high bench, huge black eyes peering at me, accusing me. When I rose to make an argument, no words came out of my mouth; the judge hammered an enormous gavel and the spectators, men with army fatigue caps low over their eyes, laughed at me as the case slipped away from me. I kept waking from the dream, getting up to touch Lauren's hand and check her breathing, but every time I closed my eyes, it came crowding back again.

TWENTY-ONE

IN THE MORNING, Chauncey and I were disheveled and unshaven, but nothing ominous had happened. The nursing shifts changed and Lauren still floated in her half-world of life. But it *was* life. And once the world stirred into the normality of day, it was possible to arrange for a guard to stay by her bed. It wasn't easy. I'd forgotten this wasn't quite a normal day. Today was Thanksgiving.

A few calls from Chauncey and the charge nurse eventually yielded an off-duty policeman who needed some extra cash. He came slouching into the ICU, and it was almost ironic that I found the creak of his leather holster so reassuring. I handed him a list of the nurses and doctors in attendance and told him, "No one else is to come near her. No one. Before anyone touches her, check that they're on this list. I don't care who they say they are, doctors, nurses, or relatives. Understood?"

"Understood."

Large and phlegmatic, he filled the small room with his bulk, suitably daunting.

Chauncey wanted me to go home with him, but there were things I had to do. I was tired, but I couldn't sleep or sit down to eat Thanksgiving dinner while someone I'd put in peril was lying comatose in the hospital.

First, I went to the office. By the thin light of morning, the sight of it was even more depressing than by the neon pink glow of night; the tarpaulin, low and sagging from further hours of rain, hung a gloomy pall over the blackened skeleton. The front part of the building, Bella's territory and the storeroom, was just twisted metal and unrecognizable shapes. The fire had burned through the adjoining walls to my room, eating the floors so the joists were exposed; what hadn't been destroyed by fire, water had finished off. The glass fronts of the bookcases in my room were shattered; law texts lay in heaped disarray, leather bindings soggy and distorted, thin fragile pages swollen into blocks of gilt-edged pulp. Father's silver tints of Springwell at the turn of the century, his framed diplomas from Columbia and the Bar, lay smashed below the ruined walls. The oak file cabinets he preferred to metal ones hadn't withstood the heat; charred contents spilled about in showers of blackened paper. The huge old safe, where the wills and other irreplaceable documents were kept, seemed intact, but the decorative paint on its front was blistered and peeling, its solid bulk still too warm for me to try the combination. At the back of the room, the desk and leather chair appeared to have escaped the worst of the damage, but when I pulled at the desk drawers, they were swollen shut and the chair oozed dirty brown water from its innards.

Already everything smelled of mildew and decay, as if it had begun to crumble back into the earth.

I picked through the wreckage in a desultory fashion and knew there was little that could be rescued from it. The task of resurrecting anything seemed insurmountable. I left the mess behind and went to check on the Ambroses. I'd have called first if there was a phone in the office, but there wasn't, of course. The telephones were lumps of distorted plastic among the rest of the debris.

The streets were deserted as I drove through town, everyone else at home enjoying Thanksgiving. At the Ambroses', all that remained of the indecency of cross burning was an ugly brown patch on the grass, but they must have been watching, because as I went up the brick path, the door opened and Angel stood in the doorway, waiting for me.

If Angel Ambrose had been frightened by the symbol of white hatred blazing on her front lawn, it didn't show. The

small head on the slender neck was proud and unbowed,
her cheekbones dusted with a silvery glinting powder, the
almond eyes outlined in blue shadow. She wore a short
bright red dress like a shout of defiance. Dressed to kill, as
though this was some special occasion. I had to remind
myself again that today was a special day.

Deliberately casual, she leaned against the doorjamb, her
arms folded, swinging one high-heeled foot. ''Just dropping
by?''

''I heard what happened. I came to say I'm sorry.''

''Yeah?'' She looked me up and down. ''Well, maybe I
believe you. I heard what they done to your office. Where
were you?''

''In California. Did I come at a bad time? Are you going
out?''

''You think we'd be going out after what happened? And
yeah, it's a bad time.''

I would have preferred to think the Ambroses had somewhere to go on Thanksgiving. The idea of them spending
the day alone in their house waiting for another outrage on
their property, perhaps on their persons, was not my idea
of a proper Thanksgiving.

''How's Joseph?''

''You want to come in and see for yourself? You've
come for something, haven't you?'' She didn't move from
the door, didn't attempt to make me welcome, merely tilted
her head back and stared down her nose, challenging me
in some way. ''You don't look so hot yourself,'' she said.

''I didn't get enough sleep.''

To enter the house, I had to pass close by her, and I
could smell her perfume, heady and exotic. I could also
feel the tension emanating from her, almost tangible, like
tiny bolts of electricity sparking out of her.

On the sofa where I'd sat the other day, Joseph was
slumped among the cushions, as though tired beyond bear-
ing. He didn't even raise his head to look at me. The pale

upholstery made his skin appear darker than ever, and though it was only a few days since we'd met in Joe's Tavern, he seemed heavier and older, distinct streaks of gray in the dense springy hair, deeper lines about his mouth. He looked more like Angel's father than her husband. The air in the room was almost opaque with conflict, visible and palpable.

"I came to see how you were both doing. If there was anything I could do to help."

His gaze didn't lift from his knees. "Ain't nothing you can do, Mr. Richards."

"Try not to be upset by that idiotic act. Whoever they were, they won't get away with it, you know. That sort of thing isn't tolerated anymore."

"That's not his problem. He lost his job," Angel said fiercely.

I looked from her to Joseph. "Lost your job?"

He sighed wearily. "Yessir. A damn fine job, it was, too."

"He should've stood up for himself. They'd no reason to fire him."

Raising his eyes at last, he blinked at me. "I knew once they got wind of this business, I'd be through. I knew it was a bad idea, suing them doctors."

I went to sit beside him and wanted to put an arm around the hunching shoulders. "Maybe it's not that. They're laying off all through the lumber trade these days."

He shrugged. "Wanna get rid of someone, you gets rid of troublemakers first."

"He's so damned submissive," Angel snapped. "All the more reason, if he believes what he says, to stand up and fight. Laying someone off the day before Thanksgiving! What sort of Thanksgiving is that?"

"Anyone said anything to you about the case, Joseph?"

Angel was scornful. "Of course they haven't said anything to him. They're not such fools as that."

"It could be tough to prove," I said, and she laughed derisively. "Everything's tough to prove, isn't it? Especially for lawyers."

"Hey, hey, Angel. There's no call for being rude to Mr. Richards. He done his best for us."

I'd done nothing for them, I thought, and Angel, with that uncanny knack of knowing my thoughts, instantly countered, "Yeah? Like what?"

"Hush, child," he muttered without conviction.

"Don't you tell me to hush up, old man."

I interrupted, not wanting to hear the irritable snapping. "Listen, both of you. I think it's time we had a talk about what's going on. We're getting into deep water around here. You had a cross burned on your lawn and I had my office burned down."

Angel said, "That scared you off?"

But at least Joseph showed some sympathy. "I was real sorry to hear about it, Mr. Richards. I sure hope it wasn't nothing to do with this suing business."

"Thank you, Joseph. But whether it was anything to do with it or not, it doesn't affect your case against the doctors. We can start all over again if we want to. What does affect us in that matter is what has happened to Dr. Woods."

Immediately, Angel leapt to the attack. "That son of a bitch!"

I put up a hand to stop her. "He had a heart attack, Angel. I'm sorry to tell you, but he's dead."

There was a moment's silence and then she laughed again, another shrill high-pitched sound with no humor in it. "Good!" she said. "That's good! I'm not sorry." Then abruptly her face changed and her voice rose. "No! No! I don't want him dead. I want him in court. I want everyone to know what he did." She cried, "If he's dead, they'll make him out to be some sort of hero. I know what they put in obituaries. He's no hero."

The false cool of a few minutes ago vanished in a flash.

Now she was taut and strained and jerky, biting the side of her cheek, mouth twisted and ugly, long painted nails digging into clenched hands, long legs quivering under the scant cover of the little short dress. A woman on the edge. The fancy clothes and the bright makeup were nothing but a travesty, a vain attempt to disguise her anguish. She should instead have been wearing sackcloth and ashes. With a piercing wail, she threw herself into a chair and pounded the arms like a child having a temper tantrum, her feet thumping the floor. The mascara smeared and blurred around her eyes, her voice became a shriek. "I want him alive! I want everyone to know about him! About this goddamned filthy town."

Joseph and I watched in silence, waiting for the storm to abate. At long last, she fell quiet, though not calm. Her eyes rolled and darted like a cornered animal seeking escape.

I said, "I think we should settle. You could have some money and get away from here."

She sucked in a choking breath. "I told you a thousand times—"

"I know what you've told me, Angel. But you're not going to get that satisfaction now Dr. Woods is dead. If I go to his lawyer, I know we can get a settlement. It could be over and done with and you could start again."

I could start again. I could get away. Perhaps I could take Lauren Watson away with me.

"No! No! No!"

"You don't want to know how much it could be?"

Beside me, Joseph asked quietly, "How much?"

She yelled across the room, "We're not going to take anything from them."

"At least two hundred thousand from Dr. Woods's estate. And we can still go after the other doctors, the hospital."

His mouth gaped open. "Two hundred thousand?"

"It's an insult," she screamed.

"But, baby, two hundred—"

"Shut up! Shut up your mouth, you old fool! Your son is dead and all you think about is money. It's disgusting."

Trying to keep an even and level tone, I said, "There would always have come a time when we'd have had to talk about money. Money was all you were ever going to get out of this. Even if Dr. Woods had lived, you weren't going to put him in jail."

"It's where he belonged!"

"In your opinion, maybe. But it's not going to happen, so we should discuss a settlement."

"We could buy a place," Joseph murmured. "Down south somewhere."

Angel beat at the cushions with clenched fists, her face contorted. "I don't wanna go down south."

"You could move away from Springwell," I suggested. "Get another house. It'd mean you wouldn't have to stay here." But they weren't listening to me.

"We could have us a little farm, Angel, back in Belvedere County. Where your folks are."

Sitting bolt upright, she strained her smeared face toward him, the veins in her neck throbbing and knotted. "It's blood money, that's what it is. You think I'd go back there and set myself up in a fine place so my folks could say, 'Look what she got for letting those white doctors kill her baby?' Think I'd do that?"

"I always did want me a little farm, a place of my own. We could have us a few hogs and grow a little corn...."

"You old fool! You think I'm going to live in the back of beyond on a hog farm?"

The pale room vibrated with her fury. She turned on me, snarling. "Now are you satisfied, Mr. Big Shot Attorney? Coming here with your Judas money? You're as bad as he is. All you think about is money. Money, money, money. That's all you fucking lawyers think there is in life, isn't it? You know what I want? I want those doctors' names in the papers, so's everybody knows just what they did. Are you in it with them? Is that it? Oh, you're so nice and mealymouthed, aren't you? Butter won't melt in your mouth, will it? Trying to pretend to help. Bet you're all in it together, aren't you? Bunch of white guys covering up for one another, seeing how they can do folks like us down. That's how it is, isn't it? Don't listen to him, Joseph. Can't you see what he is? As bad as the rest of them.''

I reeled at her attack. I looked to Joseph, but he looked away from me, eyes avoiding mine, as though in his heart he agreed with her, and I was hurt by his lack of response, offended, resentful. Suddenly, all the grief of the past two days swept over me, all the exhaustion of the night, all the worry and concern for Lauren, the shattering way my world was disintegrating. My nerves shredded like Angel's.

''Damn it! I'm doing my best for you, and that's how you thank me? Someone burned down my office and they trashed my house, and all I get from you is invective and accusations. You're accusing the wrong person. You're even accusing the wrong doctor. Woods did his best for your child, and now he's dead. And all you can do is go on screaming about him.''

''Your house?'' Joseph said slowly. ''Someone trashed your house?''

''Yes.'' I was as weary as he was. ''Trashed it and set a fire and put in danger someone who has nothing to do with any of this.''

A thick silence deadened the vibrating room. Angel stared across at me and I got to my feet. ''Listen,'' I said. ''I'm sorry about everything. Everything. I shouldn't have come here today, because I'm too damned tired to discuss these matters in a proper manner. I'll leave now and let you think things over. Let me know what you decide.''

Uncoiling out of the chair like a cat, Angel stalked across

the pale carpet toward me, thrust her face into mine. "What do you mean, 'the wrong doctor'?"

I tried to fend her off. "Don't go on about Dr. Woods, that's all I'm saying. The man is dead. He tried to help your boy. It was someone else who didn't help when he should have. It was someone else who allowed Jordan to sicken and die."

"Who?"

I was too exhausted to talk to her rationally anymore. She was wearing me out. I hesitated for a moment, but there was no reason for me to cover up for him. "The other surgeon. The one who never came—Grogan." I'd said it, out loud. "But I don't have real proof. I can only say there are other avenues to explore."

"I don't want no more explorations," she said. "I want the truth."

"Look, I'm sorry, but I've got to get back to the hospital now, Angel. The truth will have to wait for another day."

Grabbing my arm, her nails dug in painfully. She barred my way out of the house and repeated stubbornly, "I want the truth."

"You may never get it, Angel. None of us may ever get it."

The madness flared in her eyes again and she shook her fists at me. "You got to tell me, you hear? Joseph! You want to know the truth. Make him tell it."

Lifting his heavy head, Joseph looked at her for a long moment, flexed his big hands, then rubbed them along his thighs. "What I want is a bit of peace and quiet. That's the truth. Just some nice peace and quiet. I wanna get away from this place. Been nothing but sorrow and trouble ever since we came here. Sorrow and trouble."

Whirling toward him, she seemed to forget about me, brushing at her skirt in a dismissive gesture. "Okay! Go then. Or I'll go first. That make you happy?"

He shook his head slowly. "Nothing'll make me happy anymore, baby."

"Please," I said. "It's all bad enough. Please don't wreck your lives over it."

Turning on me again, there was contempt in the smeared eyes. "You think our lives aren't wrecked already? Don't you understand? My baby's gone. They're burning fucking crosses outside our house; he's lost his fucking job. How can it get any fucking worse?"

"Hush, baby," Joseph murmured sorrowfully. "Hush now."

"I ain't going to stay here and talk about this garbage anymore." Launching herself at the door, she tore it open. "You talk to him about money, Joseph Ambrose, and that's the end of you and me, understand? And you!" She jabbed her clenched fist toward me, as if it held a dagger pointing straight at my heart. "I'll find out what you're talking about. And then you'll be sorry. You'll all be sorry, the whole fucking lot of you."

She hurled herself out of the house, fuming and spitting and out of control. There was a moment's silence, followed by the sound of a car door slamming, an engine revving wildly, wheels spinning, and when I went to the window, she was driving away from the house like a bat out of hell.

I stood at the window, watching the car careen down the road. I hoped to God she met nothing en route to wherever she was heading.

"Where's she going?" I asked. "Does she mean it? About leaving?"

Crunched in the sofa, Joseph gazed at his hands. "She's one angry lady," he said in masterly understatement. "I think she means it all right. She and me's had a lot of harsh words lately. Does something to a woman, I guess, losing her kid that way. Been coming on us ever since, I'd say. But I don't know as how we'd have stuck together even if little Jordy hadn't gone like that. Just showed up the dif-

ferences, that's all. Made her mad, made me old. Now all
I want is to go away and forget about it.''

That was all? Just go away and forget about it? Easier
said than done. An awful lot of wreckage was left behind
when one small boy died before his time. A man's heart
had failed; a young woman was in dire danger; a marriage
had gone sour; my home was in shambles, my office
burned. There was the taint of hatred over a whole community. On the table by his father's elbow, Jordan Ambrose's huge black eyes glowed at me accusingly, as in my
dream. The shadow of little Jordan Ambrose stretched long
and dark over a lot of lives. He wouldn't be easily forgotten.

And all I'd had to offer for all these wrongs was money.
I knew how Angel felt. It was blood money. But it was the
best I could do, the only thing I could do.

''You want to accept the settlement, Joseph?''

His eyes were old and bloodshot. ''I don't want no settlement, Mr. Richards. I just want my boy back. But I won't
get that, will I? So I'll take the money 'coz I don't know
what the hell else to do.''

Amen. What the hell else was there to do?

TWENTY-TWO

AT THE HOSPITAL, Lauren still slept like Sleeping Beauty, as though waiting, I imagined foolishly, for a kiss to awaken her. If only real life was as simple as fairy tales. But, after all, there was encouraging real-life news; the nurses told me her eyes had opened once or twice when they spoke to her. I held her limp hand and said hopefully, "Lauren, can you hear me?" and her eyelids fluttered as though she did indeed hear something somewhere in the secret world she now occupied.

The off-duty policeman paced the room restlessly.

"Her sister came," he said. "I did like you told me. Kept her away from the bed. She was pretty upset. Cried and carried on."

"She was the only visitor?"

"Yep, the only one. She went home to have Thanksgiving dinner with her kids. Said she'd come back later."

Thanksgiving. I kept forgetting.

"You have a dinner to go to?" I asked him.

He grinned, cheerfully enough. "If I did, I wouldn't get to it, would I?"

"I'll stay," I said. "You go home, be with your kids or whoever." I didn't want to think about my home. I had nothing better to do with my Thanksgiving than stay here.

Thanksgiving makes little difference in places like intensive care units. Two new patients were admitted into the other cubicles and the staff ran frantically between them. Telephones rang and machines bleeped and a clutch of relatives arrived to peer anxiously through the glass partitions. Nurses appeared and reappeared at Lauren's bed, checking drips and vital signs, shining lights into her eyes, testing reflexes, writing on charts. They frowned at me but brought me coffee and said how terrible it was such a thing should happen to one of their own. How dangerous it was to mix drugs and alcohol. "We can't believe it of Lauren," one of them said, shaking her head. "She might take a glass of wine but not hard liquor, not Lauren. As for mixing it with tranquilizers? She's a nurse; she'd know better. But I suppose nobody thinks this sort of thing will ever happen to them, do they?"

And each time the nurses came to the bedside, they called urgently, "Lauren? Lauren? Say something, Lauren."

The eyelids flickered and sometimes opened wide for a brief unseeing second. But she didn't answer.

I wanted them to stay and talk to me about her, but they had no time to stand and chat.

Chauncey came. "Just checking," he said. But his concern seemed more for my welfare than for Lauren's. He gave her only a cursory look, briefly feeling her pulse. "You can't stay here day and night," he said.

"Why not?"

"This wasn't your fault, Noah. You already saved her life. A few more minutes and she'd have died of asphyxiation, or burns."

"Isn't there a belief somewhere that if you save a life, you're responsible for it forever afterward?"

He put a hand on my shoulder. "You have an overdeveloped sense of responsibility. When you're tired of sitting here, there's a bed at our house."

I wanted to ask him about Grogan but didn't. There'd be time enough to ask about Grogan when Lauren woke up. Nothing else seemed important. I half-expected Grogan to come blustering into the room at any moment, turn off the respirator, pull the tube from her throat, put something in the IV. Do something foolish and dramatic that would finally and decisively expose him as the villain of the piece.

He didn't, of course. Grogan let other people do the dirty work. He dealt in sins of omission, not commission.

I thought of many things in the hours I sat by Lauren's bed.

I thought of the first time I'd seen her, so fresh and young and scared. She had reason to be scared. I stared at the curve of her cheekbones and the violet circles below her eyes, at the steady pumping of the ventilator, and I promised aloud that if she came out of this, at the very least we'd go to the opera together. I talked aloud to her, told her inconsequential things like the story of *Rosenkavalier,* of the beautiful Marschallin who dreaded the loss of youth; how she, Lauren, made me think of Sophie, with all her future before her.

I thought of Janet, how I'd sat by her hospital bed like this, holding her hand, willing her to live, and I discovered that particular grief was shrinking down into a small sore spot on my heart; the grief would always be there, but it no longer overwhelmed me. I could begin to plan a future, if only to go to the opera with another young woman. Perhaps it was possible to let go of Janet at last, let her slip away peacefully, because all my energies were focused on this new struggle. I'd lost that other struggle. I was determined not to lose this one.

I thought of my father, making deals with his friend the doctor. Betraying that absolute trust I'd always had in him. I knew why there was no written conclusion among the papers of the Westing case. He wasn't perfect after all. Thank God. My father's perfection had sometimes been too much to bear.

I thought of the Ambroses and their burdens. Too many. The color of their skin a heavier burden than it was possible for me to understand. Because of the color of their skin, they suffered the loss of their child and now they suffered the loss of love. I could forgive Angel her impotent rage. If the Ambroses had been white, none of this would ever have happened. I wouldn't have shocked Carl Woods into a heart attack. Lauren wouldn't be lying here. My office and my home would not lie in ruins.

I thought of Grogan, how it all stemmed from his bigotry. How cursed this country was by bigotry. How I'd once believed that had changed and how mistaken I was. I plotted to get him—with Carl Woods's taped statement, with Nita Barnes's testimony, with Lauren's story, when she woke up—if she woke up.

I remembered that the tape from Woods was in the safe in the ruins of my office, recalled the blistered paint of the safe and doubted the fragile strip of plastic would have survived. I wondered if I'd ever find Nita Barnes again or if she'd melt back into the hidden fabric of Hispanic America.

As the afternoon drew down into darkness, I knew it was wishful thinking that I'd get Grogan, because none of it would stand up in a court of law. It was unlikely it would ever get to court. The best hope to get Grogan had died with Carl Woods. We could sue the hospital, but it was Woods who'd have damned Grogan. I wasn't sure I'd ever be able to bring a case against him. It wasn't a crime to refuse to treat a patient—not if someone else could treat him, and there had been someone else. Woods was guilty of malpractice because he'd botched the operation, and his insurance would have to pay, but at least he'd tried to help. Grogan's sin was a sin in my eyes, a sin against medical ethics, against humanity, but it was all based on hearsay and rumor and personal conviction. Enough to convince me, maybe, but to get a court to listen?

The old aphorism was true: Justice and law weren't necessarily synonymous.

When Lauren woke up, I might be able to get Gurning. I knew, in my bones, that he was the one who had put Lauren in the way of danger at my house. I didn't understand how she got there but once there, it must have been easy for him. Was it me he'd wanted to silence, or her? Maybe both of us. I thought I'd never touch whisky again, because it was sickening to picture how it must have happened—Lauren forced to swallow the pills, the scotch forced down her throat. You can force anyone to do anything if you have a gun in your hand.

He might try again—Gurning or one of his band of brothers. Maybe, after all, Nita Barnes hadn't been so far off the mark. We'd learned there are such nightmares lurking in the heartland of America.

Several times during the night, the doctor from the emergency room came in to see Lauren. I wondered when he went off duty. He told me the blood tests were improving, the alcohol rapidly dissipating with the fluids washing through her system. "Diazepam," he said. "That's the problem."

"Diazepam?"

"Valium."

My heart sank. "Like Karen Quinlan?"

He seemed surprised. "You remember the Quinlan case?"

Who could forget? Karen Quinlan had passed into medicolegal lore, the girl who never woke from a coma induced by Valium and alcohol. Her parents fought the courts to have her life support discontinued, and when they eventually won, it still took her years to die.

"We're hopeful," he said. "There wasn't that much alcohol in Lauren. We have to wait and see how much brain swelling there is. We're giving her steroids and we're trying to flush the drugs out of her system. We've got to be careful not to give too many fluids because of cerebral edema. It's a balancing act. But she could come out of it anytime."

"And if she doesn't?"

"We just have to wait and see," he repeated, and went away.

It wasn't much comfort.

Soon afterward, a woman appeared in the doorway. I knew immediately who she was. She was an older version of Lauren, a tired droop to her shoulders, a sallowness to the fine skin, no luster to the fair hair. But she had the same triangular shape to her face, the same wide forehead, and the same wariness in the eyes.

The eyes were hostile. "Who are you?" She asked.

I stood up. "Noah Richards. It was my house she was in."

"Does that give you the right to be at her bedside when they wouldn't let me near her?"

"It's for her protection."

"That policeman wouldn't even let me sit by her. I'm her sister."

"Someone tried to kill her. You understand?"

"Well, it wasn't me," she snapped. Then the defiance crumpled, her eyes filling with tears. "I know you pulled her out of the house. Thank God you got there in time." She inched nearer to the bed. "How is she?"

"The nurses think she's beginning to respond. She's opened her eyes once or twice."

The woman was close to the bed now. I put out a hand to stop her, but she wasn't the one I was afraid of. I was afraid of the person she was married to. So I let her bend down and smooth the hair from Lauren's forehead, kiss her forehead, and clutch her inert hand. "Laurie, it's Meg. I'm here. Tell me you're going to be all right. Tell me, please."

The papery eyelids fluttered; the smooth forehead creased. Her sister looked up triumphantly.

"She hears me! She hears. Please, Laurie, speak to me." Lowering her head to the covers, she began to weep, hard, wrenching sobs that somehow had more to do with herself than with the person in the bed. "I'm so sorry, Laurie. So sorry."

When she'd cried herself into silence and her head lay

against Lauren's breast as though in sleep, I reached across and touched her hand.

"You want to tell me about it? Why she's been so frightened? How she came to take Valium? What she was doing in my house?"

Raising her head, she stared blankly at me. "Valium?"

"Yes. Do you keep it at home?"

"Valium? I used to take it, a long time ago. There might still be some somewhere. But I haven't... Lauren never would take it."

"Where was she last night? Did you see her?"

"She came to the house after I'd fed the kids. I... I was going out and Lauren said she'd baby-sit; then I didn't go after all, and she left."

"You're married to a Gurning, aren't you?"

She said, "What's that got to do with anything?"

"Come on! Your sister is lying here in a coma and you're not going to tell me what's she been so frightened of?"

Picking up Lauren's hand, she pressed it to her face, closed her eyes.

"What relation is Brett Gurning to you?" I asked.

Her eyes flew open. "Brett?" She stumbled over the name.

"Yes. Brett Gurning."

After a moment, she said, "He's my husband's brother. Look, my husband and I...we don't get on. We haven't for a long time. I want a divorce, but he's been very...difficult about it. Lauren's been afraid for me, for the kids. My husband...he can be a violent man. They can all be violent."

"All? You mean the Gurning family?"

She didn't answer, just looked frightened again.

"Has she ever said anything to you about a little boy who died at the hospital?"

"What little boy?" she said faintly.

"A little black boy. A child called Jordan Ambrose. Did Lauren ever speak of him? To you? To your husband?"

"Oh, that child." Pinching her lips, she stared down at Lauren, quiet and far away from us. "There were...conversations about him. Just after it happened." Silent again for a moment, she took a deep breath. "My husband was there when Lauren told me about it, about how bad she felt and how the doctors hadn't come when the nurses wanted them. He got angry and said she was never to tell anyone else. Said that it would be the worse for all of us if she did."

The respirator sighed in the room. "What do you think he meant by that?"

"Meant?" The dulled eyes flashed into life. "Who knows what someone with those kinds of ideas means when he wants to throw his weight around? He's a bully. He wants to dominate me and the kids, wants to make us think the way he thinks, wants to make us believe the same crap he believes. He can't understand I don't feel that way. He doesn't love his kids, and yet he wants to take them and make them in his own image. He has guns, and I'm afraid of guns. You don't have to get on with people if you have a gun in your hand, do you? You can just blow someone away if they don't agree with you."

She was speaking to the converted when she spoke to me about guns. "Who's he going to blow away?" I paused. "You don't mean yourself?"

There was a fatalism in her voice, a weary resignation. "As a matter of fact, yes. One day I'll be found with several large bullet holes in me."

The fatalism appalled me. "For God's sake! Why don't you just get the hell away from him?"

"We had a plan, Laurie and me." For a second, her expression was almost hopeful. "To go somewhere safe. Just creep away one night. But you need money for plans like that. We were saving up. We had to be sure we'd get far enough away, somewhere he wouldn't follow. But they watched all the time, him or his brothers. There's four of them, you know. We're surrounded by them."

She appeared sensible enough, articulate and lucid, not stupid. How could she have married someone who made her fear for her life? But every day one heard of women afraid for their own lives and for the lives of their children, women threatened by the very men who should have taken care of them, women with nowhere to run. Society is unable to protect them, keep them safe.

Now that she'd started to talk, it seemed like a catharsis for her. "That little black kid made everything worse. They heard a rumor the parents were going to sue, and it made them more suspicious and more paranoid, if that's possible. Made them close ranks. They think the world's out to get them, you know, take away what's rightfully theirs. They're always raving on about liberals and welfare deadbeats, and they go off and play war games, preparing for Armageddon."

"They? The brothers? Or are there more?"

Wearily, she said, "Oh, I don't know. I'm not privy to that sort of knowledge. I'm treated with as much suspicion as anyone else. Except he wants the kids. It's very hard to deny him the right to see them."

"Have you ever heard them speak of a Dr. Grogan?"

"Grogan? I don't remember. They don't tell me anything anymore. Perhaps Lauren mentioned him. I've heard the name somewhere."

"Where are your children tonight?"

"At the neighbors. They're safe enough there." She smiled a little. "My neighbor's a police officer."

We were silent for a while. The whole ugly story had ended up with this, the mechanical breathing of the respirator, the slow rise and fall of Lauren's breast, the shining hair on the pillow, the plastic tube distorting her mouth, the tape pulling at her delicate skin. I felt murderous and impotent. All I could do was sit there and pray a healthy constitution would bring her through.

"Tell me about the other night," I said. "The sequence of events—what was said and when. Where was she going after she left your house? What time was it? Why didn't you go out? Did something stop you? Someone?"

Tears clouded her eyes again. They were ordinary eyes, not the intriguing flecked hazel of her sister's. "It's all my fault," she moaned. "I should have stopped her, not let her leave. If only I'd known."

"Tell me."

"It was no big deal. I met someone; he asked me to go out with him. I thought it'd be fun to do something different, talk to someone different. Lauren said she'd baby-sit so I could go for a couple of hours. Somehow, my husband found out about it. He finds out about everything, I don't know how. He came to the house and made this awful scene, and in the end I said I wouldn't go. Laurie said if I kept knuckling under, I'd never get anywhere. She said it was time I talked to a lawyer and that she knew someone who'd help. Said she'd go and tell him everything, right then."

"She said that in front of your husband?"

"Oh, no. She wouldn't be that stupid. He'd gone by that time."

"What time was that?"

She shrugged the thin shoulders. She had gestures very like her sister's. "About nine-thirty, I suppose. I said she couldn't possibly go see a lawyer at that time of night, and she told me this lawyer wouldn't mind." A rueful half smile flickered across her face. "It was you, wasn't it? Laurie trusted you. But I wish I hadn't let her go. I bet he followed her."

I'd made the phone call from the plane. What time was that? Seven-thirty or so. I'd left the message on the machine so Lauren would know I was coming back to Springwell.

It was at once a comfort to think she'd gone looking for me and a terrible realization that I might have sent her into a trap.

"You think your husband followed her? Why?"

"Because he's paranoid, and suspicious."

Not Brett Gurning after all? I was disappointed in an odd way. I'd made up my mind he was the villain, because he was a villain I knew. I said so, out loud. "Not Brett? You don't think he was the one who might have followed her?"

"It could have been Brett. It could be any of those damned Gurnings." She spat out the name. "Gurning. I wish to heaven I'd never heard the name."

Suddenly, startling us, a convulsive flailing movement erupted from the bed, a coughing and choking sound. Lauren's eyes flew open and her hands were at her mouth, tugging frantically at the tube strapped there. But her eyes remained distant and unfocused, as though she was unaware of where she was or what was happening. She thrashed wildly among the sheets. I leapt to my feet to fetch the nurse, but she was already on her way, signaled by the monitors. In a flash, she dragged the tape off and pulled out the tube, pressed the bell pinned to the bedclothes, and then the doctor came, waving us away from the bed.

I found myself holding tightly on to her sister's hand, just as I'd held Lauren's. We saw her take deep sucking breaths of her own, mutter unintelligible words. The miracle was happening. She was waking up.

TWENTY-THREE

SHE CAME OUT of it slowly, painfully, precariously. I stayed by her bed the rest of the night, and though the doctors told me not to expect any sudden miracles of recollection and speech, I did expect her to wake in an instant and tell me everything, and to forgive me for putting her in the path of danger. It didn't happen that way, of course. She returned to life in small increments: first the ability to breathe on her own, then to sip tiny drops of water and almost focus her wandering eyes on the person attending her. But not yet to speak. "And to remember?" the doctors said. "That may never happen."

Eventually, I left her to the care of the nurses and another underpaid police officer on sentinel duty and went to Chauncey and Daphne's to sleep at last. Later in the day, I talked to the police about the house and then Daphne went with me to inspect the damage.

I'd managed to put the house out of my mind. God knows, there'd been more worthwhile things to worry about than a few sticks of furniture. The police told me not to touch anything, and I warned Daphne, and myself, that things might not look so good in the cold light of day, but when we went in through the side door, unlocked as usual, neither of us was prepared for the devastation.

It was incredibly obscene, a desecration. As if the house were a living being who'd been raped and mutilated and left for dead. I understood exactly why people feel so violated when their home is burglarized. The invasion of my private and personal world was disturbing enough; the destruction Daphne and I found was deeply unsettling, as though nothing could ever be tranquil in that house again, as though there could never be laughter again in a place so vandalized. It wasn't only the destroyed furniture and the smashed dishes, or even the smell of killer smoke still lingering in the air. It was a presence, a lurking evil left by those who'd marauded through the rooms, put pitiless hands in secret places, ruthlessly and systematically torn apart unimportant objects precious to others. My mother and father spent their married lives in that house, gathered together the paintings that now were wrenched from their frames, chose those Oriental carpets, now slashed and stinking of urine. They had been given those dishes and glasses that lay in trampled shards on the floors. The very floor had been pulled apart, clothes ripped to pieces, even the few things left after my mother died—a fur coat my father couldn't bear to give away, a silk dress I could still remember her wearing.

Whoever had done this must have been possessed of a fearsome rage, and they must have taken a long time to do it.

Daphne was horrified. "Oh, Noah! It's too awful. I can't look at it," and she put her hands over her eyes like a child.

I was filled with a sudden and dreadful regret. I remembered all the secure years of my childhood in that house; my mother, who once sang in her kitchen; my father, who'd painted and mended and taken pride in his possessions. I'd not loved the house as they had done, had not kept it safe to pass on to another generation.

"How could anybody do such horrible things?" Daphne was shocked and disbelieving.

I shuddered to think of the hate that had caused this.

Without words, for there was nothing to say, we turned our backs on the filthy mess and went outside for relief, down to the dock where the dinghy was still tied up, unharmed. One unsullied relic. Pulling aimlessly on the mooring line, I drew it toward me until the bow bumped softly against the pilings. It didn't seem possible that only a few days had passed since I'd gone fishing in it.

"What are you going to do now, Noah?"

"God knows. Go back to California maybe."

She looked at me sharply. "That wasn't what I meant. I meant what are you going to do about all this? You're not just going to walk away from it, are you?"

"I don't think I could live in that house again, Daphne. The sight and feel of it revolts me. I've no place to hang my hat as a lawyer. Now would be as good a time as any to make a move, wouldn't it?"

"Noah! You can't mean it. I know you. What about that young woman at the hospital?"

"Lauren? Perhaps she'll come with me."

Daphne touched my arm with some of her old hopefulness. "Something good might have come out of all this if you've found someone at last. You wouldn't have spent all that time with her at the hospital if you didn't feel something for her."

"I hardly know her," I said. But that wasn't really true. I felt I knew Lauren Watson very well after sitting by her bedside all those hours. "I've learned a hell of a lot about this town in the last few weeks, Daphne. More than I wanted to know. I need to get away from here. Lauren Watson needs to get away. Too many bad things have happened to her in Springwell."

Daphne's mouth set in a stubborn line. "Well, Chauncey and I aren't going anywhere. We're not running away."

"Is that what you think? That I'd be running away?"

"What else should I think? What about your case?"

"Oh, they'll get a settlement whether I stay or not."

"Is that what Angel Ambrose wants?"

"Angel wants revenge. She's not going to get that."

We walked back across the grass to the road where my car was parked, past the indignities of the house. From the outside, it looked quite normal. Scuffing her feet on the path, Daphne said, "Surely they'll find out who did this? There'll be fingerprints, won't there? And your office? They must be able to prove that was done deliberately?"

"It's not so difficult to prove arson these days. Pinning it on someone is the tough part. Just as pinning little Jordan Ambrose's death on anyone is the tough part."

"I read those notes, Noah. Someone has to be responsible."

"Someone is responsible. I found Nita Barnes in Los Angeles and she told me. She told me Grogan deliberately didn't go to see Jordan Ambrose. Because he was black. Think of it, Daphne. What you thought couldn't be true— a physician refusing to see a sick child just because he was the wrong color."

Stopping in her tracks, Daphne stared into my face, and I could see more shocked disbelief in her eyes. "Nita said that? Do you believe her?"

"Yes, I do. Unfortunately, I'm not sure I can prove it. I wish to God I could stick it to the son of a bitch. But I'm a lawyer, Daphne, and lawyers have to do things in a legal way. Sometimes that's a great handicap."

"If it's true, it can be proven, can't it? Isn't that what truth is? And if it can't be proven, is it really the truth?"

"You sound like a judge, Daphne. Just the kind I'd be up against. Maybe you should take up law."

"And get my home torn apart? God forbid!"

"It's not a normal hazard of the profession," I said.

I couldn't look back at the house as we drove away.

I spent what was left of the day with the fire department. "There were definite traces of accelerent in your office," the arson expert told me. "I take it the building was insured, Mr. Richards?"

"Of course. Well insured."

"Yes?" He regarded me carefully. "I understand you were in California when the fire was set? We think some kind of timing device was used."

I didn't care for the way he was looking at me.

"What the hell?" I said. "You're not implying I set my own place on fire?"

He didn't seem to find the suggestion outrageous. "I'm not implying anything, Mr. Richards. You're a lawyer, after all."

I wasn't sure what that meant, but I didn't like the sound of it. I made an overdue call to my insurance agent.

Then I visited the hospital again, and this time Lauren recognized me. When I took her hand, she still didn't speak, but the flecked eyes smiled at me and her hand in mine returned the pressure. The rotten taste of the day fled away.

The next morning, I borrowed a tidy coat from Chauncey and went to Carl Woods's funeral.

The day was suitably overcast, clouds hanging low in a somber sky, the service in the same small Episcopal church where my father and mother were committed to the life beyond. I hadn't been inside since the day of my father's funeral. Now it seemed as though there was much to pray for.

Outside the church, a crowd clotted in dark groups around the entrance; inside, the small space was already overflowing. In the old tradition, the casket lay in front of the altar, heaped with flowers, candles burning at the head and the foot.

I squeezed into the last pew at the rear of the church. The first pews, where the relatives would be sitting, were beyond my sight, but several rows in front of me I could see the back of Chauncey's head, Daphne beside him, the smooth grayness of Lance Todd, as well as other familiar and not so familiar profiles. Most of Springwell seemed to be there, and I found myself searching for a bony face and a very light head of hair. Though my mental image of the Gurning family didn't include their presence in a church, it was still a relief that there was no sign of any of them. The congregation rustled and murmured and the organ played Handel, "I Know that My Redeemer liveth," and it was peaceful and reassuring, just as I had hoped. The service, when it began, was traditional and familiar. I stood for the hymns, bowed my head for the prayers, and did indeed feel oddly comforted.

As we rose for the final hymn, the doors behind me opened once more, a shaft of daylight flickering briefly in the dim candlelit interior. Quick clacking footsteps echoed on the stone floor, stopped near me. I glanced over my shoulder and the words of the hymn died on my lips. Angel Ambrose stood in the aisle, very close to me, ramrod straight, wearing the red jacket and short black skirt I'd seen her in before, unsuitable for a funeral, flashy, too much leg showing. Insolent and disturbing, she was an alien flame glowing in the discreet church, the velvet head arrogant on the slender coppery neck, that imperious tilt to her jaw. The muscles of her face twitched and instantly I recognized the danger signals.

She stood motionless for a long heart-stopping moment, gazing down the nave to the altar and the casket, then she turned her head to stare at those who'd looked around. I saw surprise on their faces, unmistakable disapproval at the sight of her, disrespectul among all the correct white people. Curling her lip, she faced down each and every one. Then she saw me. Her eyes widened and flashed and her shoulders hunched like a racehorse about to bolt from the starting gate. Instinctively, I reached out to grab her. She tugged away, hissing like a snake. More heads turned. The organ music swelled and the voices rose in ragged harmony, and under the sound of them, I whispered, "Angel, please don't make a scene. Stand here quietly beside me."

She made no attempt to keep her voice down. "I didn't come here to be quiet."

"Please!" But I already knew it was hopeless. Just as the other day, she was beyond listening to reason, her body quivering, the same wildness in her black eyes. She opened

her mouth as if to scream and I caught her around the
shoulders, placed a warning finger over her mouth. The
wild eyes rolled in fury and I pressed harder with my hand.
She gnawed at it with her teeth and scratched with her
hands, arms flailing, and everyone in the immediate vicinity
shifted and stirred, more people turning, the hymn beginning to fade away. Whatever it was she had in mind, I was
only making it worse. The doors were just a few yards
away; humiliated, half-carrying, half-dragging her, I hustled
her out of the church.

On the path outside, she wrestled violently in my arms,
writhing and scratching with her long red nails, kicking her
feet, moaning and grunting in her throat like an animal in
distress.

"Angel! For God's sake!" I tried to calm her down.
"What the hell are you thinking of? Have some self-
control."

I didn't know what to do with her. I could hardly drag
her like this all the way through town. On the street, a row
of black cars were drawn up under the trees and a knot of
drivers gaped at the spectacle; then two of them detached
themselves from the cars, started up the path toward us. I
bent my mouth close to Angel's ear, tried to keep my voice
low, soothing.

"Hush now, Angel, hush. Everything's going to be all
right. It's all going to be better soon, you'll see. Everything
gets better after awhile."

I rubbed my other hand up and down the twisting steel
of her spine as the men drew closer, cautiously. "It's
okay," I called. "Nothing to worry about. She's just upset.
She'll be fine in a moment."

Stopping a few feet away, they grinned. "Hysterical, is
she? Happens, you know. Some people can't control themselves."

"She's not hysterical, just unhappy."

In my arms, Angel suddenly went limp and ceased strug-

gling. Hot tears flowed down her cheeks and over my hand.
I murmured into the curving ear near my lips, "You're not
going to scream, are you, Angel? You promise? I'll let go
if you promise. Don't let them see you like this."

All at once, the rage seemed to have melted away and
she sagged against me, soft and malleable as a child.

I spoke as I would to a hurt child. "There now, there
now. I'll take care of you." I lifted my hand carefully from
her mouth. She took a deep breath, but she didn't scream,
just let the tears run unchecked down the smooth brown
cheeks and into her mouth, rivulets of anguish. Pulling a
handkerchief from my pocket, I wiped them away.

"Everything will be better soon, Angel. Soon, I promise
you."

She sobbed in my arms and I thought the storm was over.

From inside the church rose a final swell of organ music,
and behind us, the doors opened again. The casket was
slowly wheeled out, heaped with flowers, men in dark suits
and white shirts grasping the brass handles, treading sol-
emnly and decorously, heads bowed. After the casket came
the minister and the family, Mrs. Woods in a black coat,
her face pale, arms linked with two women, followed by
two small boys clutching hands.

I drew Angel to one side so the coffin and its bearers
could pass. I saw that one of the bearers was Grogan.

He raised his flaring red head to glare at us—at me, but
especially at Angel. Maybe I'd not have recognized the
look in the pale eyes if Nita Barnes hadn't warned me to
search for it; maybe the events of the past days had taught
me at last to recognize it. I had never seen hatred such as
that in anyone's face before.

I maneuvered Angel away from that look and hoped to
God she hadn't seen it. She still wept quietly under my
arm, her shoulders heaving, and I held her close as Grogan
went by. He stared into my face with furious disgust; then
he averted his eyes and resumed a suitable expression of

mourning. The coffin with its bearers proceeded gently and reverently down the path to the waiting hearse, the men retreated back to the cars, and the congregation filed from the church and gathered around. There was a breath-holding silence before Dr. Woods would be placed into the hearse and driven away, his final journey about to begin. Along this very path, my father's last journey had begun.

Maybe I was thinking of my father; maybe I believed the danger was over. I loosened my grasp on Angel. The pallbearers reached the vehicles at the end of the path, then bent to slide the flower-laden casket into the waiting maw of the hearse. And suddenly, she had broken away from me and was hurtling down the path toward them, arms wheeling, long legs flying, the red jacket a flash of startling color in the dark day, her voice wailing high in the solemn silence. "He killed my baby! He killed my baby! God will never forgive him."

The pallbearers, the family, the minister—all froze, transfixed, startled. The scene unrolled before me in slow motion: the bronze casket, the brilliant flowers, the clustering black shapes around the hearse, the white faces turning, mouths agape, the red jacket streaking into their midst like a clot of blood. "He killed my baby! I want everyone to know what he did to my baby."

I saw Grogan let go of the brass handle, his face flaming with that awful crimson rage. He whirled toward the flying Angel, his hand lifted as though to strike her. "Fucking nigger!" he shouted. "How dare you come here!"

His voice rang into the hushed gray air and the quality of the silence changed, a collective sharp intake of breath, the crowd shrinking away in fear or disgust or disbelief. Stopping in her headlong flight, Angel was tall and icy and frighteningly calm.

Grogan took a furious threatening step toward her. "Get away from here! Leave us alone! You don't belong here.

ou're nothing but trouble, all of you. Your fucking kid
as the cause of all this trouble.''

The men in their dark suits began to converge on Angel,
nd at last I stirred out of my stunned spectator role, run-
ing to get through the crowd and rescue her. Before I
ould reach her, an unseemly flurry erupted around the cas-
et and from the midst of the milling throng came sounds
ke the crack of a whip, little screams like that of a
ounded cat. In front of me, the crowd parted as if it were
e Red Sea, revealing Grogan sliding slowly sideways
own the casket, immense surprise on his engorged face.
ngel was standing over him triumphantly.

At first, I imagined she must have knocked him to the
round in some way. It took a moment to realize she was
olding in her hand the small silvery revolver I'd seen once
efore. From the barrel of it curled a tiny puff of white
moke.

"Christ!" I whispered, horrified. "Jesus Christ, Angel.
ou shot him?"

All around, people were running away. A confused up-
oar arose, the thin piercing shriek of a woman, a child
rying, men shouting, around the cars, up toward the
hurch. The coffin was abandoned, flowers cascading to the
round, heaping around Grogan.

"I hope I killed him," Angel said very calmly, handing
e the gun.

I held it away from me, between my thumb and forefin-
er, the barrel still hot. Foolishly, as though it was impor-
ant now, I said, "Why in God's name did you have to
hoot him?"

"Nobody calls my dead baby a fucking kid. Nobody."
he stared at the man on the ground, at the spreading
plotch of crimson on his white shirtfront, at the strewn
lowers and the cautiously approaching crowd. Then she
miled at me, the transforming mischievous smile of a
aughty child. "Lord knows, I feel better now."

People were jostling us, men with fearful, angry faces, grabbing at Angel, at me. "She's mad," someone said. "A mad black woman. You can't trust them."

Chauncey had fought his way through the crowd and was kneeling beside Grogan, pumping on his chest, trying to force life into him. I couldn't tell if it was doing any good. I heard the sound of sirens in the near distance.

Someone said, "The police are coming. They'll take her away."

"Angel," I said. "Did you know who he was?"

The childlike smile lingered on her face. "Oh, Mr. Richards, I'm just a poor mad black woman."

Shoving aside the angry, pushing men, I put my arms around her, held her protectively. "It's all right, Angel. I'll take care of you."

"The Lord will take care of me," she said.

I knew better than that. In spite of the system, in spite of the lawyers, justice might have been done after all. But she would need someone other than God to look after her now.

TWENTY-FOUR

THE AMBULANCE came for Grogan. The sight had become all too familiar to me, the flashing lights and wailing sirens, the stretcher and the oxygen masks, the crackling radios. As the paramedics huddled over Grogan, the police arrived, leaping out of their cars, snapping handcuffs on Angel and hustling her out of the frightened, pointing throng. I handed over the gun and let them take her, because there was no reason to prevent them.

The ambulance raced up the hill toward St. Mary's, and I still didn't know whether Grogan was dead or alive.

Dr. Woods's casket and the flowers were picked up off the ground and restored to decency, and eventually the hearse drove off and all the people went away, until only I was left in the shadows of the trees. A thin rain began, wetting the pavement and dampening the grass. Then I realized I was not quite alone. A slender figure in a neat black coat came slowly across the grass toward me, the rain slicking the soft hair onto her pale forehead. Daphne.

She came close and stood before me. I looked at her for a long moment.

"It's my fault," I said. "I told her about Grogan."

"You mustn't think everything is your fault, Noah."

"Chauncey says I have an overdeveloped sense of responsibility. This time, I really have something to be responsible for."

She gestured with one black-gloved hand at the church, the town, the white bulk of the hospital on the hill. "Who would have believed it could come to this? Who would believe this sort of thing would happen here? All this burning and this shooting and this hate?"

Poor Daphne. She was English. She believed in a world without guns and violence and revenge. She believed in justice and fairness.

I said, "You know what it means, don't you? If she knew about Grogan, then it wasn't some random act. They'll call it premeditated murder."

"He had it coming to him." In Daphne's gentle eyes was some semblance of Angel's fierceness. "I'm not sorry."

"Be sorry for Angel."

"Any mother would understand why she did it. Any mother would want vengeance."

"*Vengeance* is an ugly word, Daphne. With ugly results. She should have left it to the courts. That's why we have a legal system."

Her soft lips set in a hard, unfamiliar line. "But you said you couldn't prove it. What good would the courts have done her?"

"Good? You think what's happened now is good? At least she wouldn't have been accused of murder."

"You'll be able to help her, won't you?"

"I'm not a criminal lawyer."

"Then find her a good one. You must know whom to go to."

I put an arm around her shoulder and we left the shelter of the trees together, leaning on each other. She would always be my friend. I would always love her.

"God Almighty, Daphne. I can hardly believe I allowed it to come to this."

"You weren't the one who ignored the cries for help, Noah. You listened when people needed you."

"Obviously, I didn't listen hard enough, did I? And now I have to go and find Joseph. I have to make sure he's all right."

"Promise me you won't leave her to some incompetent

lawyer who doesn't understand. Take care of her, Noah. Please.''

''Me? You think I can take care of this now? I already screwed up, Daphne. Just like the doctors. A little mistake here, a little neglect there, and suddenly it's all gone wrong. And just like the doctors, I'm not sure I can make it right again.''

An unusual determination came over her gentle face. ''We can make it better. I know we can. All of us, if we work at it. We can make this a better place for everyone.''

It was easy to say.

But I'd told Angel I'd take care of her. It seemed the least I could do.

I walked back in the northwestern rain through the empty streets of Springwell to the ruins of my office, got in my car, and went to find Joseph. I found him at home watching television. He didn't seem surprised when I told him, just switched off the television, got a jacket out of the closet, and went with me in the car. ''She was one angry lady, that's for sure.''

At the sheriff's office, Angel sat peacefully in a dark cell, her hands folded in her lap, her head resting against the wall. Joseph took her in his arms and rocked her. ''It's okay, baby. Me and Mr. Richards will look after you. We'll be all right, you and me. Life's just a lot of trouble and strife, that's for sure. But the good Lord will see us through.''

She smiled happily. ''That's what I told Mr. Richards.''

The wildness had gone out of her eyes. There was a calmness, a serenity I'd never seen in her before.

''You didn't have to shoot him,'' I said.

''He called me a nigger. He called my Jordy a fucking kid.''

''Angel, that's not a reason to kill someone.''

Her smile was almost flirtatious. ''Guess no one's ever called you that, have they, Mr. Richards?''

No, no one had ever called me that. No doctor had refused to treat someone I loved.

There are some questions lawyers don't ask their clients, not if they don't want to know the answer. Criminal lawyers don't ask their clients if they are guilty, because then they might have trouble defending them. So I wouldn't ask Angel again what she knew about Grogan. I understood what I was letting myself in for. A new life. A different kind of law. Wasn't that what I had been looking for all along?

There was hostility in the sheriff's eyes when I placed my card in front of him, committing myself. "I expect my client to be afforded every right," I said.

I practiced my arguments on the way back to St. Mary's to find out about Grogan. St. Mary's, where it had all begun, where I had found Lauren.

Without the Ambrose case, I might never have found her. Without the Ambrose case, I might never have found out about Springwell.

In spite of all the senseless wreckage of lives and property and beliefs, there spread over me a profound sense of purpose—like balm, like salvation. I might never have to rewrite another will or prepare another real estate contract or ever take another malpractice case.

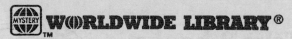

Take 2 books and a surprise gift FREE!

SPECIAL LIMITED-TIME OFFER

Mail to: The Mystery Library™
3010 Walden Ave.
P.O. Box 1867
Buffalo, N.Y. 14240-1867

YES! Please send me **2 free books** from the Mystery Library™ and my free surprise gift. Then send me 3 mystery books, first time in paperback, every month. Bill me only $4.19 per book plus 25¢ delivery and applicable sales tax, if any*. There is no minimum number of books I must purchase. I can always return a shipment at your expense and cancel my subscription. Even if I never buy another book from the Mystery Library™, **the 2 free books and surprise gift are mine to keep forever.**

415 WEN CJQN

Name   (PLEASE PRINT)

Address   Apt. No.

City   State   Zip

* Terms and prices subject to change without notice. N.Y. residents add applicable sales tax. This offer is limited to one order per household and not valid to present subscribers.
© 1990 Worldwide Library.

MYS98

WORLDWIDE LIBRARY®

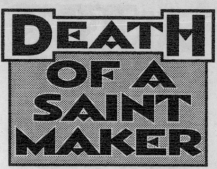

DEATH OF A SAINT MAKER

ALLANA MARTIN

A TEXANA JONES MYSTERY

DEATH IN THE DESERT

The Chihuahuan Desert between Texas and Mexico is vast, hot and empty. The borderland is home to Texana Jones and her veterinarian husband, Clay.

When an intinerant wood-carver, affectionately called the Saint Maker, is killed, a bloody pit bull named Gringo is found standing over the body. But Texana believes there's a deeper mystery involved. Her conviction leads her to the border's most dangerous edge, into the secret underworld of drugs, smuggling, poaching…and death.

Available January 1999 at your favorite retail outlet.

WORLDWIDE LIBRARY ®

ARTIST'S PROOF

GORDON COTLER

A SID SHALE MYSTERY
STILL LIFE

Nothing could have persuaded ex-NYPD cop turned artist Sid Shale to get back into the investigative groove. Until Cassie Brennan's murder.

The victim had posed several times for Sid…in the nude. To save his own neck, Sid starts sifting through the sands of Cassie's last days—from the distraught boyfriend to the shady restaurateur who hired her as a cleaning lady—uncovering a motive for murder as primal as it is tragic.

Available January 1999 at your favorite retail outlet.

Look us up on-line at: http://www.worldwidemystery.com   WGC300